A Way
to
Escape

Michelle Thompson

LMH PUBLISHING LIMITED

© 2016 Michelle Thompson
First Edition
10 9 8 7 6 5 4 3 2 1

Editor: K. Sean Harris
Cover Design: Sanya Dockery
Book Design, Layout & Typesetting: Sanya Dockery

Published by LMH Publishing Limited
Suite 10-11, Sagicor Industrial Park
7 Norman Road
Kingston C.S.O., Jamaica
Tel.: (876) 938-0005; 938-0712
Fax: (876) 759-8752
Email: lmhbookpublishing@cwjamaica.com
Website: www.lmhpublishing.com

Printed in the U.S.A.   ISBN: 978-976-8245-46-5

NATIONAL LIBRARY OF JAMAICA CATALOGUING-IN-PUBLICATION DATA

Thompson, Michelle
    A way to escape / Michelle Thompson

    p. ; cm

ISBN 978-976-8245-46-5 (pbk)

1. Jamaican fiction
I. Title

813   dc 23

Dedication

I dedicate this story to my father, Clarence, and especially my grandmother, Louise and mother, Joyce, who have inspired and shaped my life. To my wonderful daughter, Dunisha, my reason for living.

Thanks to my siblings and support, Maxine, AnnMarie, Calvin, Donald; my uncle Kirk, nieces Sasha, Suzie and Tanya (Denise), nephew Jaron, and the rest of my loving family.

To my dear friends Marcia (Cutie), Marty, Joan S., Thelma, Una-Mae, Joan (Dawn) and the Doncaster Posse; Norda and St. Joseph/St. Aloysius Alumni, Lawrence and Miranda Hill, and Pastors Orim and Judith Meikle. Thanks to you all for encouragement and support. To everyone on my Daily Word list, thank you for letting me speak into your lives.

And most of all, thank God without whom none of this is possible.

Chapter 1

Rose's mother, Mari, sat on a wooden bench inside the
Kingston bus terminal, avoiding the midday sun. She waited for
Rose. A stout, dark-skinned woman, perspiration glistened from
the fold in her neck. She dabbed the sweat and fanned with the
handkerchief clutched in her palm. Sitting near the entrance, at
the sight of a bus pulling in, her head raised in anticipation of
the twelve o'clock bus from Montego Bay. Every few minutes
she straightened the bag on her shoulder and limped with bandaged knee to the doorway. She checked her watch; the bus was
forty minutes late. She leaned against the door, and looking out,
muttered about the dangers of the country road and petitioned
God for the bus driver's due diligence. Anxiousness outweighed
the joy of seeing her daughter come back to town, to her, after
the man she married and moved away with died. A man Mari
considered not marriage material for her Rosie, as he was
'blacker dan night' with hands 'coarser dan dry brush', not to
mention him being twice her twenty-four years.

Not even garlic tea could keep Mari's blood pressure down when Rose broke the news that she was "goin' try life" on the other side of the island. The only consolation two years later, Rose was coming home with baby Audrey; more for her to love.

During the time Rose lived in Montego Bay, Mari prayed day and night for a miracle to bring her Rosie back to Kingston. She thanked God the day she got word of her only child's return. Not that she objected to Rose carving her own life, oh no, she still hoped for a 'stand-up man' for her daughter, because she remembered having only five pounds, money she saved washing 'til her fingers blue', realized that Rose's father had no plans for their future and upped and left him. She said, "Anyt'ing better dan a man widout a plan", and moved from Manchester to find life for her and Rose.

Now Mari could dream again.

The bus pulled into the terminal. She spotted Rose exiting the transportation carrying her baby at her side. At first glance, she fretted her daughter looked spent, forgetting she had been traveling from daybreak. She called out, "Rose! Rosie!" When their eyes met, her smile reassured her, flooding her heart with bliss. Her face rounded in the biggest smile as she said, "Oh, Rosie." Her arms opened wide.

Tears filled Rose's eyes. "Momma!"

"Come mi darling, come." They hugged and cried. She took Audrey. "Is dis mi likkle sweetie pie?" She kissed the baby all the way home.

With a song of thanksgiving in her heart, Mari made space for Rose and Audrey in her one-room quarters. But although good intentioned, her modest pay at the bakery could barely stretch for the three of them. Her offer to be a washer-lady again while Rose looked for work was a suggestion Rose quickly put to bed, pointing out her painful fingers. That did not stop Mari. As Rose looked for work, she spread the word that she too was ready for a new 'vencha', even with arthritic fingers.

In the mid-fifties, folks from rural areas relocated to Kingston due to scarcity in sugar cane and bauxite work. Everyone seeking new means of livelihood settled in the big city, adding to the dilemma of those already there, like Rose. But to her advantage, she had talent. She could style hair and make clothes, and was the boast of her mother. "Rosie is just like her fada, good wid dem hands." Except, Mari lamented, "Ben Crawford have no ambition, him sit on him hands, don't apply himself and expect better to find him."

Rose had gifts, only now she had to 'turn it into fashion' and let her gifts work for her. With little Audrey she considered, *if I get a job in a beauty parlour or a dressmaker shop, with momma working she couldn't keep an eye on her.* She quickly summed up the situation in the tenement yard, where more women congregated than at a market sale on Saturday morning. One woman in the yard ran a haberdashery from her one-room house in the back. Watching the traffic flow in and out she thought, *there is opportunity for me too right here in this yard.*

As the new person in the 'big yard', Rose restrained her desire to rush out and set up shop, knowing she had to prove herself. Every morning she styled her hair in the latest 'do' — flip, up-sweep or bob — and made herself seen around the yard. Soon whispers, comments and outright compliments of her fancy hairdos poured in. She bought two more pressing combs and converted Mari's room into a beauty parlour during the days.

Rose's budding business grew busier each day. She enjoyed molding and shaping short, long, and even dry, coarse hair. Women with dowdy appearances were transformed with just a hot comb and tease. And although the women wanted their hair in the latest styles, when it came time to pay, they had all sorts of hard luck stories: "Mi short dis week because one a mi baby need medicine", or a school book, or this or that. Some women came right out - after their hair was done - and begged, "You can trust mi 'til mi man get pay Friday?" You name it, Rose heard it. At the end of the day counting her earnings, for the time and dedication put into the hairstyles, she questioned its worth.

Still, hairdressing gave Rose an opportunity to hone her skills. She accepted the work she provided the women as tit for tat even though her baby needed food too and she had no man bringing pay home on Fridays.

Almost everyone in the yard had some form of daily hustling that were legitimate jobs like cleaning, sorting and delivering for nearby downtown stores. The more independent tenants sold bag juices, peanuts and other knickknacks on King Street and its surroundings. A couple of men got dressed every morning but never went further than the gate. As if mayors for the community, they knew everything and everybody and were well compensated for their underhanded observations. At the standpipe, as Rose groomed alongside other tenants preparing for work, her ears were cocked. She listened in hopes of hearing a word that someone, somewhere, had connections to a job. She knew with her abilities there was more, and she wanted it.

One day, as she worked on one of the ladies' hair, the woman told her she worked at Bend Down Market by Victoria Pier. The woman said she sold straw goods to tourists visiting the wharf. It sparked Rose's interest and she inquired about the possibility of working there. Without hesitation, the woman offered to help her set up a stall at the pier.

That night, Rose talked it over with Mari and she agreed with the shift in vocation. But after further thought, they both decided it made more sense for Mari to take the job at the market, especially with her debilitating knees.

Mari met with Mr. Chin, the owner of the bakery, the next morning. As he unpacked his deliveries, she explained that she could not take the pressure standing for long periods anymore. Before hearing her option, the slender, graying Asian man glanced at her and replied, "Ah, Mari, what pressure? You don't stand for long and you can always use di stool" as he continued to open the boxes of produce.

Mari bit her tongue, stifling what would surely have cost her and Rose the job. "Don't worry sar, mi daughter can take mi space."

Mr. Chin stopped what he was doing and faced her. "You daughter? Tell her must come, man." He was only too happy to have her younger version.

Chapter 2

Mari sold to tourists from all walks of life. She learned to say "gracie" and "bonjour", and curtsied with her wrapped knee. She lined her table with colourful, decorative straw hats, bags, fans, coasters, and place mats. She sat next to her stall and invited passersby to "try one" and to "come and have a look, man". Any tourist who showed interest, she bounced off her stool, ready. "Can I sell you somet'ing today?"

The craft market worked well for Mari. Her tips from British pounds and U.S. dollars allowed her to work at her own pace. She brought Audrey with her every day, freeing Rose to go to work. Yet, as much as she enjoyed her new venture, Rose regretted hers.

At the bakery, Rose did not start in Mari's position, nor was she paid the same. The salary amounted to not much more than a bad day at hairdressing. As the newcomer, her job was to knead dough for pastries all day, while the senior workers, like Mari was, baked icing cakes and coconut, sweet potato and cassava puddings. Rose's fingers craved to do more, as well as she needed more money for her plan.

One morning on her way to work, she slipped into the milk shop to buy a cup of scalded milk. She met an old friend from Manchester. "Oh my gosh, is who dat, Cynthia?" she said, walking toward the tall, well-dressed woman at the front of the line.

"Rosie, is you dat?" They hugged. "How you doing girl?" Cynthia touched the end of Rose's straightened, shoulder-length hair. "I see you still have your nice head a hair." And running her eyes up and down her blue and white dress, said, "And your nice little figure", slapping Rose on the hip. "Girl you looking good."

Rose knew how to put herself together, even when vanity was her least concern. "My gosh, Cynthia, it's a long time."

They sat in the windowless shop at a corner table with two chairs. They sipped their cups of milk and caught up with each other's life. Rose told her she had a daughter and hoped to find her mister right. "So what about you?"

"Misses, mi no have no luck, mi no even t'ink no good man outta street for mi," Cynthia answered, and they laughed. They swapped stories of their endeavors gaining meaningful work in Kingston. Rose confided in Cynthia that she was dissatisfied with the job she had and was looking for something more suitable that paid enough to get her own place. "Mi love mi mada, but mi is a big woman."

"Mi understand mi dear," Cynthia said. She told Rose she worked at Patel's Clothing in West Kingston and assured her, "I will keep you in mind if anyt'ing." With Rose's flair for sewing, she prayed a break opened at the clothing factory.

From time to time, Rose and Cynthia saw each other at the milk shop. One morning exiting the shop, Rose bumped into Cynthia arriving. "Lord, mi glad mi see you, Rosie." Cynthia pulled her friend to the side. "Mr. Patel taking on people at di factory. You still interested?"

The beam on Rose's face gave Cynthia the answer. She arranged an interview with her boss. Rose went about the job and got it. As she left the factory that afternoon, walking along Spanish Town Road, honking taxis and fume-gushing buses passing couldn't faze her. Hearing the words 'start Monday' both deafened and delighted her. She laughed out loud, not caring who saw, for now she could move on to the life she envisioned for her and Audrey. Planning the days ahead, she decided to finish the rest of the week at Chin's.

Rose dreaded telling Mari her plan to leave the bakery. Until now, she had not voiced her displeasure at working there. With Monday being three days away, she needed to tell her about the job at Patel's soon. Friday night after Audrey fell asleep between them on the bed, she turned to her and in a soft tone said, "Mamma mi quit Chin's." Mari laying on her back, never shifted her gaze from the ceiling. "But mi have another job now," she added. Her tone conveyed reassurance.

Mari looked at her and said, "Mi know you never happy, I could see it on you." Rose squeezed her mother's hand, her eyes filled with certainty. And although Mari was broken-hearted, she understood her daughter had long moved on.

Rose had been at the factory for a month and a half. She saved her salary and rented a room close to where she worked in West Kingston. She and Mari didn't live close, but they saw one another on Fridays when she stopped at the market after work and they chatted until Mari packed up to leave. On Sundays after church Mari visited her for dinner. Most of the time was spent with Audrey, who ran into her arms when she arrived. "Granny, Granny, Granny!" The toddler stuck to her grandmother through treats of fudge or icicle she bought her when the ice-cream man rode by.

Because Audrey wasn't of school age, when Rose had to work she left her with an elderly woman, Ms. Elliot from the same yard. Ms. Elliot took a special liking to Audrey. Refusing to accept any money for taking care of her, she said, "I would do it for nutting, Ms. Rosie." Ms. Elliot claimed her affection for Audrey stemmed from the granddaughter she imagined to look the same as her. She said Audrey was "likkle and tough", falling and bumping her head on the tiled floor and springing up, finger in her mouth, ready to go, "same way mi daughter was".

Many nights after Rose put Audrey to bed, she sat with Ms. Elliot no matter how tired she was, listening to her grieve for her daughter. Her daughter Millie moved to England and died of pneumonia a year after. She had another child, Desmond, and he visited once in a while. Desmond's actions led the 'big yard' tenants to gossip, "Only when him want somet'ing him show up". When he did come, he'd plant a kiss on her cheek and tuck a few shillings in her hand. "Dis is for you, Mada", furthering the gossip when he returned in three or four days to 'borrow' it back.

Nothing was secret in the tenement yard. One afternoon, one of the men came home and told his woman he had seen Desmond at Caymanas Park, emphasizing, "and it wasn't di first time". After she quarreled with him for being at the race track, he reminded her that was how food got on the table. Even so, she could not wait to tell it in the yard. Soon it was all over the place that Desmond was a 'no good hustler' and 'worthless', and would rather bet on horses than help his 'poor mada'.

All this 'big yard' hearsay worked in Ms. Elliot's favour. When Rose or any of the women in the yard went to the market, they brought her 'a likkle somet'ing' in a bag; from callaloo to chicken back, and a few fingers of green banana to cook a meal.

And not to mention when Joseph, the single man who ran his house better than any woman, cooked, he never forgot to bring her a plate and a glass of lemonade to wash it down.

Chapter 3

It wasn't long after Rose moved on her own that she met an admirer. He lived in the house across the street from hers. A fireman, stationed a fifteen-minute walk away, he worked shifts and had ample time to study her movements.

Rose noticed a few mornings leaving for work, the tall, trim man, 'not too dark', was either at his gate or on his veranda. He pretended not to watch her, keeping his head in his newspaper. She felt his eyes trailing her down the road. One evening as she was coming home and he was at his gate, as she passed he smiled and tipped his head. "Good evening." Keeping her eyes straight ahead of her, she slanted her lips at his words; he took it as a smile. The next evening he was there again. "Hello beautiful," he greeted her with smiling eyes. She appreciated his welcome and liked his dreamy eyes, yet, she kept going, thinking, *if he is a decent man, he will make his intentions clear.*

The following Saturday evening, coming home from the corner shop, Rose held her shopping bag close to her chest. She saw her admiring neighbour outside the shop and sensed he was waiting for her. As she walked by, he stepped in front of her. "Can I offer to carry your bags, nice lady?"

"No it's alright," she replied, as she continued on her way.

"I beg you pardon, my name is Arta, Arta Tomlinson." Arthur walked so close to Rose, they brushed shoulders.

She pulled away and looked up at him. "Nice to meet you, sar."

"May I ask your name?"

She glanced at him. "Rose."

When she got to her house, she attempted to open the gate with the grocery bag in one hand and her purse in the next. He swiftly saw an opportunity and said, "Let mi hold it for you" reaching for her bags.

He walked Rose through the gate, to her room, and placed the groceries on the table. She showed him to the gate. While he prolonged his stay, chit chatting, Ms. Elliot brought Audrey out to Rose. The first question from little Audrey was, "Who dat, Mommy?" Rose and Arthur looked at each other like children caught fooling around under the cellar.

They stood there in silence; it was time for him to go. He held on to the gate, shuffling in place, thinking of how to get his point across. Rose took Audrey from Mrs. Elliot and turned to leave. He saw his chance abating and blurted, "Is it okay if I visit you again?"

"If you want." Her response feigned disinterest, but he had ignited a flame she thought had long burnt out.

He too, had an inkling he had lit a spark, not as intense as his, but a flicker nonetheless. He would later reflect on the first morning he saw her going to work, and admitted to her that he watched her at every chance: *lovely, juicy berry, dark, smooth and cool, like not a day in the sun…your fancy dresses show off your coca-cola shape. You mesmerized me, I had to have you.*

From that evening walking Rose home, Arthur schemed to make her his wife. He bought her the basics from the neighbourhood shop, and when she 'trust' fish or cow foot from the handcart vendors, he saw to it her promissory notes were paid on time. On his days off, he met her after work and escorted her home, or they went for walks at Kingston Parade and Race Course. One night, at his suggestion, they stopped at the neighbourhood bar. Entering the smoky room, they followed the psychedelic lights to a table for two in the back and sat across from each other. He shouted over laughter and high voices to order two beers. "None for mi, t'anks," Rose told the young woman tending their table.

"Oh, come on, Rosie."

"No, don't drink, not starting now."

"Why? You is a church woman?" he asked, half-jokingly.

"Not really." She set her purse in her lap and leaned forward.

"You 'fraid you get drunk?" He tugged on her fingers.

"Dat's right. I tried it one time and never like how mi feel."

"How?"

She sat back in her seat. "Mi head never feel right, man."

"From one beer?"

"No, it was actually rum and coke, but it just turn mi off liquor." The server recommended a ginger wine. Rose turned it down. She'd had ginger wine before and liked it. The truth was, she wanted to keep a sober head with a man she was just getting acquainted. She had a ginger ale instead.

A man standing next to the duke-box filled it with coins and selected Alton Ellis, The Paragons and The Heptones. As Arthur sipped his beer and Rose her ginger ale, they eased into conversation. He asked, "So you t'ink you will get married again and have more children?"

"Anyt'ing is possible if di right man comes along."

After some hesitation, he asked, "So you t'ink I could be dat man?" His eyes were penetrating. "You know I have feelings for you."

"And I like you, but I don't really know you dat much. I mean I know you're a fireman but- "

"What you want to know?"

"For one, are you a mass murderer?" He laughed and caressed her fingers, trying to soften her up. "How mi never hear you talk about your family?"

Arthur took a long gulp of his beer and said, "Suppose mi don't have none." His lips slanted, pretending to smile. Rose read his joking as a cover for a sensitive issue, but continued, "No man, mi serious." She surmised he had plans for them, and if so, she had to be satisfied she knew him well enough. He had told her his mother died and he may have other siblings on his father's side, but not much else. She needed details for when Mari asked.

"Well, mi never married and mi don't have no children."

"Yea, but which part a town you come from?"

Realizing her persistence, he spoke up. "Mi born a St. Mary." She folded her arms, searching his eyes. He straightened his shoulders, picked up the bottle cover and ran his fingers around the jagged edges. "Mi come a town from mi was a young man. Mi live wid Sergeant Pritchard and him wife, is him get mi on di force." He took a drink. "Dem was good people, but dem gone to England now."

"You was a police?"

"Yeah, for t'ree years, den mi get into di Fire Brigade." He put the bottle to his mouth and guzzled the last of the beer. Then he waved to the waitress, pointed to the empty bottle and turned to Rose. "Want another ginger ale?" he asked.

"Let mi see." She brought her hand to the blue neon light above her, checking the time on her watch. "No. Mi have to go get Audrey. Ms. Elliot must ready to turn in."

On the weekend he took her to the pantomime at Ward Theater to see *Miss Lou* and *Maas Ron*. As the two comedians bantered, laughter drew them closer and Rose cozied up to him. Before the night ended he learned she had a birthday the following month. He told her Sam Cook was coming to Jamaica at that time and asked if she'd like to go. "He's my favourite singer," she told him.

For the special event, he bought a new shirt and tie, and 'put a likkle somet'ing' in her hand for the beauty parlour. And for her birthday and the show, she made herself a floral hobble gown that accentuated her curves.

The night of the concert, Sam's romantic crooning enhanced the mood, and after the show they walked home arm-in-arm. Rose hung a sheet to separate Audrey's sleeping area, and he stayed the night.

Slowly his belongings melded with hers. His toothbrush was placed with hers in a cup, his comb on her vanity, and a shirt in her laundry. At three months the relationship showed no fizzle. He brought liveliness to her life. They shared expenses and his financial contribution meant for her, less time at work and more with Audrey. She felt secure. She no longer hid his things under the bed when Mari visited, and agreed to his moving in. He sold his few furnishings, gave up his room and brought his little suit-case and transistor radio to live with her.

Rose had hinted to her mother she had a suitor. She disclosed the extent of their relationship in bits to shield her from possible disappointment. But the time had come for Mari to know the man her daughter had taken a chance on.

She invited her for Sunday dinner — cow foot, rice and peas and potato salad with carrot juice. Arthur stocked the icebox with liquor. The three of them huddled at the two-seat dinette set; Arthur used the stool from the vanity. Audrey sat in her grandmother's lap as she ate and fed her. After dinner Rose cleared the table and Audrey went to ride her tricycle, leaving Mari and Arthur alone. Mari sat quietly, her countenance pleasant as she listened to Arthur reveal his heart for Rose. He sipped his beer. "Yes, Momma, mi love Rosie. Mi love her and have plans for mi and her." Mari nodded, he sounded ambitious. "Mi good to her, you nuh, Momma." He walked to the icebox, opened another beer and sat down again. "Mi good to her, man, she don't tell you?" He rambled, and Mari wondered if his rambling was undying love for Rosie, or the alcoholic brew he feasted on.

When Rose walked into the room, Arthur leaped to his feet, set the bottle on the table and held her hand. "Rosie, my darling Rosie," his mouth quivered, "right here, before you mada and God, I want to ask for you hand in marriage."

Rose, eyes and mouth wide open, laughed. Nervousness overtook her. She blinked. "Is what dis?" The words she'd hope to hear, astounded her. She glanced at her mother, equally taken aback, and replied, "Well, okay, I mean, yes."

It took a couple more months, but before the year ended, his plans came through: Arthur Tomlinson married twenty-five year old Rosemarie Crawford, his blackberry, ten years his junior.

Chapter 4

A couple of months into the marriage, Rose was pregnant.
With their growing family, they rented two rooms in a house on
the next street, and a few months after, welcomed a baby girl
into their lives. Excited about his first child, Arthur readily
helped with changing dirty nappies, bathing and rubbing olive
oil on her new-baby skin. She was breastfed around the clock,
and grew chubby fast. He and Rose often joked that she would
soon outgrow Audrey. The paternal care he had for Audrey
never lessened – he adopted her – even though their playtime
did. When he came home from work he went straight to the crib
for his baby daughter. He'd throw her up in the air, blowing
bubbles on her belly as he caught her mid-air. At meal times he'd
bounce her on his lap as he ate. He held her until she fell asleep
in his arms. He called her his 'little princess', said she was the
spitting image of his mother, a light-skinned woman he knew
only from pictures as she had died giving birth to him. Out of
adoration for a mother he loved through his imagination, he
named the baby Maureen after her.

Arthur rarely talked about his upbringing, even with the most innocent probe. One day as he went through the chest of draws, he came across some pictures he sort of buried. He removed the rubber band. A picture of his mother was on top, triggering a heavy sigh. As if knocked to the bed behind him, he sat staring at the faded black and white photo. Audrey trekking behind him asked who was the lady in the picture. He shook his head, remaining pensive. He contemplated life without his mother, a life with adopted parents who treated him like their yard boy. Many days they kept him out of school to tend to their fowl business, and when they had biological children, he had to tend to them as well. When he got the chance at seventeen, he fled to Kingston. He sighed, wishing the woman in the picture knew how things had worked out for him, how he now had his own family.

With Audrey in kindergarten, Maureen creeping and gradually weaning off breast, Rose could go back to the factory, except, Arthur disagreed. He objected to her leaving Maureen with Ms. Elliot to go to work. He argued, "Dat old woman need care herself and you wan' leave my child wid her? You must be outta you mind."

Rose reasoned that her employer allowed only a few months off before he hired someone permanent in her place. She pleaded, "Di extra money wouldn't hurt and God knows we could use it." Nevertheless, Arthur's strong disapproval prevailed. He persisted that home was where she should be with the baby. She gave in, and convinced herself that Ms. Elliot's arthritic knees would give her too much trouble caring for a leaping, teething child, anyway.

To prove he was serious, Arthur bought Rose a sewing machine and put a sign in the front yard announcing she was open for dressmaking. Arthur knew erecting a sign without checking with the landlord could cause an eviction, but said, "If di landlord give mi hell, I will warn him, him risk getting nutting at all." His grounds was, without his wife's earnings they could not afford the rent, and he would stop paying it all together until he found another place, and when that would be, he couldn't guarantee. The landlord ignored the sign since the rent had not been late so far, justifying the matter a wait and see.

Chapter 5

Two years after Maureen's birth, Rose had a son named Donovan. From birth the baby sucked two fingers, his index and middle as one. Arthur made fun that he came out the womb hungry. A proud father, he strutted like a king to the veranda when his fireman friends came by. He introduced the new heir to the Tomlinson throne. "See mi boy yah, see him yah." As he grew, he'd sling him around his neck in a donkey ride. When he started walking, it pleased him to watch him clunk up and down in his shoes, pointing to his feet, "Ook Dada, ook." If Arthur had to run to the shop for Rose, he took him, enjoying comments on the street. "You boy favour you, Mr. Tom." One of his neighbours stopped him to say hello and she pointed out, "Watch him little ears, just like yours", referring to the small ears he and his children had. "Rose never tell a lie." Like most men around town, he gleamed with pride from the look-a-like comparison.

Things were looking up for the family. Rose's sewing business was not only popular in the community; word spread of her specialty in embroidery and ladies from as far as other parishes brought clothes to have decorative needle-work done. And Arthur, he finally got the promotion he sought as head driver at the station.

With the extra money coming in they disputed how to spend it, as each had their own idea on improving the family's living conditions. Arthur felt transportation was paramount and Rose thought with an expanding family, they needed their own house.

Although buying a house made the most sense to her, she knew it stood to impede how she earned a living. She weighed her options: *With all the customers I have, how can I move from the area that brings me steady work?* It meant relocating, which was chancy at this time. With mixed feelings, she plowed on. She worked late nights to meet deadlines with one goal – owning a family residence.

Arthur was unable to convince her otherwise and plotted behind her back. One night, as she worked on the last piece of clothes for the day, she heard a rumbling at the gate. She went to see. It was Arthur, he had driven home a Zephyr Six. Shock glued her to the doorway as she watched him park the car at the gate.

He walked pass her at the door. She followed him, waiting for him to say something. When he didn't, she asked, "Arta, is whose car dat?"

"Mine," he said, and then as if caught himself, "our own."

"Our own?" Her eyes widened. She shook her head. "No, dat is not mine." He sat on the chair and pulled off his shoes. She stood over him. "How much you pay for it?"

"Not much," he answered, looking pleased with himself.

"Because it probably not wort' much."

"It's a good car, di fellow just bought somet'ing else, dat's why him sell it."

"But we can't afford it. Take it back." Her anger stewed. She paused, then as it simmered, quietly said, "Remember, my money in it to."

He grumbled, "You see dis rahtid woman", pushed his feet back into his shoes, stormed out the house, got into his car and sped off.

Later in the night, after she tucked the children in bed, concerned, she waited in the front room for him. When she heard his car stop, she peeked through the curtains and watched him park. *Thank God*, she mused with a sigh. As he stepped into the house she got up. "Arta, where you was?" she asked, both relieved and furious.

He staggered through the house reeking of rum; she got her answer. She followed him. "Arta, did you ask di landlord if you could park di car in di yard?" He mumbled something about not leaving it on the street, as he kicked off his shoes. His rum scent was too much to ignore and she said, "Arta, is so you drive home?"

"How you mean?"

"Drunk!"

"Who drunk?" He frowned, dragging off his shirt. "You don't see mi reach home?"

"Somet'ing coulda happen to you on di road!"

"Well nutting happen, so stop worry."

"But I don't understand you," she said, arms folded, head tilted and brows knitted. "You come in here dis time a night, stink of liquor. What wrong wit' you, Arta? You forget you have work in di morning?"

"Stop you talking and leave mi, man!"

"Yes, go on 'til you lose di work." He raised his hand at her. She ducked, scurrying to the children's bed. "You better gwaan," he warned.

Rose stayed with the children for the night. She couldn't sleep, being distressed over his drinking that could cost him his job and the family's livelihood.

From that night, she realized any comments about the car roiled him and their arguments made the children cry. She pondered what to do, and even thought of leaving him. But with three of them, where would they go? Mari had no space. And involving her might skyrocket her blood pressure. The dilemma overwhelmed her. She resolved, "When you hand in a lion mouth, you take time draw it out", concluding that "in all honesty, Arta never left mi and di children hungry". She convinced herself that things wasn't that bad and would eventually get better.

Weeks went by without her passing judgment on the car and as a result, peace reigned. If he had a few drinks, he kept it from her, and if she had a whiff he had, she kept it to herself.

They decided to work with their accommodation for the time being. Donovan had outgrown sleeping with them and had trials with Audrey and Maureen in their bed. Adding a growing boy, especially at the rate Donovan sprouted was painful for the girls. On the days he slept with his sisters, his feet woke them in tears, gaining him the nick-name 'baby big hoof'. Rose said, by the size of Donovan's feet, he no doubt would rival his father's six feet by his teen years, because, "when chicken a go big, you see it in a him foot".

She upgraded the single, folded bed to one that fitted all three children and any more to come. She sold the bed to one of her customers, made up the difference and bought a double bed. But they had difficulty finding the perfect space for it. It was too big for the space the smaller bed occupied in the living and dining area. So Arthur moved the fridge to the kitchen, forcing it beside the stove. This prevented the kitchen door from properly opening, so he took off the door. Rose's reminder that he wasn't allowed to remove the kitchen door in a house he did not own, went through one stubborn ear, and out the next. He leaned the door between the fridge and the wall. "In case," he said, "di landlord come for him rent and come 'round di kitchen for likkle water and notice di door take off." Rose shook her head and bit her tongue. It seemed Arthur was banking on the landlord collecting his rent without doing his usual 'just let me use the bathroom' surveillance through the house.

The kitchen shrunk to a size only Rose could reasonably fit into. If she wanted she could stir a pot on the stove with one hand, while rinsing a vegetable at the sink with the other. The good thing with being dense, was that it discouraged the children from wandering in. Even her sewing machine got caught in the rearranging of the house and was designated to the back veranda. But despite what appeared inconvenient for her customers, worked out in the end. Instead of the ladies traipsing through the house, glaring at their private living quarters, Arthur posted a sign directing customers to walk around. He hung a long mirror on the back wall so they could spin and swing and admire themselves from head to toe.

As soon as everything found its rightful place in the home, and the family of five settled, Rose was pregnant again. From her first trimester this pregnancy was different from the others. This baby brought on morning sickness unlike the others. Rose threw up constantly, not even water stayed down. Her feet were swollen and her back hurt, landing her in bed. Audrey became 'mommy's likkle helper'. She ran to check the pot on the stove and chased after Donovan who played football with anything laying on the floor.

She was pregnant during the Christmas and New Year's season. Although her customers said they sympathized, they used fruit cake and sorrel laced with sweet talk to cajole her out of bed. Thankfully, her sickness eased and enabled her to grant their 'bashment' outfits. Working over the holidays augmented the family's finances, and both Rose and Arthur agreed to the down payment on a house.

Chapter 6

A baby girl was born to Rose and Arthur three weeks before her due date at the Victoria Jubilee Hospital. Two days later, in chemise, hat, socks, and wrapped in a blanket, she and Rose were driven home by Arthur.

The new four-bedroom house on Barton Place, Doncaster, was three miles from their previous home. It sat on a five-house dead-end, running east to west. Green, pink and purple crotons with a blend of hibiscus hedged the home. A promising mango tree kept the veranda cool. Doncaster, an expanding community, was located in the East-end of Kingston. Its main avenues ran south to the sea; and some homes closer to the seaside were still under construction. Trees lined the streets of the lush neighbourhood, shading front yards and barking dogs on guard.

When Arthur drove up to the house, two dogs, Rex, a Labrador, and Rover, a German Shepherd mix, lay at the gate. Rex and Rover were pets, as well as security. Arthur said his family deserved more than burglar bars for protection. At the sight of his car, the dogs barked and wagged their tails. He got out, patted them and sent them to the backyard.

Screams echoed from inside the house. "Mommy come!" "Mommy come!" "Yeaaa!" Out dashed Audrey, Maureen and Donovan with Mari limping behind, clearly no match for the race to the gate. As Rose exited the car with the infant tucked in her arms, her clamouring brother and sisters asked, "Make mi see her? Make mi see her?" Audrey carried her mother's baby bag and Arthur took her small suitcase to her room.

Donovan and Maureen tripped over themselves following their mother. They knelt beside the bed and reached for the baby's face. She blocked their hands with hers. "Let mi see oonuh hands?" They stretched their palms up to her. "Dem not clean. Go wash oonuh hands first."

The two scooted to the bathroom and returned flashing water from their hands. "Mommy mi can touch her now?" Maureen asked. "Mi can touch di baby, Mommy please?" She let them touch her covered up body.

"What she name, Mommy?" Donovan asked.

"Marceline, but we goin' call her Marcy."

"Dat's what Granny name," seven-year old Audrey giggled, "she goin' have Granny name."

By her sixth week, the baby was christened Marceline Frances Tomlinson. Marceline was her mother's middle name and her grandmother Mari's, first. The baptism took place at Holy Divinity, a neighbourhood church the family occasionally attended.

For the first few months, Marcy was the new queen of the house. She dethroned Maureen now four, going on five. No long crying for her. At any sign of discomfort, one of her siblings ran to her crib checking for 'wee-wee' or to stick her soother in her mouth. The longest she cried was at six months old. Rose and

Arthur took her to get her ears pierced, like her sisters, at a store downtown. At the first jab she screamed and twisted out of Rose's lap. Her hollering got the attention of a sales clerk who bought ice cream and Rose swiped some across her lips. The cool, sweet, treat pacified her, and the jeweler got the little gold knob in both ears.

Chapter 7

At three years old Marcy still needed continuous care. Her grandmother moved near the family, two streets outside of Doncaster. She brought all sorts of concoctions to cure her. She'd force strange tasting home-remedies down her throat and sapped her face and body with bay rum. If she ran out of bay rum, she looked in the bottom draw of the cabinet where Arthur 'hid' his white rum, to his chagrin.

After a while, her tonsils were taken out and the 'fleshy t'ing' kept in a jar in the medicine chest, behind the Ferrol, Scott's Emulsion and Seven Seas Cod Liver Oil.

Mari never left the children's recovery to pure bush and bottle potions. 'A woman a God', she often had her Bible and was quick to pray over them; practices learned from Billy Graham and Oral Roberts sermons. She mumbled prayers throughout the home, out of Arthur's range. She knew he wasn't against prayers. She had seen him insist his children prayed before meals, but Rose told her he often grumbled, "I just don't want you mada feel she can take over dis house."

Mari visited their home and stayed longer on the days he was gone. On the Sundays he worked, she brought dinner for the family. She hemmed or ironed for Rose, while she sewed. They gossiped as they worked, mostly about Arthur's drinking, often peppered by a disgruntled Mari's comments, "mi know, man" and "damn rum head". If any of the children roamed near, either woman whisked them off, "go play over so" or "not now, we having big-people talk".

Due to Marcy's delicateness, even at four years old, she anchored around the adults inside the house while her siblings played outside. Once, as she knelt beside the sewing machine playing with her bundle of scraps, she saw Mari wagging her finger at Rose. "You hear wat mi saying Rosie, you can't trust him wid you future, so you make sure put up your likkle money."

"Okay Momma, okay!" Rose said, and sighed.

The two women got worked up, and Mari left the house annoyed.

After her grandmother went home, Marcy told her mother she wished they wouldn't quarrel, and "I wish granny didn't have to go."

"She has her own house, Marcy."

"But why she can't live in our house?" Rose explained that they did not have enough room. "But Mommy, we have room," she said, and pointed to the other side of the house that had become available.

"Your fada goin' rent it, baby."

Arthur had given their tenant, Winston, notice when he caught him smoking marijuana at the back of the house. Even though he was pleased that he paid his rent on time, now it didn't matter. His 'reckless behaviour', possessing the illegal substance in his home, was inexcusable. He questioned, "What kinda rahtid man come 'round my pickney dem wid ganja? Him must be lose him mind." He was livid and vowed, "No more old nayga" coming through this gate again. He kept the house empty until Keith and Sonia Palmer and their seven-year old daughter Denise came to view. When they mentioned they were Seventh Day Adventists, although not much of a church man himself, he was overjoyed. He shook Mr. Palmer's hand like it was the Pope moving in. Both high school teachers, he said that's who he wanted, "decent, hardworking people" that would respect "mi house". Arthur always referred to the family home as "mi house", as if Rose didn't have equal vetoing power.

He rented the smaller side to the Palmers, which were two rooms; they turned the front room into a living room – a bathroom and a kitchen. Unlike the Palmers, the bigger side had separate living and dining rooms. Arthur and Rose were in the front bedroom, the bathroom in the middle, and the girls bedroom on the other side. The living room doubled as living and dining. At nights, Donovan laid his bed in the dining room and in the mornings he folded it and put it away to give Rose sewing space.

Marcy slept with her mother and father until she wasn't as sickly. Then she moved into her sisters' room and slept between them, her head at their feet. One night Maureen turned in her sleep and her foot struck Marcy's face; the blow sent her running to her mother's side for a few more weeks.

By this time, Arthur had taken to sleeping in the couch. It had become routine when he came home late that Rose ordered him to take a shower before coming to bed. He'd row and carry on, causing her to lock him out. After knocking the bedroom door in vain, he would stumble to the couch until daylight where she had to wrestle with him to get him up and get ready for work.

One afternoon, a longtime customer brought a couple of dresses for embroidery. Rose, with Marcy at her side, walked the woman to the gate. They stood talking about the old neighbourhood. The woman brought up what Rose had presumed. "You know say we have a new dressmaker in di area."

"Oh, yeah?" Rose answered, as if surprised.

"Yes, a woman start up a likkle business in her house, same like you."

"Dat's why nobody hardly come." Her voice trailed off then she heaved a quiet, "Ah boy" and looked away with a blank stare.

"Mi dear, dem bellyache say you gone too far."

After the woman left and Marcy sat with her mother on the veranda, she saw her face grow long, and the dress she was sewing dropped to her lap and her face lined with worry. She laid down her bundle of cloths and followed her mother's eyes as they searched the sky.

Arthur drove up. Rose's eyes diverted to the dress in her hand and she started sewing again. Marcy ran to him. "Daddy!" He picked her up.

Passing the lawn he said, "Boy, oh boy, not a drop a rain, di grass a beg for likkle water."

Rose answered, "Everyt'ing dry. Mi just here saying to my-self how t'ings slow bad."

He turned and looked askance at her. "You don't see while you at home building your likkle sewing business, di clothes business outta street take off." He said it as if he had observed all along what she had suddenly discovered.

He left to get the garden hose from the backyard. When he returned he said, "All we have to do is put up a open for business sign."

Rose told him,"I don't see not one auto-body, shoemaker or hairdressing sign in nobody yard. Up here is not like when we downtown."

Arthur lowered the hose and stared at his wife. "Rosie," his brows knitted, "A whose yard dis?" She didn't answer. "As far as mi know, dis is our yard, so we free to do whatever we want as long as we not growing ganja… and even den," he persisted, "is still our yard!"

Rose gave up disagreeing with him.

After he knocked the signpost in the lawn, he said, "So di ole world can see," he huffed, twisting the post to face the street, "and know dis yard open for business!"

The sign, erected in the yard on a dead-end street didn't direct much traffic to Rose. Only a couple of domestic helpers from the houses next door were interested. With those two, her steady customers were Mrs. Palmer and Denise, one of Mrs. Palmer's co-workers, and a handful of women from the old neighbourhood.

One day, the dogs barked nonstop in the front yard. Marcy followed her mother to the gate. A towering woman, knees bandaged, asked, "Good afternoon, you're the dressmaker?"

Hope leaped inside Rose, for she knew 'one, one, coco full basket', and every customer counted. She answered with a pitch in her voice, "Yes, Ma'am" and rushed Rex and Rover to the back.

"My name is Mrs. Pendergast, your neighbour at number three." She pointed to the house across from theirs. She lived there for over a year, and they waved hello to each other at times. "I have some dresses and things you see," she pinched her waist, "need some taking in."

Marcy caught herself staring at her strapping neighbour. Her thin, grey hair was in two braids, each rolled in a bun tucked behind her ears. When she glanced down at Marcy, she lowered her head, noticing her two big toes curled onto the toes beside them. She burst out laughing, still looking at Mrs. Prendergast's feet. Rose grabbed her hand. "What is di matter wit' you child?" She giggled uncontrollably until her mother said, "Go sit on di veranda!"

The elderly woman explained that since her husband died she had no one to take her to the dressmaker, and she could not climb the steps of the buses due to her knees. She smiled broadly and told Rose she was glad she was close by. Rose was equally delighted, seeing that she had brought a plastic bag filled with clothes to be altered.

Mrs. Prendergast was the only new customer for a long time and Rose got fed up with the dribble. She knew the 'good old days' was just that - old, gone, never coming back. It was time to find other ways of keeping the family afloat. *Because Arthur money alone can't do it. And what if anything happen to him and him can't work?*

The next day after dinner, when the children had left the table, with trepidation Rose voiced her fears to her husband. They sat at separate ends of the table. He turned sideways in his seat and listened, as if to say, *I know where this is leading.* Before she finished, he turned to face her. "Is because higglers go Miami and bring back cheap t'ings come sell to people who don't see how dem making t'ings worse." His response surprised her, but she didn't interrupt. "And shopkeepers in di mall can't keep up, and run go make knock offs and sell it for ten times di price. You don't see what going on? Everybody a rip off everybody to get rich."

When he paused, she said, "Everybody want foreign t'ings." She took a deep breath and added, "So I t'ink it's time I did somet'ing new."

Arthur refused to hear Rose's point and continued, "Di government should clamp down on how business run in dis country because it's always di legit small man get squeeze." He hissed, and grumbling, left the table.

Chapter 8

As work trickled in, Rose's spirit lifted. For every order she gave God thanks no matter if only to put in two darts. Because every mickle make a muckle, she consoled herself.

Her 'hallelujah' moment materialized when Ms. Brown moved in next door. Within the first week, the young woman noticed her on the veranda doing needlework. She started a conversation across the fence and went to see her embroideries; she had just starched and ironed a batch of doilies. Ms. Brown liked the doilies and bought two sets. As it turned out, she worked at HoChoy's Furniture, one of the largest furniture companies in the city. When Rose heard this, her eyes darted back and forth with possibilities. "Oh, so maybe you can take some to Mr. HoChoy for mi?"

Ms. Brown nodded and said, "Mi can do dat yes", running her hand over the stiff, rosebud-designed, threads.

"If him interested let him know mi can give him a deal."

"Dem nice man, him will like dem."

Ms. Brown took some samples to her employer. As predicted, he saw the quality in them, as well as the benefit to his business.

He agreed to meet with Rose. They met, and Christmas being two months away, he ordered doilies on consignment for the holiday season.

That evening, Arthur came home to a smile on Rose's face that put aside any expectancy of bad news.

Even the children were elated. Although they did not fully understand the extent of the financial gains, they knew it had to do with the amount of gifts their parents were able to provide at Christmas.

On Christmas Eve, the children were in jitters for the big day to follow. They sung along with carols on the radio and, *On the first day of Christmas,* each inserted their desire from Santa. In bed, whispers of the toys hoped for delayed their rest.

In the morning, when they should be awake, they were fast asleep. Rose barged through their door. "Get up, get up, come get ready. Oonuh fada leaving at eight." Luckily, she had combed and tied their hair from overnight, so the two older girls readied themselves while she tidied Marcy.

Rose had made three white dresses; Maureen and Marcy's had a red bow on the front of their waistband and Audrey's, only a red waistband. The younger sisters pointed out their bows to her plain waist band. Audrey boasted, "Because I'm not a baby anymore."

Marcy twirled before the mirror in her frilly dress; it was her first time going to Christmas market.

Filled with the spirit of gifts to come, none of the girls wanted breakfast. After dressing, they rushed to the veranda. Their mother came and ordered them to the table, just as the Palmer family was leaving for Christmas holiday in the country. "Bye, safe travel," she said. "See you in a week." Then she led the girls inside. "Come put somet'ing in oonuh belly."

A few minutes after eight, she and Donovan, with his new fire truck under his arm, waved from the veranda to Arthur and the girls off to Christmas shopping.

As they entered the bustling downtown parade, Audrey and Maureen ran ahead. Marcy pulled from her father's hand and ran after her sisters. "No, no, no, come back here," he shouted. Their eyes lowered to the ground, they scuttled back to him. "Stay close to mi. Audrey hold you sister hand." He held Marcy's and they strolled together.

The streets buzzed with higglers bartering for a sale. "Papa, over here, over here", "Mi can give you a good price, t'ree for two" and "Nice girls, come look at di pretty dollies, pick which one you like". Audrey chose a paper, cut-out doll with clothes, a snake and ladder and Jax sets; Maureen a doll, colouring books and crayons.

For Marcy, the array of dolls and dolly accessories were a buffet of her favourite things. Her eyes zipped back and forth, there was so much to feast on. She pulled her hand from her father's and pointing to Barbie, yelled, "Dat one daddy, dat one. I want dat one!" She also picked a chubby-cheeked baby with bushy hair, a cup and saucer set, and a comb and brush, which she used to brush their hair all the way home.

Arthur bought a kite for Donovan. Before dinner, he took him to the open field at the end of the road where the boys flew their kites. Marcy went with them. Arthur brought the folding chair for her and she sat with her dolls in her lap, watching him teach Donovan to fly his kite.

She never left her dolls behind until the New Year.

Rose and Arthur planned their first family outing to Dunn's River Falls on New Year's Day. Everyone had to wake early for the trip. The children fussed but were excited. Rose finished preparing the food she had started cooking the night before. She packed it, the icebox with drinks, and swimsuits and towels in the trunk of the car. They left home in the chilly hours of the morning for Ohio Rios, St. Ann's. The children shivered in the back seat and muttered one after the other that it was cold.

"Why oonuh never bring oonuh sweater?" Arthur chided. They looked at each other. How were they supposed to know it was going to be so cold at 6:00 in the morning?

"Audrey and Donovan, oonuh roll up di windows," Rose said, and they promptly spun the handles on each side. "Not all di way up. Make likkle fresh air come in."

As daylight ascended and the sun poured in, the children loosened up. Donovan rolled his window down and poked his head outside. Maureen, sitting next to him, shouted, "Donovan take in your head!"

Rose glanced back and offered him some stern advice. "Donovan, watch it! Chicken merry, hawk near."

"Boy, don't let mi have to stop dis car for you," Arthur warned. In a flash Donovan quit fooling. He knew his father would have no trouble finding a piece of switch from the many trees around.

Passing the hills and valleys, the children peered outside the car at the lush countryside, and in agreement they marveled, "Wow" and "Ah".

Further along, Audrey pointed. "Look at the little houses up there on the hill."

"Suppose a storm come and blow them down," Maureen said.

"No. You think them make out of straw?" Audrey answered, in a big sister know-it-all fashion.

"Look at the ones down in the bushes. I wonder how they get down there?" Donovan asked no one in particular, but Audrey answered.

"Roads run down there, you know."

"How you know that?"

"Because I just know," she answered, firmly. As his eldest sister, she expected him to accept her wisdom and he didn't refute.

Going around the corner, the car neared the precipice. Marcy shouted, "We goin' fall! We goin' fall!" and covered her eyes.

"Don't be a big baby," Donovan said.

"Shut up, chatterbox."

"Big baby, big baby."

"Both of you stop it," Rose said.

"This road so winding, though," Audrey said. "I never see a road like this."

"We're on Mount Russo, love."

Approaching Flat Bridge the traffic crawled as the cars crossed the narrow plank one at a time. "What a tiny bridge," Donovan said.

"It look rickety," Maureen added.

"It don't look so strong," Audrey concluded.

Their words made Marcy's heart pound. She slid from Audrey's lap onto the seat. Gripping the vinyl, she imagined the Zephyr Six slipping off the bridge and landing in the water. "Lawd Jesas!" she hollered.

Rose turned in a snap and laughed. "Likkle girl, you sound like you granny." She stretched her hand behind her and rubbed Marcy's knees.

"No, you know what you sound like? Like alligator about to swallow you," Donovan teased, then he thought. "No, more like a shark." He twisted in laughter.

"Stop it, Donovan."

"Boy, for di last time, shut up!" Rose scolded.

Arthur drove up to the bridge; it was his turn to go over. To the family's surprise, the oncoming vehicle entered at the same time. "Wait, what happen to dat man, him don't see you coming?" Rose asked, frowning.

Arthur put his head through the window and yelled, "What happen sah, you don't see mi?"

The children sat on the edge of their seats, only Marcy shrunk into hers. Her heartbeat accelerated. Doomed thoughts swirled: *This is it now. Off the bridge we go. Into the water we sink.* She squeezed her eyes shut until she felt the car speed up and realized they hadn't drowned.

The other driver had reversed and prevented a stand-off, saving Arthur a waste of time when he was eager to get his antsy, loquacious brood to the falls. He announced as he left the bridge, "Alright, we soon reach now." The children sounded a unified sigh and quieted as he gripped the steering wheel with both hands. With doggedness, he conquered each twist and turn, never stopping until he reached Ocho Rios.

"Oonuh wake up, wake up, we reach." Rose leaned over and shook the children who had fallen asleep.

Arthur pulled onto the grounds of Dunn's River Falls and the children clapped and cheered. "Yeah!" One after the other they stepped from the car, shaking their legs. Audrey observed her surroundings. "Not much people are here."

"Dis is why we had to come so early, but wait man, di crowd soon come."

They changed into their swimsuits and joined a line at the foot of the falls, behind two people speaking a different language.

They caught Marcy's interest. She nudged Audrey who stood next to her and gave her a puzzled look. Without looking at her Audrey said, "Foreigners."

"Tourists," Rose said from behind.

Marcy pretended not to watch the tourists, glancing sideways at them. She checked the paleness of their skin and patches of red. Then she looked at her skin, dark, with no redness. She searched her skin some more and saw green lines running through her arms, and glanced back at theirs, noticing they had green lines too. She kept looking for patches of red on her skin, and frustrated she didn't find any,   tapped Audrey on the arm bringing her focus to the couple. "How dem have red skin?"

"That's because them white," she whispered.

"White?"

"White people!" Audrey said, brushing her off.

Audrey's voice drew the woman's attention. She turned her head and smiled, which caused Marcy to stare. *She remind me of my Barbie, skinny and pretty, same long, yellow hair. I want to touch it. I wish I could comb and brush it.*

As she imagined playing in the woman's blonde mane, a burly looking man, the colour of roasted breadfruit, in green swim trunks, disturbed her wishful thinking. "My name is Elroy," he told the group. "I'm your guide today." Elroy instructed them how to climb the falls and punctuated each tip with a smile. "Hold di hand of di person beside you," then pointing to himself, "And everybody follow me." He studied the group. "Di likkle ones should hold on to an adult." Elroy headed the line. "Everybody ready?"

They all echoed a joyous, "Yes!"

Elroy grinned.

The fifth person after Elroy held Arthur's hand. Arthur, leading his family, gripped Marcy's, then she held on to Donovan, then Maureen, Audrey, and Rose at the end. Donovan pretended to rub his nose, letting go of Marcy's hand. His face full of mischief, he watched her scream.

Arthur warned, "Donovan!" and carried Marcy the rest of the way.

When they came off the falls, the beach was mostly vacant. They chose a leafy almond tree and spread the tablecloth and utensils for a picnic. Rose laid out chicken, rice and peas, potato salad and juice. She dished food for Arthur, then the children beginning with Marcy, and served herself last.

Arthur finished his soursop juice, rubbed his bulging belly and said, "Full to di brim!" The children laughed at his 'kangaroo pouch'.

The huge almond tree was their shady retreat and after eating they relaxed to the sea breeze.

By midday, as Rose had said, families and friends flocked the beach. Four young men and women beat another group for the space next to them. One of the men carried a boom-box at his ear. His booming music vexed Rose. She spoke so only the family heard. "Bring him blasted boogie yagga music come make noise in a people head."

"Di beach is not for you alone, you nuh," Arthur reminded her.

"Mi know dat," she snapped, and settled into the reality, although not without giving the young man a have-some-respect look. Not long after, he lowered the volume.

Arthur's solution was, "Let's go for a swim" and the children ran ahead of him. He told the girls to stay near the shores while he took Donovan out for a few laps. They bobbed around until he returned, and took turns floating over his outstretched hands. Donovan tried to impress his sisters with his newly learned skill, swimming to where only his head was seen. They cautioned him, alerting their father who was teaching Marcy how to swim. "Come here mistah!" he called, and Donovan swiftly swam back. "Listen to mi, don't make mi catch you doing dat again, you hear? Stay right here!" His sisters laughed at 'Mr. Showoff' being restricted to shallow waters.

The children grew tired under the boiling sun and everyone returned to shore. They watched two teams compete at volley-ball while finishing up leftovers. In no time they were under the spell of the sea and sun and lay spread out on their towels. When they revived, Arthur and Donovan took another swim and Marcy left to scout for sea shells. "Don't go too far," her mother told her. "We leaving soon."

By the time they rinsed off at the water stand, the sun had gone down. "Hurry up, hurry up," Rose said. "We want to get in off di road before night."

On the country road home, Arthur drove by fruit vendors, including children. They ran alongside the car balancing their produce on their heads. He pulled to the side and they rushed each other to reach the car. "Buy somet'ing from mi, nuh?" They stretched mangoes, oranges and sugarcane inside the car. The least aggressive peddlers stood back, watching and hoping their quiet desperation was seen. In the end, he bought a little of everything.

Soon the three older children drifted off to sleep. Donovan and Audrey sat at the window again. Their heads bumped on the windowpane with every jerk. Maureen, slumped over Donovan, jumped as he jerked, but none of them woke. Only Marcy was awake. She imagined crossing the 'rickety' Flat Bridge and plunging over the precipice on the winding road. Fearful, she leaned on her mother's arm.

Rose felt her head resting against her. She turned. "You not sleeping, baby?" Marcy's drowsy eyes gazed at her and she rubbed her head until she dozed.

But it wasn't long that the children awoke to their parents' anxious voices and saw the car halted on a dark road. "Cho rahtid, man," Arthur cursed. He hissed and hit the steering wheel.

Rose muttered, "What a place to break down." Turning to Arthur she asked, "So what we goin' do now?"

He sighed and exited the car into passing vehicles. The drivers honked at him. "Arta, watch di cars!" she yelled.

He searched the car trunk for anything that might solve or lessen his troubles. A few drivers slowed to see if he needed help. He shook his head and waved them on.

The children stared from the backseat, their faces awash with fear. Marcy asked, "What daddy doing Mommy?"

"Him trying to fix di car," she answered, her eyes following Arthur.

"What's wrong with it?" Maureen asked.

"I don't know, it look like one of di light burn out."

Arthur returned to the car with the flashlight and held it out the window. "You have to flood di road wid di light," he said, demonstrating Rose's part in getting the family off the dark corner of the hill.

The children leaned forward, all eyes on their father inching around narrow, hilly precipice to descend the country road. Rose held the flashlight like an Olympian carrying a torch, safe and steady, until the streetlights took over, and everyone sighed. For the rest of the way Arthur steered his weary family home without further incident.

After the long, eventful excursion, the children turned down supper, and under their mother's watchful eyes, brushed their teeth and tumbled into bed.

It was less than an hour into sleep that the girls awoke to loud voices from their parents' room. Startled, they sat up in bed and listened.

"You don't see di problem we have on di road tonight?"

"Of course I see it. But I don't know why you can't just fix di light?"

"Is not just di light, di whole t'ing a bruk down."

"Well, we can't take on no big expense right now, not when di house not finish paying for. And don't forget you suppose to carry dem children down a Bata to get new shoes."

"I don't forget," he said, brushing her off.

"And wit' all di expenses, remember you not getting di same pay no more."

"Yeah man, yeah man, bring dat up."

"But it's true. And anyt'ing can happen to any one of di children and hospital no cheap."

"Woman! Keep you frigging money!"

Although they had a joint account, they needed both signatures to access the funds. This infuriated Arthur. But this was the only arrangement Rose would agree to, considering the coaxing from Mari.

Arthur fumed and left the house, slamming the door behind him.

After he was gone the girls went back to sleep, although not for long. He returned home drunk.

His anger thundered through the house and frightened them from sleep. In a daze, they slid out of bed and peeped at him pounding his bedroom door. Rose answered, "Arta, you not coming in dis room with no liquor smell tonight."

"Open di damn door!"

"Go back where you coming from."

"Rose, mi say open di door now!"

Donovan ran to his sisters' room, his eyes bulging from fright. The four siblings watched their father curse and hit the door until he collapsed to the floor. Donovan ran to help him up, and his sisters followed. Rose heard them at the door and came out. She held one of Arthur's arms and told Donovan to hold the other. They drew him on the floor into the living room and left him on the rug to sleep.

Chapter 9

Rose worked nonstop between sewing clothes for her customers and decorating doilies for the furniture store. Once the children were off to school, she anchored down at the machine with Marcy pretend-sewing nearby. When she got up to cook, or do chores around the house, Marcy skipped along. At lunch time, she often let her sit in her lap and they ate from the same plate. When the day got too hot and the breeze from the fan wasn't cool enough, Rose took a shower and bathed Marcy right after. She sat on a cushion with her back against the door, mending clothes, while watching her play with her dolls in the tub. She taught her to spell words like rag, door and floor. One day Marcy surprised her by remembering how to spell 'bubble bath'.

"Gal, you have a good head," she praised her, "and you outgrow you sickness, you ready for school now."

Rose enrolled Marcy, age five and a half, at the Holy Divinity Preparatory School, the school Donovan attended two blocks from home. She walked her and Donovan to school, and also Denise Palmer, as she attended the same school. Rose picked up all three after school and Denise stayed with them until her parents came from work.

One afternoon Rose was cooking dinner and she needed Donovan to get a pepper off the tree. She called, "Donovan come here... Donovan" and "Where are you boy?" But no answer from Donovan. She called again from the kitchen door, "Donovan! I wonder where dat boy is?"

Marcy sat on the floor outside the kitchen, practicing long-hand writing in her exercise book. Rose asked, "Marcy, you know where your brother is?"

"No, Mommy," she answered, without raising her head.

Rose decided to get the pepper herself and to check if Donovan might be with Rex and Rover. Normally, he played with the pets in the yard after school because his father said, "Dogs don't belong in di house no matter how much they're loved". So he romped with the dogs outside, and refilled their water and corn-meal codfish mix that his father made before going to work.

Donovan was not with the animals. Rose wondered where he was as she carried on to the tree. The pepper tree was next to the fence, by the Palmers' side of the house. When she bent the corner, her eyes caught sight of the Palmers' bedroom window. She could not believe what she saw happening inside. For a few seconds, she stood staring, her mouth ajar, then these words sprung out, "Donovan and Denise, what di two of you doing?"

Marcy heard her mother's shout. She looked up in time to see Donovan speeding from the Palmers' room, hauling his pants over his bottom. Out of breath, he squatted on the floor next to her, avoiding her gaze. Then he picked up her pencil, his hands shaking as he examined it like he had never seen a lead pencil in his life. Marcy watched him, wondering what he had done that nearly caused their mother a heart attack. Whatever it was, it had to be bad, she thought, as her brother's eyes bulged from his head same as his tadpole's from its bottle.

On her way back to the kitchen, Rose conked Donovan on his head and said, "You wait 'til you fada come tonight."

Marcy laughed, showing no mercy for her brother. Afterward, she listened for Audrey and Maureen to come through the door to give them the score. She kept peeking at the clock on the living room wall, counting down to 4 p.m. She knew it took her sisters roughly half-hour to get from downtown after school dismissed.

When she heard the knob turn on the front door, she sprang off the floor and ran to meet them. "Stop running in di house, Marcy," her mother called out. She slowed and skipped instead.

"Something smells nice," Audrey said, sniffing the air as she passed her in the living room. The beef soup spices saturated the house, and her mouth watered and her tummy rumbled. "What's for dinner, Mommy?" she asked.

"Go wash your hands," her mother replied from her room.

"Wait, wait, wait," Marcy said, catching up to her sisters. Walking backwards, facing them, she delivered her news. "Donovan goin' get beating when daddy come home tonight!" At the thought of him being flogged, she smiled, her eyes closed, and added, "Mommy soaking daddy belt now."

"Marcy! Who give you news to carry?" her mother asked.

She clasped her lips in shame. But that did not stop Audrey and Maureen from pursuing. "Why?" Audrey asked, as she sat on the bed, taking off her shoes and socks.

"What him do?" Maureen queried.

"Mommy say is somet'ing wit' Denise," Marcy whispered.

There were two duties their father held that made them run and hide: one was with the belt and the other was aloe vera juice.

He'd pick a piece from the plant in the backyard and squeeze droplets down their throats. Both he claimed were for their betterment.

The belt though, brought the most fear. Her sisters stared at each other, their mouths wide open. They changed out of their uniforms and rushed to their mother's room. They circled her and Audrey asked, "Mommy, what Donovan did today?" Rose turned to look at Marcy and she dodged behind Audrey. Rose shook her head. Meantime, a car screeched at the gate. She brushed the curtains aside and they peeked through the window. They watched Mr. Jones from the fire station, with one hand under Arthur's arm helping him into the yard. By the time Mr. Jones brought Arthur to the veranda, Rose was there to open the front door. She pointed to the couch and he lay him down. The children hovered in shock. Donovan, sure to be spared a beating, knelt beside him and took off his shoes.

"Lord Jesus Arta, what happen?" she asked, leaning over him. He barely lifted his head.

"Him fall down at di station, Ma'am," Mr. Jones answered.

"How you mean fall down?"

"Him drop coming off di pole."

"How dat?"

"We not sure. Him say di pole was slippery." His slanted mouth betrayed belief. "Him must be lose him grip."

She thanked him for bringing Arthur home as he headed to the door. He paused and said, "Somebody will bring his car tomorrow."

Rose eased Arthur out of his bloody shirt and put a cushion under his head. "You want some soup?" He shook his head slowly.

The children sat on the floor by the couch. They stared and asked if it hurt and how they could help. He didn't speak, just nodded and shook his head.

"Children let your fada rest. Come have you dinner." They said they weren't hungry and she gave them more time with him.

They were happy to be with their father, even if not in the best state. He was home with them before dark and that mattered.

Later that evening, Mari stopped by the house after work. She entered the home and saw Arthur laying on the couch looking weak and pathetic. Anger, fear, worry and confirmation froze her lips in place. She made no comment except to Rose. "You have any Epsom salt?" Rose did, and set a bath. The two women raised him off the couch and helped him to the bathroom. Afterward, Rose fed him soup and he went to bed.

As they lay in bed, Rose tried to find out what happened. "How you fall down Arta?" An answer she deduced, but not one she wanted to take for granted. Arthur sulked and turned to face the other way.

The next day he stayed in bed most of the day, getting up for more soup and a shower. And before the children came from school, he left.

This became a habit. He left for work and returned when everybody had gone to bed. Even on his day off, he left early and came home late.

One afternoon, while Mari sat with Rose as she sewed on the veranda, Audrey, Maureen and Marcy were in the living room watching television. As if the grownups had forgotten the girls were close by, they discussed 'di hell' Rose was undergoing with Arthur. "You know him not head driver no more?"

"What?" Mari leaned closer. "Dem bump him?"

"It seems so," Rose said, her eyes on the dress in her hand.

"So you know wat goin' happen next," Mari said.

"Dem might fire him." Rose sighed. "Ah, boy."

"My God. Rose, wat oonuh goin' do?"

"I don't know, Momma. I talk to him 'til I blue," she said, pulling the needle through the hem of the dress.

"I hope you realize you can't depend on him."

Rose shook her head. "I don't know what goin' happen to Arta."

"No worry 'bout Arta, worry 'bout you and di pickney dem, for at dis rate oonuh sure to end up a wokhouse." She breathed heavily. "For your money alone can't carry oonuh."

"You don't hear di half." Mari's eyes narrowed, fixed on Rose. "Mr. Palmer give notice," she said, not looking at Mari.

"Same t'ing, mi say, I bet you is 'cause a Arta."

"Could be, but Sonia pregnant and dem want a bigger place."

"Lawd help oonuh." Mari shook her head and looked to the tiles under her feet.

Rose ran out of the variegated orange thread she needed to complete the embroidery on the dress and the conversation took a turn. The girls faced each other with uncertainty. Marcy, more than her sisters, was not fully aware, but sensed the family was in trouble.

Audrey and Maureen muttered in bed about ending up in the poorhouse, causing Marcy more anxiety. She eventually fell asleep to thoughts of doom. When she heard beating on the door, she thought she was dreaming of life in the 'wokhouse'. But what jolted her from sleep was her father rattling the bathroom door. Her mother had locked herself in there and he was threatening to break it down. "Open di door, Rosie!" he demanded. "Open di blasted door!"

Arthur brought the sheet he pulled off the bed, spread it at the bathroom door and told his wife he was going to stay there until she came out. Rose responded that she was not coming out as long as he was there. This angered him more, and he cursed and pounded the door harder. He became so enraged, he vomited.

Rose heard him throw up at the door and opened it. "Oh my Lord," she said, stepping over him.

The children came from hiding in their room. They looked sad at the sight of their father lying in his spew. Maureen cupped her face and cried, triggering Marcy's tears.

Rose told them to get back. She bent over him. "Get up, Arta, get up." He did not move. She went to plug the bathtub and let the water run. Then she called Donovan. "Come, help mi get you fada in di tub." The other children grabbed a hand or a foot. "Not you Marcy, stay out di way."

As Rose scraped the soiled sheets off the floor, she sent the children to bed. "Go now, oonuh have school in di morning."

The girls tossed and turned, unable to sleep. They grumbled among themselves about the disturbance, especially Audrey, who had begun high school that year. "It's not mommy's fault anyway," she said, comforting herself and her sisters.

Every second or third night the children awoke to their father's violent uproar.

This night, however, while they slept, it was their mother's scream that woke them. They sat up in bed yawning and rubbing their eyes when she ran to their room in a panic, quickly shutting the door behind her. They watched her spin in the dark. "Oh my God, oh my God." She picked up a shoe and crouched in the corner.

Marcy started crying, then her sisters. Audrey cried out, "I can't take this no more, I can't take it!" Donovan woke and came to the room terrified.

Rose heard Arthur's feet approaching the door. "Rosie, you see how you wake up di pickney dem? Come outta dem room."

She rushed to the door and slammed it, but it had no key to lock him out. He pushed the door and barged in. "Come outta di pickney dem room and come in a your bed!"

As if she had had enough, Rose screamed, "Lawd God, Arta, what you want wit' mi? What you want wit' mi Arta?"

He moved towards her and she threw the shoe at him. It missed. She tried to run. He grabbed her by the hair and punched her in the head. "Is what you a do, fight mi? A mad you a get mad?"

Audrey stepped in front of him. "Leave her alone, Daddy. Leave mommy alone."

"Shut you mouth and go to you bed."

Still holding her hair, he shoved her into their room. Audrey followed them. He turned to her. "You hear mi, go!" She made one step back, staring daringly at him. He came at her and she bolted into the hallway with the others. He stood at his bedroom door and ordered them to go to bed now.

They dragged themselves to bed and cried as they listened to their mother's plea, "Woi! Woi! Don't kill mi Arta, do, don't kill mi", until they fell asleep.

The next morning the children woke up late for school. Realizing their mother had not come to wake them, they went to her room. Their father had left. "Oh God, Mommy," Audrey moaned, seeing her mother's bruised forehead and the marks on her arms and legs. They sobbed and climbed on the bed with her.

Rose eased herself onto her elbows. "Oonuh go get ready for school." Her voice was hoarse.

"No Mommy, I not leaving you," Audrey said through tears.

"I don't want oonuh miss school," she insisted.

No matter what Rose said, her children wouldn't leave her side.

When she tried to push herself out of bed, Audrey took action. "Lie down Mommy, lie down." She made her a cup of black coffee, brought it in a tray and laid it beside her on the bed. Following their mother's instructions, she and Maureen prepared scrambled eggs, toast and tea for the four of them, and later, she warmed up the leftovers for dinner.

Mari stopped by the house after work, going straight to Rose's room. She was tired with shopping bags in both hands, and took the closest seat. Seeing the children in bed with Rose, she joked, "Any space on di bed for mi?" She had not seen her daughter's bruises yet. When Rose raised her head to greet her, shock replaced her grin. "Rosie, what do you?" Her legs weakened and she sunk to the bed. "My Lawd, is what happen to you?" Her chest heaved and her eyes watered. She drew closer, examining her welts. "Talk to mi Rosie. Is Arta do dis?"

Although Mari knew Arthur could 'act like a drunken fool', this beating was unacceptable, even from a drunkard, and one she would not expect her daughter to tolerate. What Mari didn't know, was that Rose hid the physical side of their conflicts for fear she would've insisted she leave him. Not that she wouldn't. But as Mari often told her, "Hen wid chicken can't climb wall", and Rose had four.

Mari raised Rose's chin. "Jesus Rosie." She inspected her face. "Dat rahtid serpent, you see." Temper swelled the veins in her neck.

The children went to the living room to watch television, giving Rose and Mari time to themselves. The hallway separated the living room from their mother's room. Audrey turned down the volume and her ears on full pitch to eavesdrop on the adults. When she couldn't hear, she left the couch and sat on the floor with her ears on the wall. Even with the television on low, and her ears an antenna, she picked up fuzzy vocal signals from Rose's room.

As Mari collected her bags to leave, Audrey heard her footsteps and dashed to the couch. Passing the children in the living room, she took gizzada and coconut cake from her bag and handing it to them, quietly said, "Oonuh look out for oonuh mada, you hear?"

Not long after Mari left, Arthur came home, a surprise to everyone as the sun had not yet gone down. Going by he mumbled a greeting. "Good evening," they replied, as if in mourning and sat up in their seats. He said he brought ice cream, which was another surprise, as that was reserved for birthdays. He dished the frozen dessert in bowls and called them to the table. They weren't that hungry as they had eaten supper and gobbled up the treat from Mari. Still, it was ice cream. They ate in silence.

When he filled a bowl of ice cream and took it to Rose, Audrey's curiosity was again alerted. She hastened to the living room, her siblings behind her. Maureen, Donovan and Marcy stood at the entrance of the hallway. They watched Audrey walk back and forth to the bathroom, glancing at her parents' room each time. Lucky for her, the door was wide open.

Donovan asked, "You see anything?"

"Yeah, him sitting on the bed beside mommy."

"I'm going to look." Donovan ran to the bathroom and back.

"What you see?" she asked.

"I couldn't see anything."

"Then how you must see if you run?" she lectured him. He frowned and went to sit beside Maureen on the couch.

Audrey and Marcy knelt behind the door, straining to hear their parents. But nothing was being said, because Rose ignored

Arthur and the bowl of ice cream he had placed between them on the bed.

Since his attempt to redeem himself failed, he got up to leave. The two spies kneeling beside the wall signaled to their two cohorts on the couch that their father was coming, and all of them ran to the table, tumbling the chairs on the floor. He entered the dining area with his head hung, the bowl of watery ice cream in his hand. Oblivious, or pretending not to notice their shenanigans, he went to the kitchen, dropped the bowl of uneaten ice cream in the sink and hissed on his way out.

Before the children could return to the television, he grunted that it was time to go to bed. They were upset and murmured that bedtime wasn't for another hour. He heard them and said, "Well, pick up a book." They pouted behind his back on the way to their room.

"Audrey, you can tell us Brother Anancy story?" Donovan asked, following the girls. "Me not ready to go sleep yet."

"No Donovan." Audrey shook her head. "I'm not in the mood for no Anancy jokes now. Just go to your bed." As they prepared for bed, Audrey packed three shoe boxes with shoes against the door to keep it open 'just in case of anything'. But instead of sounds of ruckus, the soothing sound of Otis Redding's *When a Man Loves a Woman* flowed through the house.

It was rare to hear records playing in their house of late. When Arthur first bought the record player he played it for months; now, he only did mostly at Christmas. He sat in the living room by himself, listening to love songs.

He was the daddy they missed, who came home with treats before their bedtime.

One evening he brought home peppered shrimp and crab. "Daddy, these taste nice," Donovan said, crunching the shells.

His sisters concurred, except Marcy. The spicy seafood nauseated her with just one bite; even the smell made her queasy.

"Maybe you allergic to shell fish," he told her, and her mother fixed her mint tea and tucked her in bed.

Arthur was good all week, but regardless, the children restrained the impulse to run and jump on him at first sight. They watched him first, checking his mood. If he played his music in the living room, the girls wandered to their room and Donovan played outside. He noticed their coolness and after a few times of them leaving the room as he walked in, one Saturday he cornered them. As he entered the living room, they picked up their books to leave. He said, all cheery, "Sit down, where oonuh going?" and put on a record. "Who know dis one?" he joked, giving them a lesson on each song.

He advanced his improvisation by suggesting a dance competition and two pence for anyone who took the challenge. The children leaped off the couch. "Me Daddy!" and "Give me!" He told them they had to earn it and put on one of his ska songs. They shook and shimmied, tripping into each other and the center table. Rose yelled from her room, "Not in di house!" They wiggled and jived to the veranda. There he offered 'thruppence' to whomever 'break a leg'.

The sound of fun and laughter drew Rose to the veranda. She smiled, their happiness warmed her heart. Mari stopped by in the midst of the excitement; she stayed at the gate. She wasn't pleased and showed it. She never waved, nor said 'howdy' to Arthur, neither did he acknowledge her. Rose met her at the gate and they talked in the front yard.

The competition waned as the children grew tired. Arthur reached into his pocket. "Alright, alright, everybody win." He dropped a couple of coins in their hands. Then they ran off to their mother and grandmother. He went inside, got a beer, changed the record to Otis Redding, and sat alone in the living room.

Arthur's rebound lasted under two weeks.

One afternoon Rose went to visit Cynthia, her longtime friend. She saw to it the children bathed and had their dinner before leaving, warning, "Stay inside, or else!" Their father wasn't home, so she asked the Palmers to keep an eye on them.

He returned sooner than expected. Luckily, the children were where they should be - inside the house. Donovan and Marcy lay on the rug close to the television. As Arthur passed he said, "Mi don't have money to buy eyeglasses." He believed sitting close to the TV caused blindness. "So get up and sit in di chair." He shot a warning glance at Audrey and Maureen sitting with their feet on the couch; they quickly straightened up. Watching television in the daytime was against his rules; after supper and homework, for two hours maximum. He believed reading a book, always being in a book was what would take them far in life. Playing and watching TV were low on his list of priorities. If it weren't for their mother there wouldn't be one in the house. So, it was their 'laying around idle watching TV' that caught his attention. "Oonuh don't have anyt'ing to do?" Audrey got up and turned the television off. He continued walking through the house, then suddenly turned back to the living room. "Children, where oonuh mada?" No one answered. His face grim, he asked again.

This time Audrey answered. "She went to Ms. Cynthia, Daddy. She said she soon come back."

"From what time she leave?"

"Ahm, Ahm," Audrey stuttered.

No one knew the exact time Rose left. She said she'd be back soon, and that was that. Only, that was not good enough for Arthur. He wanted a full run down of her activities. The children searched each other's eyes for answers, and finding none, they said nothing.

"Children, don't get mi rahtid mad in here today. Somebody answer mi!" His spit sprayed.

Both Donovan and Audrey started speaking at once, and Donovan stopped and let Audrey carry on. She stood up. "Maybe about… about half hour to an hour, Daddy." Her voice quivered.

"How she gone and leave oonuh alone in di house? What if I never come home?"

"No Daddy, Mrs. Palmer is here."

"Don't tell mi nutting 'bout Mrs. Palmer!" he shouted. "Mrs. Palmer is oonuh mada?"

Audrey hung her head, avoiding his spitfire eyes. He stormed out the living room mumbling, "Your mada act like it's she alone live in dis house. Well, we goin' see when she come!" Terrified, they stared at one another, not making a move.

Arthur walked through the house grumbling, "I wonder where she really gone?" and minutes after, said, "I soon come."

The children sat still, too scared to turn the television on. Mrs. Palmer came over. "I thought I heard oonuh father. Him gone already?" They nodded. She looked them up and down. "What you children up to? How oonuh so quiet?" Her eyes circled the room on her way out.

Not long after, a car stopped at the gate. They thought it was their father, so no one got up. "Look is who that, Marcy," Audrey said.

She peeped through the window. "Is mommy! Is mommy!" she screamed, and they raced to the gate.

Their mother stepped from the back of a car. Ms. Cynthia was in the front with her friend, the driver. Rose leaned in the window to talk to Cynthia. Marcy called, "Mommy come." She wanted her mother to hurry in before her father returned. As Rose waved goodbye, Audrey opened the gate and they ran and latched onto her. "Oh Lord, oonuh really miss mi." Rose smiled at her brood clinging to her side. "Everyt'ing okay?"

"Yes mommy, but-"

"But what? What oonuh do now?" she asked, her tone cheery.

"Nothing Mommy," Donovan replied.

"Mrs. Palmer goin' give mi bad news?"

They walked with her to her room, each talking over the other to tell her about their father's behaviour. It wasn't but a few minutes Rose was in the house changing her clothes that he returned. "Rosie! Rosie!" He called coming into the house.

She met him in the hallway, buttoning her house dress. "Yes, Arta?"

He charged at her with his hand in the air. "Hey Rosie, a which man carry you home?" He landed a blow to the side of her head. "Is man you have?"

"Jesus, Arta!" Rose screamed, holding her head. In tears, she tried to convince him. "Arta, it's Cynthia and her friend drop mi home. You know that she live far."

He raised his hand to hit her again, and this time she blocked it with her hand. The children screamed for him to stop. When he hit her another time, ruckus broke out in the house. Audrey and Donovan grabbed cushions and hit him, and Maureen and Marcy held on to his shirt, pulling him away.

Mr. and Mrs. Palmer heard the fracas and rushed over. Mr. Palmer told him, "Mr. Tomlinson, stop it! You can't do this to your wife." He forced between them. "Have mercy man, watch how you making your children cry. You can't do this to your family, man." He blocked him from Rose. His wife helped her to the chair and went for ice in a towel for her face.

Arthur ranted that Rose had gone out all day with a man. "Dat is a lie, Arta, I told you yesterday I goin' look for mi friend," Rose said, through swollen lips.

"Den why she never come in and say good evening or somet'ing?"

"But you wasn't here Arta."

"She wouldn't know dat 'til she come in."

"Arta, you not making sense." Rose pressed the cold towel to her face.

"Yeah man, mi no have no sense, mi no have nooo sense. But you new man have sense?" he said, and stepped towards her.

The children yelled for him to stop. Mr. Palmer reminded him, "Regardless of how you see the situation, there is no proof, so give your wife the benefit of the doubt."

Arthur shrugged, then hissed and left the room.

The couple waited with Rose until he drove off. Mrs. Palmer asked, "You think you'll be all right now?" She nodded, and thanked them for being there at that crucial moment.

"Don't be afraid to call us," Mr. Palmer said. She nodded, shifting the ice-packed towel on her face.

Mrs. Palmer added, "We mean it, Rosie."

Once Rose seemed less pained, the children went to their room. Audrey stacked the shoe boxes at the door. They watched and listened, none of them could sleep. Marcy huddled between her sisters and said, "Me feel so 'fraid."

"Me feel shame, the people them have to know our business."

"I don't care," Audrey said. "At least them help mommy. What if them wasn't here?"

"You're right," she answered, softly.

"Next time is the broom I goin' use on him." They chuckled.

Marcy fell asleep with a picture in her head of Audrey knocking sense into their father with the broom.

Around midnight she jumped out of her sleep, not to Audrey going after him, but to their mother, wailing. "Help!" "Murder!" "Somebody help me!" She and her sisters scurried out of bed. Donovan met them at their parents' door. The four of them banged on the door, calling, "Mommy! Mommy!"

"Go sleep!" Arthur answered.

"Help! Murder!"

"Shut up!" He hit her.

The children screamed, kicked and pounded the door. Mr. and Mrs. Palmer came running. The dogs barked at Ms. Brown at the fence. "Rose you alright?" she asked.

Arthur yelled, "Move away from mi property and mind you own business." His voice wobbled.

"Mr. Tomlinson," Mr. Palmer said. "Mr. Tomlinson, open the door."

"I say, oonuh leave mi!"

"Mr. Tomlinson, this is serious what you doing, man."

Arthur hissed. He came to the door and stuck his head out, and as he did, Rose pushed passed him, tearing the door wide open. He grabbed at her, but she was too swift for him. She fled in only her underwear to the bathroom.

"Mr. Tomlinson, what happen now?" Mr. Palmer asked, with a frown.

"Just go back to you house, dis is between mi and mi wife."

"I don't mean to get in your business, but your wife bawling for help and murder." Mr. Palmer was annoyed at sounding like a broken record.

Arthur shook his head as if he too was tired of repeating himself. He pointed, "Please, go back to you house and leave mi and my family."

"No, don't leave, him want to kill me," Rose said, through the closed door.

"Mr. Tomlinson, you can't see you causing them grief."

Arthur hissed.

Mrs. Palmer put her head to the door. "You all right Rosie?"

Arthur shoved Mrs. Palmer to the side and kicked the bathroom door. "Rosie, you a mi wife, and I want my wife tonight!" He shook the door knob and demanded she come out. She kept quiet. He continued shaking the door. Then he cried out, "Rosie, you a mi wife, you a mi wife Rosie, and I want you in di bed, I want you in di bed Rosie." He shook and shook the knob. Still no response from her. Everyone stood around him just watching. Bracing his forehead on the door, he said, "I love you Rosie, I love you, you's mi wife." Tears ran down his face as he cried his heart out to her.

He bawled until he dropped to the floor, half naked in his underpants. The Palmers fought to get him off the floor and into bed. Audrey whispered through the door that he was gone. Rose came out the bathroom. She stood at their bedroom door with her children surrounding her. She observed his inebriated body sprawled across the bed, his snores vibrating through the room.

Mr. and Mrs. Palmer quietly returned to their house, the children to their room, and Rose went to sleep on the couch.

The following day, Arthur slept most of the morning, showered, then left. Mari appeared right after he was gone. She passed Marcy playing with her dolls on the veranda. "Granny!"

"Not now baby."

Audrey and Maureen were doing house chores when she slipped by them to their mother's room. Audrey put the broom down and Maureen stopped dusting. They looked at each other. It was unusual for their grandmother to be there midday on a Saturday, and operating so sneakingly. Audrey tiptoed to their mother's partially open room and peeped through the crease in the door. Her sisters crept up beside her and she ushered them to the hallway.

"What you see?" Marcy asked.

"Shh. Talk soft."

"What you see?" she whispered.

"Mommy put some things in a bag."

"What things?

"Things from her paper draw, you know, her important documents." Marcy had no idea what documents were, but knew 'important'.

Mari slipped out as she slipped in, in secrecy, setting the girls' minds on overdrive.

Maureen and Marcy followed Audrey to their mother's room. They could tell she had lots on her mind; she never looked up when they entered. Her eyes and hands moved swiftly. She folded and packed customers' clothes, wrote their names on a piece of paper and pinned it on a package. She packed doilies in a box marked HoChoy's. "Children get up off di floor" was all she said going by, her hands filled with the box and packages. She took the items to the girls' room and hid them in the corner. "Don't touch!" she warned her daughters at her heels.

The next day, she gave the box to Ms. Brown to take to the furniture store, and subsequent days, the owners came to get their package of clothing. She didn't take new orders, just finished the ones she had started.

At the end of the week, the Palmers had prepared for moving. And on Friday evening, they brought home fried fish and bammy for a little celebration. Everybody was home except Arthur. They waited for him, and after an hour Rose said she doubted he'd be coming home soon, so they carried on.

Rose set chairs in the backyard, Mr. Palmer put on his taped music, and after they ate, the children frolicked while the adults chatted.

Sharing a last meal for the two families was like ingesting bitter herbs, good for you, yet difficult to swallow. They lamented on losing each other. "Remember we'll only be two streets away," Mrs. Palmer said, making light of the heavy mood. She and her husband had bought a small three-bedroom house in the same neighbourhood, and they had a helper coming in from the country for the new baby. "We're just a stone's throw away. And you and Donovan will still see Denise at school," she told Marcy.

"Only for a few more months, Mommy," Denise said, as she had passed her common entrance for high school.

Mrs. Palmer wrapped a fish and bammy for Arthur who hadn't come home at the time they were turning in. "Put this up for Arthur," she said handing it to Rose.

After Rose closed the door, she turned to the children. "Well..." She sighed and continued, "All good t'ings must end, and all good friends soon part."

The next day was moving day for their longtime tenants, their 'saviour', as Rose called them. It started grim for the girls.

Marcy said, "It feel like a rainy day" even though the sun streamed in through the window. "I don't want to get up today." She lay on her side, her hands propping her head. Maureen had the covers drawn over her head.

Audrey gazed at the ceiling. "What we going to do after them leave?"

"I wish we could go with them," Marcy said.

"Yeah, and leave daddy."

When they heard the truck rolling to the gate they hurried to the veranda. Rose went as the truck backed in. The reality of their leaving hit her. She leaned against the wall looking as helpless as her children. As the men moved the furniture to the truck, her heart tugged with each piece. When they packed the last one, Mr. and Mrs. Palmer and Denise stopped on the veranda to say goodbye. Rose and the children walked them to the gate. The families hugged each other and fought back tears. Marcy cried, remembering her mother's words, 'good friends soon part'.

Mr. Palmer lifted her. "Marcy", he wiped her face with his hand, "Don't cry, we'll come and visit, okay?" She nodded and hugged his neck. He kissed her cheek. "Good girl."

Arthur drove up as the drivers finished loading. He came over quickly. "I want to wish you and you family all di best, man." He shook Mr. Palmer's hand.

"Thank you Mr. Tomlinson, you too."

He said goodbye to Mrs. Palmer and Denise, and got in his car and left.

They waved goodbye and the dogs barked as the truck pulled away. When the truck turned from their sight, Marcy's eyes watered and she held onto her mother's hand. Rose looked at her last child, her 'wash belly', and bit her lip, forcing back tears. She stroked her little face, wiped her eyes and pulled her close. She then let out a long sigh.

"Oh fada God."

Chapter 10

All day, Marcy wondered who their next tenant might be and how soon they would come. At night she prayed: Dear God, please send another saviour soon.

Deep in sleep, she heard a voice. *Answer to my prayers*? It took a moment as the voice got louder for her to recognize it wasn't God answering, it was her father insisting that her mother, "Come outta mi house woman! Leave right now, right now!" She sat up, trembling. Her sisters stirred from sleep, sat up as well. They listened. Marcy thought, *Why mommy not answering? Why she not telling him she not leaving? I wonder if him do something to her? I wonder if...I wonder if him strangle her?* Terrified, she sprung off the bed and said, "Something happen to mommy."

"Stop it, Marcy, don't say that," Audrey said, her face equally disturbed.

Donovan burst into the room. "What happen now?"

"Daddy and him foolishness. Him telling mommy to leave."

They gathered outside their parents' bedroom, listening to sounds of feet shifting and hangers clanging on the floor. "Stop flinging mi clothes on di ground, Arta."

"Mommy! Mommy! Mommy!" Marcy called, and they thumped the door.

Rose opened it and they swarmed her. Her clothes were scattered on the floor. They helped her gather and put them in the open suitcase next to her. Arthur stood over them, glaring. He said to the children, "What oonuh doing in here, go to oonuh room!"

Rose got between him and them. "If mi leaving, my children coming wit' mi!"

"You must be flipping mad! My pickney dem not leaving here." Another word, and the veins in his neck would burst.

Marcy felt dizzy at the thought of living with him and not her mother. She gripped her mother's hand.

"Make mi see how long you can last widout mi," Arthur said with a smirk and backed away.

Rose warned, "Arta, every dog have him day." She knew his time would come.

He called Marcy. "Come over here likkle girl."

"No Daddy, I want to go wit' mommy!" she yelled, clutching her mother's hand tighter. He scowled. His knitted brows were a silent reprimand; she lowered her eyes.

Audrey tearfully said, "Daddy, don't let mommy leave, please, Daddy." She wiped her eyes. "If mommy going, I going with her."

"None of you going anywhere!" He shoved them out the door and locked it.

They cried and kicked the door. He opened it with his belt in hand. Shaking it, he said, "Oonuh want somet'ing to cry for?" He slapped the wall with the belt. "I will give oonuh somet'ing to cry for." He flicked the leather strap in the air and made after them. They cried and ran to their room.

Donovan stayed with his sisters. They couldn't sleep; they listened out for their mother.

Before long, they heard the veranda gate open then close. The dogs whined, and the front gate opened then closed. They knew then that she was gone. And like the stray cats under their window, they bawled like babies into the night.

Marcy cried until her eyes were sore. She doubted she would live to see morning. But she survived, along with her brother and sisters. She lay staring at the beige, finger-smudged wall, wishing her mother's leaving was a dream. Neither she nor the others wanted to leave the room, to face the truth. Audrey, whom her siblings depended on, was staring at the light bulb above her, her right leg shaking as she seethed.

"I bet mommy out there. How much you want to bet?" Donovan said, trying to cheer his sisters.

"Audrey, can you go check?" Marcy nudged her big sister.

Without saying a word, Audrey rolled off the bed, flung the door open and her brother and sisters lined up behind her. She led them to their parents' room, peeped in, then turned and shook her head. Disappointment dashed their hopes; loss weighed down their faces. Their little hearts were broken. They dragged on. Marcy swallowed the lump settling and willed her feet to keep up. Nearing the kitchen, the aroma of soup greeted them. They looked at each other; their father never cooked. The possibility of hope realized broke a smile on Marcy's face. *Could it be?* Audrey motioned them to keep coming. Marcy's heart sang. *It must be.* They crept further and rounded the corner of the kitchen. "Mommy!" "Mommy!" "Mommy!" Mommy!" They shouted and jumped all over her.

"Shhh." Rose put her finger to her lips. "Oonuh keep quiet."

Marcy, swinging her mother's hand, almost in tears, whispered, "Mommy, please don't leave again."

"No baby, when mommy leave again, you coming." She pinched her cheek. "What time oonuh fada leave?" They said they didn't know. Audrey told her she kept their door shut.

"I don't t'ink him gone far, so I not staying long."

"Mommy, you leaving again?" Donovan asked.

"No, don't leave again, Mommy," Audrey said.

"I coming back for oonuh later, don't let oonuh fada know. Pack up oonuh school books and t'ings."

"Where we going Mommy?" Maureen asked.

"Don't worry, just bathe and put on some clothes. Hide oonuh t'ings under di bed. And Audrey, comb Marcy hair. "

Rose moved jittery, glancing behind her at the slightest sound.

The children surrounded her. She hugged and squeezed each of them. "I see oonuh likkle more," she said, and left incognito as she came.

They stayed at the window for a while, until Audrey pushed them to get ready.

As Marcy packed, she mumbled that her clothes were missing. "Stop complaining and pack your things," Audrey told her.

Audrey took charge. She shared the chicken foot soup her mother brought, made sure they bathed and brushed their teeth. "And don't forget to pack oonuh toothbrush."

She combed her hair, then Marcy's. Marcy tensed up as she pulled her hair. "Stop acting like a big baby." She didn't hold her hair at the root and comb to the end, like their mother did, causing Marcy's head to feel tender long after. Only this time, when she yanked the comb through Marcy's 'natty head' she bore the pain, reminding herself that her mother would take over and Audrey won't have to comb her hair ever again.

They waited on the veranda for Rose. Audrey got the jax set to quell their anxiousness. She and Maureen sat on the warm tiles facing each other, going back and forth in the game. When the ball bounced away, they sent Marcy for it. She wasn't satisfied being their ball catcher and asked, "Why can't I play too?" Audrey obliged her a game and showed her how to throw the ball high, in time to gather the jax before it came down. "I understand, I understand," she said. Donovan, in the chair above, chuckled. She gave him the 'eye' and proceeded, even though her hands were too small to catch the ball and the wire prongs at the same time.

Donovan cleared his throat. "I have a brilliant idea," he said, and stooped beside Marcy. "Whoever lose the most games," he looked at his little sister, "not going with mommy."

"Donovan!" she said, and elbowed him.

"Donovan stop troubling her," Audrey warned.

Their father drove up and Marcy let go off the ball and jax. Audrey snatched them and stuffed them in her shorts pocket. "Go in the house," she whispered, and the four of them scrambled off the floor and went into the living room. They sat shoulder to shoulder on the couch; none dared turn on the television. Arthur entered the room. He looked at them bunched together and asked, "Oonuh don't have nutting to do?" Walking away, as if he remembered things had changed since the night before, he asked, "Oonuh eat anyt'ing from morning?" They said yes. He continued on.

From the kitchen he called out, "Oonuh mada come here today?"

The three younger ones looked at Audrey. She answered, "Yes, Daddy."

He came to the living room. "Did you mada say anyt'ing?" he asked Audrey.

"Like what Daddy?"

"Like if she coming back today?"

"I don't remember mommy say anything, Daddy." He went back to the kitchen.

She heard him opening the pot and handling the dishes; she frowned and muttered, "Him hate mommy, but him still eat her food."

"Since we can't watch TV, you think we should get our books?" Maureen asked Audrey.

"No, him might catch us going under the bed for it."

They didn't have to sit numb like a piece of furniture for long, because the gate opened and they dashed to the window. The dogs barked and wagged their tails; it was their mother and grandmother. Audrey put her finger to her lips to conceal their excitement and not notify their father that they had arrived.

Still, Arthur heard the dogs. He came to the living room as the women entered the house.

Mari stood behind Rose in the doorway. She looked serious, carrying something wrapped in a crocus bag.

Rose said, "Arta, mi come get mi t'ings and mi taking mi children", her voice more stern than her look.

Arthur's face contorted. "Rosie, you have nutting in dis house."

"Look Arta, mi not warring wit' you, mi come to get mi children and leave." She held his glare.

Mari's eyes were fixed on him. She stepped between him and Rose, pointing the bag in his face. "Arta, don't start nutting you can't finish." He sensed that she was set for war. He hissed and stepped back. "Mi daughter just come to get her pickney dem and leave you ass, so don't joke today."

He narrowed his eyes and his nose flared; it seemed any minute he would hit her. Instead, he said, "As a matter of fact, dis is my house and you trespassing, so leave!" Spit flew from his mouth.

She reached into the crocus bag and pulled out a machete. All at once, the children leaned back in their seats at the sight of the long, shiny blade. "You t'ink you can beat mi like how you batter my pickney?" She shook her cutlass in front of him.

"No Mama, no!" Rose shouted.

Mari's voice trembled. "I will chop you up, I will chop you up, Arta. I will kill you in here today." He stood against the wall, staring coldly at her.

Rose moved between them and said, "Arta, just make mi get mi t'ings and leave you house", and eased by him, held frozen by the sight of Mari's machete.

"Children come, get oonuh t'ings."

Rose made a quick run through the house. She took nothing with her that evening, not even her precious sewing machine. The children got their bags from under the bed. One after the other they marched out the door and only Maureen looked up as she passed her father. He did not return her glance. Marcy wanted to say goodbye, but followed the others and stayed silent.

Rose led them to an awaiting van. They piled in. Marcy looked back as the van sped off. Her father wasn't there.

Chapter 11

They did not drive very far before reaching their destination behind a zinc fenced gate. The driver, Mr. Bertram, 'Mr. B', mostly for 'Bossman', owned many local shops. He was Mari's landlord. Upon reaching the gate, she got out the van and spread it open for Mr. B to park in the yard. The children recognized the house. Marcy said, "I know dis house, is Granny house." They had been there a few times, in better days, when their father took them to church and left them knowing Mari was there. He would pick them up after Sunday school and give her a drive home. They'd run into her house for treats as he said, "Make it quick." But they never stayed overnight - until now.

Mari's one-room house was crowded; a cabinet in the corner, a dresser on one side, a vanity and stool on the other. Next to the door was a big, brown suede chair with a leg rest and doilies covering the arms and head. Rose called it a recliner and Mari, a 'lazy bwoy'. Everybody wanted to stretch out in it, but Donovan beat his sisters. They settled for the arms, leaving Marcy standing with a pout.

"Marcy, go on di bed, baby," Mari said. She stuck her tongue out at her brother, behind her grandmother's back and flopped on the bed. It was the same size as theirs. She ran her hand over the frilly sheet and wondered if all of them would fit.

"Granny, where everybody goin' sleep?"

"On di bed."

"Everybody can hold?"

"Yes, baby, wi just bungle up and make wi self small."

After she put on her night clothes, her grandmother reminded her to pray and she said the *Our Father* prayer. She fixed herself against the headboard, making room for the others.

When she turned in the night and her eyes opened, she saw all of them, including her mother, laying side by side across the bed. Everybody's feet hung off, except hers. Her grandmother slept in her big chair.

At daylight, she woke to movements and voices and for a second, shook her head to get acquainted with her surroundings. Then she smiled.

She lay taking in her new life. The whole family was awake and adjusting accordingly. Her mother and grandmother were shifting suitcases, bags and furniture to make space in the room.

As Rose sorted the children's clothes, Maureen said, "Mommy, I was looking for that dress."

Marcy noticed hers and Audrey's matching dresses and said, "Oh, Mommy, is you did have it."

"Yes, and oonuh goin' put dem on dis morning."

"Where we going, Mommy?" Audrey asked.

"We going to church wit' you grandmother."

It was a long time they had gone to church on Sunday morning, due to the commotion on Saturday nights. "Gee wiz, Mommy, me feel tired," Donovan said.

"Mommy, can we go next Sunday instead?" Maureen asked.

"We have to go today, Mommy?" Marcy added.

"We have to go today," she said, firmly.

She chased them out the bed. "Di shower situation different here, so get up now." She followed them and stood at the bathroom door so they could tidy before the other tenants came. In total, five people lived downstairs and shared one kitchen – at times, some used their coal stove in the back yard – and an inside and outside bathroom. A big house it was, with the landlord, his wife and two grown children upstairs.

As Rose and the children readied, Mari prepared a light breakfast of tea and boiled eggs.

Walking to the bus stop, Audrey admired her mother. "Mommy, you look so nice." Rose wore a white dress with yellow patterned flowers on the bottom, and a white belt hugged her waistline. She raised the corners of her mouth and her sad eyes belied her smile.

"It's true Mommy," Marcy chimed in, gripping her mother's fingers. "You look pretty."

Donovan first saw the top of the metal-looking Jamaica Omnibus Service (JOS) bus at the stoplight and announced, "It's coming." The west-bound bus pulled up. An elderly woman in a broad rimmed hat, with a purse over her arm and a Bible in her hand, entered first. Next, Mari braced one hand against the door and mounted the bus, landing gently on the weak foot. Rose guided the three older children in and said to her youngest, "Watch you step, Marcy" as she helped her in; it was her first bus ride.

Rose wasted no time looking for work. One of the places she applied was the JOS company. Ms. Pottinger, the neighbour opposite Mari's room, worked as a custodian for JOS. She advised Rose the company was hiring. Rose went to JOS the next day expecting to get a job as a custodian but was hired as conductress. As conductress, issuing tickets for cash fare, she would earn more than a cleaner.

A few weeks living with Mari, everyone soon adjusted to six people living in her one-room, and each had a chore. Maureen and Audrey worked together. They shelled peas and picked through rice grains for 'clean' ones. Donovan ran errands to the shop, which he enjoyed, as it took him out the house. Marcy tagged along with Mari wherever she went.

She followed her to the corner shop to buy '50 ice' – half a block of ice to stock the icebox. Sometimes, she sat in the backyard with her as she fired up the coal stove to roast a breadfruit, or cook 'tough' meats like pig trotters and tripe. Now and then, on a Saturday evening, Mari brought home a chicken. She tied the chicken by the foot to a tree, and fed it corn until she changed her clothes. Once she got the bucket, a knife she sharpened on a stone, and a cigarette at the end of her lips, she untied it. Marcy drew nearer then, peeping through her fingers. This was the only time Mari smoked, during the killing and cleaning of the fowl. She plucked it and used the fire to singe the feathers, then took a long drag off the cigarette. Sometimes she turned the lit cigarette inside her mouth, puffing, as she focused on the job in hand – Sunday dinner.

Since Mari had no television, the children listened to her nightly programs with her. Her two favourites were *Life in Hopeful Village* and *Portia Faces Life*. When the shows ended, she and Rose went to the gate to talk, and sometimes they were joined by Ms. Pottinger.

Ms. Pottinger lived in the room across from Mari's with her common-law-husband and daughter, Marcia. Marcia lived with her father and visited on weekends.

Marcia was Marcy's company. They played skipping and hide and seek around the yard. Since their names were so close, they called themselves the girls from Mars, one and two. Marcy was number two because she moved in the yard last. When Marcia wasn't there to play, her mind wandered to the things she missed, like the family having their own bathroom, and taking bubble baths with her dolls.

She dreaded going to the toilet at Mari's. Most of the time, someone other than her family was there, and she had to go outside, which was the real problem. Once, using the outside toilet, she didn't realize there was no paper and she had to call out for someone to bring a piece. She had sweated having to 'broadcast her business' to the yard. On top of that, it was scary in there as the bulb was dim and couldn't prevent her from seeing 'duppy man' come through the walls.

Her bathing alone in the outside bathroom was off bounds, unless one of her sisters was bathing too. Not only because she was afraid, but her mother said it would save time and water. Although in the shower, Audrey and Maureen whispered that their mother never liked the guy in the back room, sitting in his doorway, 'just watching'. Even so, she did not mind bathing with her sisters as they helped to wash her back. One day she told Audrey she missed bathing in a bathtub. Audrey conked her on the head and said, "Well your home is different now, and so is the bathroom, so stop complaining."

Marcy and Donovan were enrolled in St. Matthew's Boys and Girls, the same public school as Audrey and Maureen. They switched schools because Rose could not afford the preparatory school fees on her own. It bothered Marcy for a while, but soon she met two friends, Claire and Antoinette. They both lived downtown, near school, except that Claire, who was Chinese, lived above her parents' haberdashery. Marcy joined the Spelling Bee Club with her friends, and they sat under the big tree in the school yard practicing their spelling while having lunch.

In the evenings after school, Marcy sat on the sunny veranda and did her homework. Hardly anyone stayed out there because of the sun. Mostly Marcy did, as from a baby she felt chilly easily and savoured the sun on her body. Also, being on the veranda she saw when mangoes fell from the tree by the gate, or tamarinds at the fence. The landlord's son, Denton, also loved the veranda. He stayed there any time of day. Sometimes he listened to cricket playing in Jamaica, or somewhere around the world, but mostly, it was his horse races that fastened him to the steps. He carried a white paper in one hand and the other held a transistor radio to his ear. Her grandmother called him a 'time waster' and a 'leech', because 'him live off him fada and won't work'.

Denton would seek her out on the veranda, and finding her he'd say, "Hey likkle girl, pick a horse for mi, nuh?" Beaming, she would, thinking she had special powers. Sometimes he came back the next day saying as he grinned, "Baby girl, you always pick a winner", handing her the paper to pick another. He would ask, "Who you say today?" and read the names. She would choose the one that sounded the funniest, strangest, or agreed with the one he hinted. Call it luck or 'special powers', the ones she chose most often won.

One day, as they were on the veranda, ears fixed on the galloping horses, she heard a voice calling "Marcy " from the street. She glanced behind her and saw her father at the gate.

"Daddy!" she yelled and ran to him. He stretched his hand through the iron rod gate and touched her face, staring crossly over her head. She looked back at Denton, busy with his horses; he didn't see her father 'killing him' with his eyes.

"Daddy how you know where we are?"

"I just figure, baby."

"Then why you never come?" She hadn't seen him since they left.

He didn't answer her question, he just said, "Where everybody?"

She told him her mother and grandmother were at work, and went to get her siblings.

Audrey came to the veranda and merely waved at him. She didn't smile or speak to him. Donovan and Maureen, teary-eyed, came together. He reached through the gate and wiped her tears with his fingers. He stood staring at them through the iron rod gate. His 'dreamy eyes' as Rose called them in their courtship days, were now droopy and remorseful, 'poor t'ing' eyes. The children stared back, equally disheartened. They scrutinized his black hair sprinkled with white, his face unshaven and his frame as if he had hardly slept or eaten since they left.

Unsure of the time the adults were due home, he shifted and asked before leaving, "Oonuh mada working now?" Maureen told him yes, although she did not know where, going off her mother's instruction: "If oonuh fada ask, oonuh don't know anyt'ing". Even if he didn't believe they knew nothing, he made no fuss. He only muttered how much he loved and missed them. Before he walked away he said, "Go inside now" and locking eyes with his youngest daughter, warned, "Marcy, don't sit on di veranda alone." She wanted to say, *I wasn't on the veranda alone, Daddy*, but his stare said, *Hush!*

He continued to visit when Rose and Mari weren't home. Each time he came it was the same: face dragged, clothes rumpled, and talked of how much he loved their mother, that he never meant to hurt them and he wished they were together again.

One night, as Rose ironed her uniform for the next day, Audrey gave her an update on his visits. Without taking her eyes off her ironing, she said, "Him have plenty time now. Him don't tell oonuh him not working?"

"Him lose him job Mommy?" she asked, surprised.

"Yes. Dem fire him."

"Why?"

"Must be him drinking."

"That's why him look so," she said, seeing the bigger picture.

"Poor daddy," Maureen said, softly.

"Daddy mash-up now," Donovan said.

"Hmph, him don't see mash up yet," Rose said, putting away the ironing board.

Chapter 12

The job at the bus company went well for Rose. After three months she had enough saved to consider moving. One Saturday morning after Mari left for work, she and the children sat at the table having breakfast. As she sipped her hot cocoa she told them she was going to look at a place, news their ears longed for.

Audrey asked, "What you mean Mommy, a place for us to live?"

"Well, dats what I hope."

"You going today?"

"Dis afternoon."

"We goin' get our own house again, we goin' get our own house again," she sang.

"Yeah!" Marcy clapped her hands.

"Hold on, hold on," Rose said, puncturing their dream with reality. "I said I'm going to take a look, I never said we had it yet."

While Rose went to view the place, at home the girls lay across the bed penetrating the ceiling with daydreams of the move. For the most part, they had accepted life at their grand-mother's. Nevertheless, they longed for television entertainment.

Audrey and Maureen missed shows like *Bonanza, Beverley Hill-billies* and *Gilligan's Island,* and Marcy missed seeing Tabitha wiggle her nose in *Bewitched.*

"But you know what I really miss?" Marcy asked. Her sisters waited to hear. "A bubble bath." A smile spread across her face.

"Bubble bath?" Maureen sneered, and she and Audrey laughed.

She waved her hands in circles. "Yes, and make big, big bubbles." Her sisters kept laughing. "And me and my dollies would play in the tub."

"I'm just picturing you."

"Yes, you know, with the bubbles filling up the tub, covering up my whole body."

"Okay, if you say so."

"Yeah, bubble girl, come back to dry land," Audrey said, chuckling.

The news from Rose that evening deflated their high hopes. The house wouldn't be ready for another two months. She was disappointed, knowing their expectations. Despite the letdown, she continued spreading the word she was looking for some-where to rent.

The next day, coming home from work, Mari met a neighbour on the bus. As they walked home she mentioned her daughter was looking for two rooms. The woman told her she saw a 'house for rent sign' two doors from where she lived.

Without delay, Rose and Mari went to see the landlord. He offered her the house on the spot. She packed and was ready to move by the weekend.

The morning of the move, they called a taxi and loaded their bags, suitcases and a small two-burner stove; their fridge and bed would be delivered later in the day. The four children sat in the back of the cab and Rose in front with a bag in her lap. Mari planned to be there after work.

In less than five minutes the taxi reached the house. There were two houses on the property and the children followed Rose to theirs in the back. Walking to their house, Marcy thought, *I won't have any view from behind here, no veranda view,* and looking around, *and we don't have any fruit trees, like at granny.* Although the yard lacked charm, she kept quiet, waiting to hear from her sisters. And as they entered the two-room house, Maureen said, "Daddy won't find us behind here." She quickly nodded in agreement.

Rose and Mari had cleaned the house from the night before. All that was needed to be done were little things like putting away groceries, utensils, and hanging curtains. As they hung the front room curtain, the landowners from the front house came to greet them. "Come in," Rose said, and introduced Mr. and Mrs. Henry to the children. They resembled siblings, being light-skinned, petite and silver haired alike. "Sorry I can't offer you a seat," Rose said, smiling, and explained she had furniture coming. They stood in the middle of the empty room as Mr. Henry gave a brief history of the house. He told them he built the two-room house for he and his wife, expecting their son to take the main, four-bedroom house, but his son got a 'big lawyer job' and built 'a rahtid mansion' up Beverley Hills for him and his wife. His face rounded and his eyes softened with pride. With their only child out the house, they rented two of the rooms to a common-law couple, Roger and Simone, and the other, more recently, to Bongo.

Bongo, a thin, dark-skinned man, did odd jobs for the Henrys and other neighbours. He saw the children watching out for the delivery, and offered to 'lend a hand' when it arrived. At midday the delivery truck drove up to the gate. Bongo assisted the men in bringing the fridge, double bed, and a single folded one to the back. And after the men left, he assembled the beds for the family.

A television was not priority for Rose, but she grew tired of pleas and long faces and gave in. So like the beds, she 'trust it', paying the bill a little at a time.

The morning of the television delivery, the children paced at the front. Bongo offered again to keep an eye out. He helped the men unload the TV when they arrived and directed them, "Come dis way, keep coming, 'round here so."

That evening, Rose divided the show times so that Audrey and Maureen wouldn't 'hawk' the television for themselves. They sat through Marcy's *The Flying Nun*, and she watched with them Little Will try to make it back to earth in *Lost in Space*. Later they gathered with their mother for the *Carol Burnett Show*, and went to bed around 9 p.m.

Because Rose worked early shifts, she woke as a habit every morning before dawn, so waking early the following morning was her norm. What was different, however, was the shuffling, scraping movements at the front door. Alarmed by the sounds, she grabbed the flashlight; she normally used it that early in the morning to save electricity and not to wake the children with the overhead light. With it in hand, she tiptoed to the front. As she neared the door, she switched it on and almost fainted at the sight of a man running out the front door. She dropped the flashlight and screamed, "T'ief! T'ief! T'ief! T'ief!" and ran to the children still screaming, "T'ief, t'ief, somebody help!" She turned on the overhead lights, flooding the rooms.

The children rose shaken and confused. "What Mommy? What happened?" Audrey asked.

Using her head, she gestured to the front door and whispered, "T'ief come in a di house."

"You see him, Mommy?" Donovan asked. She shook her head.

They huddled, looking out the door the man left open, waiting for help. In no time, the light went on in the Henrys' home. Relieved, Rose sighed. Soon her neighbours converged on the veranda to examine the damage. "Don't touch anything Rose, let it stay for the police," Mr. Henry said.

"No mi just checking… it seems him take out two glass from di window."

"Yes, see them there," Mr. Henry said, pointing to them on the veranda railing.

"You see him face?" Roger asked.

"No, it happen so fast," she said, still shaken. "'Cause as him see mi, him just turn back and run. Him sorta likkle body... not too tall."

"Try remember what you can for di police."

"And you know, a just last month dem break in a dat house," Simone said about the house behind theirs.

"So we definitely have a thief in the area," Mrs. Henry added.

"Rose, my dear, you tell the police all you can when they come," Mr. Henry said.

Roger turned to her. "I leaving for work now, I can report it at di station on mi way." Rose asked him to tell Mari as well.

Mari hurried to the house. She went directly to the kitchen to make Rose a cup of black coffee, and waited with them on the veranda for the police. Eventually, two policemen came with a small crowd trailing them. The older policeman said, "Stand back" and a few of the onlookers checked the scene and left. As he inquired who was involved, Mari escorted the children inside to let the police 'do dem work'. In no time, they quietly returned to the veranda.

The police took Rose's report. She explained how the man must have taken out the two window panes. She believed he placed them out the way, then put his hand through the open space to unlock the door and let himself in, and luckily, she woke in time to catch him sneaking through the door. She said, "Him take foot and run" when she flooded him with the flashlight.

The police spent close to an hour completing their investigation and told her they would contact her with their findings. Before they left, two women standing to the side asked to speak with them. The women stated what they believed, talking over each other. The younger, more muscular police officer said, "One at a time, please." The more talkative woman explained that 'talks have it' Bongo was suspected in break-ins in the area. One of which was the home Simone mentioned. The woman said somebody told her they saw him running from that direction 'di same time as di robbery'. The police asked the women to describe the person they knew as Bongo. Although the description was similar, he said he would weigh it with Rose's, and other notes he had on robberies at the station.

Mr. Henry returned to the house after the policemen left. "So what goin' happen now?" he asked Rose as he replaced the panes in the window.

"Dem say dem will get back to mi."

"We can only hope they find out something fast, because who knows where this criminal will end up next."

"You never know, him might be right here under your nose."

Mari made porridge for breakfast. She blessed the meal and gave thanks the situation wasn't worse, and suggested they catch the ten o'clock service. The children were frightened of the thief coming back and she consoled them. "If oonuh worrying 'bout di t'ief, him gone long time."

"Especially if it's Bongo," Rose said.

"You know him not goin' show him face in di area for now."

"Or never," Donovan said.

"Oonuh just lock up di place and come."

"I don't know, Momma, I don't know if I have di energy for church dis morning."

Mari convinced her that today of all days she should be grateful and show her gratitude by going to church. "Go and give God t'anks!"

She went home to get ready.

They got a drive to church from the Henrys. Although the seniors attended Kingston Parish Church, downtown, they made a detour to their church, Holy Trinity Cathedral at North Street.

By the time church ended, it appeared Rose's fears had subsided. She made pleasant conversations and even smiled, showing no visible signs of the morning's predicament.

They left church and went to Mari's for the afternoon.

Marcy asked her mother to let her play with Marcia for a while and they played with her dolls on the veranda. Marcia told her she heard a little bit about the burglary and now wanted to get 'di full score'.

"I don't even remember what happen," she said, not wanting to dredge up what she had put aside.

But even with her reluctance to discuss the incident, Marcia urged, "Tell me man, it's true you mommy chase the thief with a flashlight and him run and scream for help. It's true?" She realized that account made her mother fearless, like superwoman, and liked that description better, so she grinned and nodded.

When it was time to go home, Marcy, laying on her grandmother's bed, yawned and asked, "Mommy, can I sleep here tonight?" Audrey and Maureen, lounging in the recliner, had the same thought. "Please, Mommy please?" Audrey asked. "I don't like down there anymore."

"Yes Mommy, let us stay here tonight," Maureen said.

Rose glanced at Mari and they went to the gate.

After they left the room, Audrey said, "I don't feel good 'bout that house."

"Me too," Marcy answered.

"What if the thief come back?" Donovan asked and chuckled. "Is now it goin' be scary."

"Stop saying that, Donovan."

"I just know daddy must be wondering where we are," Maureen said.

"I not goin' back, I goin' stay with Granny."

"Mommy never said you can, Marcy," Audrey said. At that moment, Rose and Mari walked in the room.

"Mommy never said what?" Rose asked. They kept quiet.

"Oonuh come, we going down di house."

"We goin' back Mommy?" Marcy asked, with a frown.

"Just come."

Mari stayed. The children followed Rose to the garage where Mr. B, Denton and his friend waited in the van. Mr. B drove them to the house. Rose directed the men to take the fridge and television, and the children, their school things. They waited in the van while she spoke with Mr. and Mrs. Henry. Mr. Henry walked her to the gate and as he closed the gate behind her, said, "I understand, Rose, I understand." That was the last time the children went to the house.

Mr. B. stored the fridge and television, and Rose and the children lived with Mari for another month. The children picked up old routines as they counted down the days to having more room space. Rose continued to go to the house and little by little brought back their belongings. She gave up the house at the end of the month, with plans for Mari to join them when they moved again.

One evening as the family finished dinner, Mari's sister Diane, and her son Lascelles, made a surprise visit. "My heavens, Di, what bring you a town?" She waved at Donovan to give up the chair to her older sister.

"T'anks mi son" and taking the seat she said, "Mi not staying long." She rested her cane against the chair.

Mari offered them a drink of soursop juice.

Rose called Lascelles to a chair at the table. "Mi just bring momma to Kingston to see Dr. Rodriquez." He explained that his mother's sight had deteriorated and her doctor recommended that she see a specialist, one of the doctors from Cuba.

Diane suffered with diabetes for many years and had poor circulation in her legs and limited vision in one eye. "Him say mi sugar no better, and di eyes gone from bad to worse", she rubbed her eyes, "dem cloudy and mi can't see a t'ing, especially a night, but apart from dat mi a manage by di grace a God."

Mari updated her on their situation and the impending move. "So you come at di right time, mi love."

"But you know where to reach dem children, right? You still have Millie and Lorna phone number at work?" Mari assured her she did.

After she finished the juice, Mari took the glass and she straightened her cane and said, "Mi want to reach home before it get too dark, come Lascelles." She held the cane and he held her arm. "If anyt'ing mi will send word wid one a dem children."

She caught sight of Marcy sitting on the bed, with her mother. "Rosie, a di lickle one dat grow so big? She favour you sah. Come here child."

Marcy sashayed up to her. Diane ran her hand over her head and lifted her chin, "How you do?" She smiled, looking into the child's eyes.

"Fine," she answered, looking up at her grandaunt's blurry eyes.

"How old you is?"

"Seven, but I'll soon be eight."

"Soon be eight, going on eighteen," Rose answered.

Diane opened her little change purse, took out an icy mint and gave her. She looked at the sweet, wanting to unwrap it; she looked behind her at her mother. "Not now," Rose said. She clinched the mint tighter.

Mari held Diane's hand and they walked to the gate; Lascelles, Rose, and the children followed. They said their goodbyes and Mari told her, "Mi will pray for you, mi sister."

"God bless you, mi love."

As Lascelles helped his mother into the car, she reminded him, "You give dem di tings?" He hurried to the trunk for a box. "Auntie Mari, momma bring all kind a fruits for you, lots of Ethiopian apples that you like." Rose took the box inside.

"God bless you mi sister. Oonuh gwaan now, drive safe."

Back in the house, Rose sat beside Mari on the bed. Mari's mind seemed far away, as if thinking of her own health. Rose asked her, "Momma, you taking you pressure pills everyday?"

"Now a days mi don't feel too bad, you nuh."

"But you still have to take it. You can't stop taking it just because you feel good."

"Sometimes when mi can't reach di pharmacy, mi just chew likkle garlic."

"Momma, no worry wit' di garlic. If you can't go, tell mi and I will go for you, but you have to take di medicine." Rose leaned close and rubbed her back. "You know Momma, she have her seven children and dem will look after her. Don't worry yourself, Diane will be alright."

Chapter 13

Within days of moving to their next home, the children realized that what was their landlady's castle was their curse. For one, its lush fruit trees were off bounds. While they could eye the low hanging Julie mangoes and the juicy plums on the tree, that was it. She warned, "You children are not allowed to pick the fruits!" Even the ones that fell, and enticed, were left for the ants. She complained to their mother, "They must wait for me to give them."

Mrs. Hernandez, a retired teacher, lived on the bigger side of the house. She had been on her own since her daughter, Heather, an intern at the College of the West Indies, moved to live near the institution.

In the second week of living at Mrs. Hernandez's, the girls sat on the veranda floor doing their homework. They ate peanuts as they worked. She came to the doorway, looked around and took a seat in the chair. "Don't forget to pick up the trash when you're finished." They glanced at each other, she'd said the same thing the day before when they ate icicle, even though they hadn't made a mess. She suddenly started talking about Heather. "Heather is a paediatric doctor, you know." The children looked at her without responding. She went on, "She doing research on bottle fed babies versus breast fed ones." They looked at each other, puzzled. Audrey knew who a paediatrician was, Maureen wasn't sure, and Marcy, definitely not. It was a topic of no interest to them. But Mrs. Hernandez was clueless to their boredom. In a softer tone, almost to herself, she said, "Heather only takes the forty-minute drive to East Kingston to see her mother at Christmas." Then she jumped up. "Oh Lord, I forgot the pot on the stove."

At which, Audrey shook her head. "Maybe she using Heather fat to fry us."

Even Rose questioned Mrs. Hernandez's motives. Before moving in she told her the amenities were included in the rent. After they moved in, she changed the agreement, stating that Rose must pay for water and electricity separately. Rose wondered if having the six of them there, she intended to get rich off their desperation, or simply wanted them out. Mari figured her as an 'ol' ginal', not to be trusted. As much as Rose objected, she had little choice and concluded, "Place not easy to get now a days, so we just have to tough it out."

The daily drudge of work and the responsibilities of home weighed on Rose. She worked extra shifts to meet the bills, moving quickly and constantly going or coming from work. Sometimes she fell asleep where she sat at the dinner table. The busier she got, the less she smiled. And this scared Marcy. When her teacher announced a trip to Hope Gardens, she and her friends were excited to see the animals and planned to bring their money the following day. Her friends did, but she was afraid to approach her mother and waited all week. She built up the courage one night as she sat at the dresser putting rollers in her hair. "Marcy, since you know from last week, why you take so long to ask me?" She sulked. "I don't have di money tonight, you have to wait." She teared up. "Stop di crying, you might want it now, but you won't die if you don't get it." She ran off to bed and cried herself to sleep.

Luckily, the next day her teacher said all those who didn't have their money could bring it the morning of the trip.

That evening, she bypassed Mrs. Hernandez on the veranda and found a new place in the backyard, one she was sure her landlady wouldn't disturb as she never sat out back. The woman disliked lizards zipping across the yard even though the little reptiles were just trying to get away. Only mosquitoes buzzing for fresh blood deterred Marcy. She leaned on the tree, reflecting on her mother's words: *You won't die if you don't get it.* She knew it made sense, but wished it wasn't so. Soon thoughts of life with her father crept in. Joyful memories brought a smile, and unpleasant ones saddened her. As she wondered if things would get better for her family, she gazed over the neighbour's yard at fowls grazing. Two roosters attacked each other and she shooed them to stop. They chased to the fence, butting at her. She shooed again, and they butted and scratched under the fence. She laughed at them trying to get to her, and stuck her tongue out. The more they clucked, the more her body twisted in laughter, until her grandmother called her for dinner and she ran inside laughing.

Arthur visited the children's school at least twice a month, usually at lunchtime. Sometimes he went straight to the boys' side to get Donovan, but mostly, he looked for Maureen or Marcy first. He went to see them the week they were moving from Mrs. Hernandez. The girls were on the playground and ran to him at the gate, and afterwards went to get Donovan. He took them to the patty shop near school. Although they had brought sandwiches, they welcomed the treat. They spent the time talking about Maureen's last year at primary school and her success at passing her common entrance. Tears filled his eyes as he praised her. After they finished their patty, meatloaf, and chocolate milk, he walked them back to school. Before they got to the gate, Maureen said, "Oh Daddy, I forgot to tell you, we're moving on Saturday."

Chapter 14

Almost two years after leaving their family home, they moved into a house on Summerfield Road, Doncaster, not far from their original home. It was a rented house and they were the first people to live there. Mr. Lau, their landlord, and his family, lived above the dry goods store they owned on the main street. The day Rose told the children she found a new place to live she prefixed it with, "And we won't have to see di landlord" because she or Mari would take his rent to him every month, to which the children cheered.

The morning the movers came, Marcy danced on the spot as the truck backed into the yard. Everything was packed and ready, so the men loaded the truck and took their possessions to the new house. When the driver stopped in front of the house and she saw its hedging - croutons, Joseph coat and shame-a-lady - she wiggled: *This is my new house, this is my new house.* The driver reversed and parked in the driveway and one of the men lifted her off the truck. She flipped open the green letterbox strung to the gate and peeped in; she hadn't seen a letter box before.

She dashed into the house behind her brother and sisters. Sliding on the red and white tiles, her mother called out, "Oonuh stay outta di man dem way." She crept around the movers as they laid the furniture against newly painted walls, and onto the kitchen where her eyes fixed on the bright, shiny sink. "Watch it baby, watch it!" One of the movers startled her as they brought in the new four-burner stove. She slipped into the corner until they passed, then eased out the door to the bathroom to see the tub. *There it is, so clean and white.* She traced her fingers on the inside, the white chalk on it, now on her hand. *Maybe if I show mommy my hand, she'll let me take a bath, then I'll be the first one to bathe in it.* She giggled.

She heard laughter coming from outside and skipped to the backyard. It was her sisters stoning guineps off the tree without success, until their grandmother showed them the stick from the clothes line. "Use dat, nuh," she said, pointing to the stick next to them. Their laughter went up, as they pulled the fruits down.

"We have guinep tree," she said, rushing to grab the ones that fell.

"Watch di seed," her mother said. "Chew it up before you swallow it."

"See a Blackie mango tree there," Maureen said, pointing at the neighbour's tree, its branches hanging over their yard. "And see, we have ackee too."

Donovan came from the side of the house with a mouthful of his findings. "The cherry tree next door hang over our fence," he said, with some stuffed in his pants pockets.

Mari picked ackee for dinner and went to the kitchen. There, she sorted the kitchen stuff. Everyone else chipped in to unpack and arrange the furniture. Audrey assigned the wardrobe space, taking the two top draws, Maureen the two middle ones, and Marcy, the bottom two. The two mirrored sides were for dresses and Donovan used the built-in closet. He had the same setup for sleeping, opening his folded bed in the cordoned area of the dining room.

During the organizing of the home, a car horn sounded at the gate. Donovan, closest to the window, looked out. "It's a man in a van."

"Oh, oh," Rose said, leaping to her feet. "Dat must be Mr. Garrison, him moving in today." Their tenant, Trevor Garrison, had the small side of the house.

The children followed Rose to the veranda. She opened the gate for him to back in the Volkswagen van. Among his belongings were stacks of LPs and 45s. Rose's eyes rolled when she saw his sound system. *I wonder how that goin' work with my sleep.*

The new house was spacious and Rose filled it with fine furniture. The children didn't have to crowd on the floor before the television anymore. She bought a black leather sofa with matching side chairs, a stereo, and a six-seat dining table. The day the sofa came the children, playing, dropped themselves on it. She reminded them, "Take care of it 'cause it nuh done pay for yet."

Most of what she bought was on credit, to be paid off when she got her 'pawdner draw'. Both she and Mari who now worked at Coronation Market still selling straw goods, had accounts at the bank, and she also had an account with a credit union. But each week they saved a good sum of their money in 'pawdner', with a group of mostly women. 'Pawdner' was unofficial banking, with savings collected every week over a period of months, even up to a year. Each week the money collected went to one person. Sometimes two people put together as one, which was the case for her and Mari, to clear off the furniture bill long before it was due.

The second week arriving at Summerfield Road, Marcy met her neighbour. She was in the front yard with her grandmother working in the garden and noticed her in her yard. She looked about her height, close in age, and hoped they could be friends. She stared, trying to make eye contact, but the girl's eyes were locked on where to place her feet in a game of hopscotch. When she stopped hopping, Marcy moved closer to the fence. "Hey," she called. The girl saw her and smiled. "Come here," she said. She slid her body through the shrub and came right up to Marcy at the fence. "What's your name?" she asked.

"Sandy."

"My name is Marcy, I just move here."

"Who and you live over there?" she asked, looking at Mari.

Marcy told her, and asked, "You have brother and sister too?"

"No," she said, and then shook her head as if trying to get her words straight. "Yes. I mean, I have a brother and a sister on my father side. They live in St. Elizabeth."

They stood at the fence getting to know each other. She told Marcy her real name was Sandra Newman and she was nine years old. "I am older than you," Marcy bragged, although only by a few months.

Sandy, standing akimbo, replied, "Well I am almost ten."

"What month?"

"November."

She ran it through her head. "That's not now, that's five months from now."

She flipped her braided ponytail, light coloured to match her skin, and said, "It don't matter."

Not wanting to upset her new friend, she changed the subject. "You have white in your family?"

"Yes, on my father side." Her mother called. "I have to go now, bye."

She did not see Sandy much after that. Her mother Norma Pierce owned a beauty salon and after Sandy left the private school she attended, she stayed at her mother's salon close by. They came home together at seven o'clock in the evenings, and on Saturdays, she went to the salon with her for the whole day, so Marcy only saw her on Sundays.

Over the months, Ms. Pierce and Rose became neighbourly, and Ms. Pierce allowed Sandy to come to their house. After a while, she let Sandy stay with them on Saturdays instead of going to the salon. Sandy never cared for the sunny veranda like Marcy, and talked her into sitting under the ackee tree. One day when they were in the backyard, Rose came and told Sandy her father was at the gate. Marcy followed her to the front. "Daddy, Daddy," Sandy said, and ran into his arms. She resembled her father; the two were light-skinned, with wavy hair and dimples.

"How is my big girl?" he asked, lifting her off the floor.

"Fine, Daddy." He sat on the veranda railing with her on his lap.

Marcy peeped from the corner as he kissed her and she hugged him.

She fidgeted as he handed her the shopping bag he brought. "This is yours, sweetie."

Sandy's father caught Marcy watching. "Are you Sandy's little friend?" he asked.

Sandy answered before she did. "Yes Daddy, she's my friend, Marcy."

"Hello Marcy."

"Hello," she said, moving closer.

"I'm Sandy's father, Mr. Newman." He smiled and the dent in his cheeks deepened.

Sandy held her father's face and turned it back to hers. "Daddy how you know I was here?"

"I went to your mother's shop."

Sandy and her father began talking about the things he brought. Marcy saw they were happy to see each other and thought she was probably in the way, so she went inside.

Seeing Sandy so loving with her father made Marcy think of her father for the rest of the day. It was going on two months he had not come to see them at school, and even though he had their new address, he never visited. Bad memories or not, she missed him. She thought often of them living as a family again, and since they had a nice home now, maybe he could get a job and help her mother take care of them.

It sounded like a good idea, and she was excited to bring it up at dinner. "I wonder how daddy is?"

"Yeah, I was thinking how him don't come for a while," Maureen answered.

"What if he's sick?"

She sighed. "I hope not."

"Sometimes, I think...I think," her sisters eyes on her, "what if daddy was to move into this house with us?"

Audrey's eyes narrowed and she squinted as if baffled. "You know mommy and daddy got a divorce, right?" Her sisters' faces hung.

"How you know that?" Maureen asked.

"I don't believe you, Audrey," Marcy said.

"Why is it such a surprise?"

"Who told you?" Maureen asked.

"I heard mommy and granny talking yesterday. I was in their room putting rollers in mommy's hair."

They got quiet.

Then Marcy said, "Oh boy, daddy's chance with mommy gone."

"Yeah, that kinda sad," Maureen said.

"What wrong with the two of you?" Audrey frowned. "Daddy's chance with mommy gone long time. Him never stop drinking and lose him job."

"But he works," Maureen said.

"Where?" Audrey asked, doubtful.

"He works for Mrs. Franklin at the bar."

"That little work can't help," she sneered.

"It's better than nothing."

"He probably doesn't even get any money." Audrey chuckled. "She probably pay him with rum."

"Yeah, but if he was to come back, he could get a better job."

"Be real, who goin' hire a drunken man?"

"He's not drunk all the time."

Audrey hissed. "Anyway, stop dreaming 'cause mommy wouldn't want him back."

"You don't know."

"Yes, Audrey, you don't know," Marcy added.

"Not after all the beatings he gave her."

Maureen left the table and was quiet for the rest of the evening. In bed that night Audrey tried to make friends and told her, "Me never mean to say that about daddy." That didn't satisfy Maureen.

The next day she was still not speaking to Audrey, so Audrey brought up what happened to their mother. She sent her to get Maureen and Marcy and had a talk with all three of them. When she rectified their squabbles, she told them they could visit him if they wanted.

In the afternoon, they went to find him.

Audrey suggested stopping at Franklin's Bar first, as he might not be home so early. Maureen went to see him there before and led the way. Franklin's Bar, a renovated house, looked more like a family home than a bar with trees and flowers in the front. And that it was in the days when Mr. Franklin was alive, and he, his wife and their children lived as a family.

They stood at the gate as a few men went in and out. An older man, watching his steps as he walked towards the gate, asked, "What you children want inside here?" Audrey told him they were looking for their father, Arthur Tomlinson. He smiled. "Oonuh is Arta children?"

They nodded, and Audrey said, "Yes, you know him?"

"Yes man, he's mi friend."

"You know if he is here today?"

"Yes," he said, and turned. "Make mi go call him."

A few minutes after, Arthur came. He smiled and hugged them. Marcy looked him over. His clothes were wrinkled, but he was not drunk. She smiled and gripped his hand tighter.

They walked beside him, two on each side to his house a few streets from the bar. Four little mongrels lining the gate barked as they reached. He shushed them and they scattered, then returned growling. He led the children behind the main house to a one-room house, once a maid's quarters. While he dug his key from the coins in his pocket, Marcy gazed at the callaloo growing in the backyard, surrounded by avocado and breadfruit trees, and thought, *at least he has food.*

Entering the room, the first thing that stood out was its tightness. She recognized the bed, fridge and kitchen table from their house. The table next to the door stocked his Milo, a tin of corn beef, three tins of sardines and a loaf of hard-dough bread, his transistor radio and hotplate tucked in the corner. "Sit down, nuh," he said, showing them the bed. "Oonuh want likkle syrup?" he asked, opening the fridge to take out the syrup and water. The door bumped into the bed and the children giggled at his nimbleness in trying to get the bottles out.

The children snacked before coming and told him they weren't hungry. "Have somet'ing to eat, man." They tried to explain their bellies were filled with crackers and cheese, and that their grandmother would have dinner ready by the time they got home. "Come on man, oonuh must want somet'ing now," he said, spreading the corned beef on the hard-dough bread. They did not want to hurt his feelings, knowing he only wanted to feel in charge again, so they went along. Surprisingly, when they were finished, nothing was left on the plate.

He sat on the bed with them, and they asked why they hadn't seen him for a while. He was silent, as if thinking, then said how badly he felt that their mother had divorced him, and he wanted to make up for all his mistakes. He said he tried many times to get her attention when he saw her going home from work, but she pretended not to see him, or shouted at him, drawing stares from people on the street. All he wanted, he said, "Was for mi and her to talk." The children listened, although it was a story they heard from their mother when she came home from work aggrieved that he 'lay wait' her at the bus stop.

When he changed the topic from their mother, he asked, "So how school?" Donovan gave him good news about his common entrance and plans to go to Calabar High. He commended him. "Mi glad how you stay outta trouble and keep you head in di books."

Audrey butted in. "That's because mommy don't joke with him. He has to put down the ball sometimes."

"And he can't sit on the fence with his friends and let mommy see," Maureen added.

"You stop talk. Who ask you anything?" Donovan shouted at Maureen.

"Don't talk to your sister like dat."

"But Daddy, she telling pure lies."

"And is those boys them say beat up another boy, because him act like a girl and him homosexual."

"No, none of my friend's would do that."

"Don't let mi see you wid dem boys on di corner."

"So what about you, Miss Maureen? Look how much time I see you and that boy, following you home."

"He's not following me home, he's going home, 'cause he lives down the road," Maureen said, giving Donovan a bad eye.

Arthur took a deep breath, hung his head, and after a minute or so, said, "Well mi glad oonuh alright, mi don't know what mi woulda do if anyt'ing happen to oonuh."

By the time the children were ready to leave, the sun had gone down. He walked them home. They stopped at the gate and he hugged them, holding on as though he was not letting go. He didn't seem to care if Rose or Mari saw him. He hugged them one last time and waited until they went inside the house.

Marcy and her sisters went to their room and she said, "Daddy look lonely."

"I know him lonely, especially now since it really over with mommy," Maureen said.

"But the way him talk is like him don't really feel so."

"Well, too bad, it is *so*," Audrey said. "In a way, I'm glad we got to see him and spend time with him, but honestly, I don't want to see him any time soon." She shifted her eyes from her sisters. "Because all daddy do is talk about the same things over and over, and I know mommy would rather die than take him back."

By the time Rose came home from work, they had gone to bed without getting a chance to tell her about their visit. The next day she was home early. They sat the dinner table and they talked over each other to paint her a picture of his life. She listened and shook her head a few times. "And he talks like he still wants you back Mommy, he wants his family again," Audrey said, getting her mother riled.

"Please!" She frowned. Her face hardened. It was a look that grew more stern and unhappy with each day. "All I ask is dat him just leave mi alone." She hissed. "Him a walk behind mi a sing *Consider Me*, and..." she squinted, trying to remember, "Oh, *When a Man Love a Woman*, like him a damn fool."

Arthur was dogged in his desire for Rose, hunting her at every chance. As the children watched TV one night, and Mari was in her room, they heard a knock on the mailbox. Donovan checked to see. "It's Ms. Campbell from up the road."

All four children went to the veranda. "Your granny is here?" They told her yes. "Tell her come now."

By this time, Mari, whose bedroom was in the front of the house, came out. Ms. Campbell, speaking quickly, hands flying, said, "Come, fight broke out with Mr. Tomlinson and another man up the road."

"What?" Mari's heart fluttered.

"You have to come now."

"Rosie alright?" she asked, opening the gate.

"She want you up there now."

"Oonuh stay," she says to the children, closing the gate.

As soon as she was half way up the road, they slipped out behind her.

People surrounded Arthur sitting on the sidewalk. "See him children a come," a woman said. His shirt had drippings of blood on the front, and he held a rag to his bruised head and his top lip was swollen.

"Daddy!" Marcy rushed to him. The children bent over him, checking his bruises. He pushed them away and mumbled, "Don't call mi nuh daddy, call mi di man! I'm not daddy. I'm di man!" He tried to stand and stumbled, slumping onto the sidewalk.

Rose saw the children and called out to them. They ran to her on the other side of the road where a smaller crowd gathered. Frightened and confused, they rallied around her. She stood with Mari and another man they did not recognize. She and the man talked with a police officer. She squeezed her hands together as she spoke. Audrey asked, "Mommy what happen?"

"I tell you when we get home."

Around twenty minutes later they were home. They went to Rose and Mari's room and Rose went to the bathroom. The children surrounded Mari as she described the commotion the way she understood it. She told them that because their father lay waited their mother at nights, she got fed up and planned with a co-worker, Jerry, to walk her home. He saw the two of them come off the bus together and trailed them. In his 'drunken, foolish, jealous state', he sneaked up on them. He slapped Jerry on his back.

Jerry turned to see what was the matter, and without giving Jerry a chance, he raised his hand to hit him again. But Jerry was quicker; he punched him in the mouth and the two of them wrestled to the ground. Rose screamed for help and people crowded. Two men squashed the fight, but by then Arthur had suffered wounds. Someone called the police who were not far away. Apart from the blow to his back, and a few scrapes, Jerry did not have serious injuries.

Listening to Mari relay what happened was surreal to Marcy, like getting an update on a radio drama, and not her real life. As much as her father fought with her mother, a street fight was inconceivable, and the horror on her brother and sisters' faces said the same.

As they were transfixed on the story Mari told, a wail resonated from the bathroom. "Woi, woi, woi, help mi Lord Jesus, help mi fada God." The children scrambled off the floor and ran to their mother in the bathroom. They teared-up watching her sob. Their grandmother sat on the side of the tub, holding her as she bawled.

Back in her room, Mari lit her prayer candle and read the 27th Psalm over Rose; the children watched in silence.

Later that night, they went to sleep under a blanket of grief, as old wounds opened up again.

Since then, Marcy was ashamed to walk to the corner; she took the long way to the bus stop. If anyone looked at her for long, she thought they were thinking of the night her father got beat-up in a fight. Well, that was the word Patricia White spread at school. She lived on the same road as her and watched the fray from her gate. Rose had warned, "Don't play wit' her, her mada too cantankerous." Which was true, as nearly every day

Mrs.White had a quarrel with somebody on the road. Even on Sundays after church, before entering her home, she could be heard yelling over something as simple as someone leaving the gate open. Patricia was the same at school, getting into trouble 'with her mouth', saying something out of line, or outright lying about another student. Marcy stayed far and ignored her taunts of "Marcy father is a rum head".

Months passed and the children had no contact with their father. They never went looking for him, and he didn't lurk by the house trying to glimpse them in the front. No one wondered out loud for him either, or spoke his name in the house. From 'that night', it was like he had died. That was how it appeared at home. Nevertheless, Marcy guessed like her, they all wondered how he was.

Rose had to go to court, as he filed charges against Jerry. The morning of the trial she fretted about testifying against him. Luckily, when she went, he never showed up. She presumed he probably knew nothing would come of it since he had caused the problem in the first place. She went home relieved and shared the good news with the family. It was the brightest Marcy had seen her mother's eyes in a long time. "If I don't have to see Arta as long as I live…just be outta him life for good." She shook her head. "Only God knows how happy I would be."

Her friend Cynthia visited in the evening. They sat on the back veranda talking and laughing. It pleased the girls to see their mother relaxed, and they hankered near. Cynthia took notice of them. "Di girls dem growing nice, man." After Cynthia left, their mother told them she was going to Canada the following week. Marcy felt sad that her mother's renewed joy was short-lived with Cynthia leaving, and asked if she was coming back.

She replied with a smile, "She may or may not, it depends." It marveled her that her mother's good friend was leaving and she looked so happy.

Around midday one Saturday, Marcy was by the fence talking with Sandy when a long, blue car stopped at the gate. Arthur stepped out and she waved bye to Sandy and sped off. He put his finger on his lips. She knew his signal and said, "Mommy and granny not here, they gone to work." He came closer; she glanced up and down. He looked as if he had put on a little weight, his face wasn't as drawn and he had shaved and trimmed his graying hair. "Where you were so long, Daddy?"

"I was in di country, baby. I bring back somet'ing for all a you." He went to the car and brought back two boxes. She opened the gate and he laid them inside. "What's in them?" she asked, prying the box open.

"Goodies for everybody. Go call Donovan to come get dem."

She knew Maureen and Audrey would want to see him too, so she shouted from the veranda, "Daddy is here! Daddy is here!"

He smiled when he saw them running to see him. Maureen asked, "Daddy, where you were all this time?"

"I was in Clarendon doing some work." He looked at Donovan. "Son, take di boxes inside, give dem to you mada when she come."

"What's in them?" Donovan asked, lifting a box.

"All kind a fruits. Cassava, Jack fruit, star apple, sweet sop, 'hole heap a t'ings, son."

They talked for a few minutes then he said he had to go.

Donovan asked, "Who that man waiting for you, Daddy?"

"Who, Mr. Fitzy?" He glanced at the car. "Is him I work wid. Him own di house where mi live."

"The yard with the whole heap a noisy dogs?" Marcy asked, giggling.

"Same one."

He explained that he worked with Mr. Fitzy in the country on his farm, and delivered the produce he sold to different parishes. Mr. Fitzy's wife was sick, so this trip was cut short. Before leaving, he checked on how they were, and asked, "So oonuh mada alright?"

"Yes, she's all right, Daddy," Maureen answered.

"Anyway, I have to go now, Mr. Fitzy waiting."

"So when you coming again?"

He rubbed their heads and said, "Oonuh goin' see daddy often man, don't worry."

Later when Mari saw the boxes of food he brought, she had nothing bad to say, and even put aside some cassava to bake pudding and 'blue draws'.

But it was different with Rose. She was crossed. "I don't want dat man 'round here," she quarreled. "I have a mind dash dem 'way."

"No Rosie, you can't do dat. It's food di children can eat. Don't make him upset you dat much and work up you pressure," Mari said, trying to cool her daughter's temper.

Even in anger, the children knew she wouldn't have thrown out the food. She had taught them to 'eat up' and always be thankful because 'plenty African children starving and would love to get what oonuh don't want'.

Afterward, Marcy went on the veranda and took a book to read, but her mind stayed on her parents. *If they could only talk to each other and live in peace. If daddy could accept their divorce and not provoke mommy, that would keep her blood pressure from rising and him from shrinking away, that's all I want.*

But life rarely granted what we want.

Chapter 15

The children had just had dinner and were in the living room watching a gripping episode of *The Fugitive*; the police had closed in on the one-armed man. Their mother was resting and their grandmother came and sat in the living room. The television was not her entertainment as she normally fell asleep no matter how intriguing the show, yet none of them made big of her sitting there. As the show went to commercial, Audrey rolled her shoulders and said, "I can't stand all this tension."

Marcy said, "It's true. Me 'fraid to watch the last part."

"Don't forget, it's only a TV show," Donovan mouthed.

While they waited for the program, discussing how it would end, Mari muttered something. They didn't notice, so she spoke louder, "Oonuh hear mi?" They turned to her. "Mi say oonuh mada going away Friday." Friday was the day after next. They stared at her, shocked and confused. Her face was solemn and her eyes were heartache red.

Marcy got up and turned down the television. "What you said Granny...mommy going away Friday?" She wished her hearing was bad. Mari nodded. "To where?" She squinted, trying to decipher if her grandmother's nod was a definite yes.

Before she could answer, Donovan, in shock like his sisters, asked, "Where mommy going?"

"I can't say yet, I just want oonuh to know."

"That can't be real," Donovan said. "How mommy going away and never tell us?" His eyes narrowed. "No, no, this can't be real."

"But how mommy could be leaving in two days...well not even two days, 'cause the day almost over," Maureen said.

"So we will have only one more day with her, then she's gone?" Marcy asked, sinking into her seat at the thought.

"I don't believe it," Maureen said. "I don't believe mommy leaving us. No way! She wouldn't."

"It's true, mommy going away," Audrey said, her voice low and shaky.

Maureen and Marcy stared, their mouth agape. Donovan asked, "What you saying Audrey, you knew mommy was leaving and never said anything?"

"It's true, Audrey?" Marcy asked, wishing hard she would say *Got you! Got all of you! Me and Granny was only making a little fun.* And then they'd double over on the floor in laughter.

"Yes, she is," she said, not laughing. "Mommy told me, but she don't want us to tell daddy. She don't want him know before she leaves."

"That's why she never tell us? She think we would tell daddy? Mommy think we would really do something so stupid?" His eyes watered. "And because of that we just hearing mommy leaving in another day? This can't be real."

Neither of them cared anymore if the one-armed man got caught or not, so the TV became background noise and Audrey turned it off. They followed their grandmother to their mother's room, and she left them to talk. They sat on the floor, looking up at her on the bed. She took a deep breath and said, "Oonuh granny tell oonuh?"

"It's true Mommy?" Marcy asked. She breathed hard and begged her heart to be still. For although her mother had grown distant, she'd rather have her distant and at home, than faraway in another country.

They quieted. Waited. Hoped. Wished. Then Rose broke the silence. "Yes, mi going Friday, but mi might come back in two weeks."

Their wish and hope shattered, they remained quiet, until Donovan said, "Or you might not, Mommy?"

She told them that if she did not return in a couple of weeks, it meant things were going as planned. "And," she said, "If I get a chance to stay and work and carve a life for oonuh, I goin' take it."

Marcy steadied herself on the floor and studied her mother. *Even with sad, puffy eyes she's beautiful, her skin so clean and smooth, and waist, like she never had four of us, she doesn't even look like forty. I goin' miss her so much.* She wanted to hold this sight forever in her mind. When the thought occurred that her leaving didn't mean she would never see her again, she asked, "You mean you will send for us?"

She said it was her plan to do so, if given the chance. "It not so easy, you have to get work permit and landed papers, and all dat." Marcy drew closer, resting her head on her mother; her scent, coconut and lemon, she vowed to remember.

When she woke the next morning, her mother's leaving had not fully sunk in. She lay in bed, fumbling through hazy thoughts of things happening so fast. *Why us? Why now?*

Her mother came to their room and gave her and Maureen the okay to stay home from school. Audrey had it harder because she had one more year in high school. She begged, "Please, Mommy, I wouldn't be able to concentrate."

She was strict about their education, wanting them to excel to college or university. Having the four of them in her room, she reminded them of her expectations. "I don't wan' hear any of you get in wit' no bad company, or skipping school, and coming in late at nights, oonuh hear mi? And do as oonuh granny tell oonuh!" She latched eyes with theirs.

Like four little shadows, they followed her the whole day. It was as if she had been to Canada, and just got back. They were her babies again, like the early days at Barton Place.

Mari stayed home as well. Rose gave her a cooking break and prepared breakfast. After breakfast they cleared the kitchen sink so she could wash Rose's hair. Rose told the girls to watch what their grandmother did, "Especially you Audrey." Audrey moved closer. "So you can learn, and help your granny." The girls hovered as their grandmother pressed and curled her hair and put rollers in to keep the curls for the next day.

It was late September, and Cynthia wrote that the fall season had started in Canada. She informed Rose that it was cool, which for her 'just coming up', meant cold.

As she packed her small suitcase, they helped her bagged the clothes she was leaving with instructions for whom to give if she didn't return. Cynthia advised her to bring a sweater for the plane, and that she would bring a warm jacket to meet her at the airport. After she packed, she placed the sweater over the suitcase and set it by the door.

"You're staying with Ms. Cynthia, Mommy?" Marcy asked.

"Yes, and if Canada grant mi di work permit I can work and get mi own place."

"Then you will send for us?" Donovan asked, his face bright with expectation.

"Yes," she nodded, looking from one to the other. "But first I have to work and get a place for us to live."

That night in bed, the girls expressed how they felt about their mother's going abroad. Audrey and Maureen were excited for the gifts to come at Christmas. Marcy's heart wasn't ready and she was offended. "Gee, how oonuh act like oonuh not goin' miss mommy?" Her sisters looked at her as if she had said something strange. Maureen answered, "What you talking about, of course we going to miss her, but what we going to do?"

"We have to accept it, because if it work out for mommy, it will work out for all of us in the end," Audrey added.

"Yeah, but —"

"Look Marcy," Audrey raised on her elbows, "We all feeling it that mommy going away, and who knows when we'll see her again, but I'm glad she is happy for a change, so we just have to pray that things work out in Canada so she can send for us soon."

The room got quiet. Marcy buried her face in the pillow until sleep came.

By daylight the girls woke and went to their mother's room; neither she nor their grandmother were there. Her suitcase with her sweater thrown over the handle was still at the door. The sight of the ready suitcase stirred Marcy. She closed her eyes and garnered the courage to remain calm, like her sisters.

They went to the kitchen where the women were; Donovan was with them. Their mother was making 'punch'. Punch was her favourite drink she used to prepare for her and Arthur, and would occasionally give the children a sip, as it was made with Guinness Stout and Wincarnis Tonic Wine. They remembered the taste and salivated as she poured each of them a small cup.

"Mommy it taste a little different, not as strong," Maureen said.

"I didn't have any Wincarnis to put in it."

"It still nice though." She licked her lips.

"I love the condensed milk taste in it," Marcy said.

They gathered at the kitchen table and the conversation led to Arthur. She asked if they had seen him lately. "No, not for a week or so, so you know he might come today," Audrey said.

"Hopefully by then mommy gone," Donovan said.

"Mommy, you know daddy goin' ask where you gone, what we should tell him?" Maureen asked.

"You can tell him anyt'ing you want. I won't be here so it won't matter." She paused then said, "Just as long as nobody give him di address."

She told them she would write as soon as she was settled, hopefully in a few days. She took a guess that her letter might arrive in seven days, because that's how long Cynthia's letters took. She reminded them their grandmother was in charge, not that they'd forget, but she wanted to make it clear with Mari sitting there. "Don't t'ink she can't discipline oonuh as she sees fit."

It was Rose's first time travelling. Her flight was 1:30 p.m. and she wanted to get to the airport at least three hours earlier. She fussed, "We have to leave early in case of traffic, or if dem have papers at di airport for mi to fill out." They lived less than half hour from the airport. Nevertheless, she hurried the children from the kitchen. "Go, go get ready, I don't wan' be late."

Every few minutes she peered out the front window for Mr. Garrison; he had promised to take them to the airport.

As time crept up, Marcy went to her room. She stuck her head inside and saw her before the mirror putting on lipstick. She stepped back to catch her breath, and thought of the last time she saw her mother in lipstick. She couldn't remember. She had on red pants, with a red and white striped, long sleeved blouse tied in a floppy-bow at the neck; her hair was teased, in a flip - *That's my beautiful mommy looking gorgeous.* It was a long time she had seen her dressed up, and regardless of the occasion, she was proud.

At exactly 10:10 the family boarded the VW van and left home. Anyone watching would not know they were on their way to the airport, and one of them wouldn't return.

They reached the airport with no delays and Rose sighed in relief. As Mr. Garrison drove up to Departures, Mari told him they were waiting to see her off. He agreed to come back.

Four Red Cap porters rushed over as they stepped from the van. Rose had only a suitcase and a shoulder purse and said a courteous, "No, t'anks" on her way into the building.

As she went through the doors, everyone else following, a heavyset, middle-aged man with a bag strapped across his body, and a bag in each hand almost knocked her over. "Pardon me, Madam," he said, racing through the airport as the airlines announced flights departing.

"Bwoy, it busy sah," Mari said as she observed the people moving purposely about. Audrey and Maureen pointed to Air Canada's red and white maple leaf banner and they joined the line. When they got to the counter, a light-skinned Jamaican attendant said, "May I have your passport and ticket?" Rose handed her the documents and she checked her in. Then she directed her to customs and immigration and explained that once she went through the doors, she would not be allowed out again.

Rose had a couple of hours before her flight but thought it was best for her to go. The children circled her. She hugged and kissed them, giving each her own personal goodbye. Marcy held on, and she wiped her tears. "Don't worry mi baby." Afterward, she hugged and squeezed her mother; Mari's eyes watered. "Momma don't start crying now," she said. She pulled away and threw them a kiss as she said, "Bye, bye" and sped off.

The children cried out, "Bye, bye Mommy." In no time her red and white clad frame faded at the last door, and she was gone.

They went upstairs to the waving gallery. Their view was blocked by the people at the railing. Little by little the crowd dwindled as Air Jamaica flights to Miami and New York departed. They moved forward and Mari remained seated. As the announcement was made for passengers to begin boarding Air Canada, they got excited, anxious to see their mother walk to the plane. Marcy left the railing and went to her grandmother and the two sat pensively beside each other.

The passengers came into view in single file and Donovan and his sisters playfully shoved each other out the way for a glimpse of their mother. "Granny, Granny, come now," Audrey called.

Mari rubbed her knee. "Call mi when she come out." Her voice was cracked, it told that more than her knee was hurting.

Donovan shouted, "See her there, see her there, see mommy there."

Marcy helped her grandmother off her seat. "Oh Lawd, give mi strength," she murmured, and fixed her bag on her shoulder. They got to the railing in time to see her waving. The children cried out, "Mommy!" "Mommy!" "Mommy!" They didn't care if she couldn't see them from the runway. "Bye bye, Mommy!" "Bye, bye!" They waved and called until she walked up the steps and entered the plane. They didn't move until the plane ascended into the clouds and disappeared.

Chapter 16

For the drive home no one spoke. Mr. Garrison, a man of little conversation, kept his eyes on the road, and the others, locked in their own thoughts, focused outside the van.

Audrey, the one her siblings expected to keep them buoyed, broke down once inside the house. She cried out, "I want my mada, I want my mada." Mari sat next to her on the sofa and embraced her. "Ah mi child." Maureen went to bed, covering her face with the sheet. Donovan never spoke. He changed his clothes, got his soccer ball and left the house. Marcy, whose heart was already broken, felt for them, but was helpless, so she wandered to the side of the house. She stopped at the cherry tree and gazed at the ripe fruits; none tempted her to pick, her mind had drifted miles away.

Loud music soon pumped from Mr. Garrison's side, exactly what the house needed, prompting from Bob Marley and the Wailers to *Lively Up Yourself*.

As an army reservist and a mechanic, Mr. Garrison worked at a mechanic shop on his days off. At nights, he played his music low for his own entertainment. Though on Saturdays, after Mari left, he turned it up for the neighbourhood, especially now that Rose was not there to remind him to "be considerate, man".

He had the girls pondering the new Mr. Garrison.

One Saturday morning after their grandmother left and his music was at its height, they took a break from their chores and reflected on the different man. They sat on the floor, the clear polish and cleaning rag in the middle. Audrey said, "What a way him bruk out?" Her sisters agreed. "But you know, for a single man, me never see a woman come visit him yet," she said, as if carefully thought through.

"Maybe he's funny," Maureen said, and chuckled.

"No, I don't think so," Audrey replied.

"Why? He could be homosexual, yes."

"No, man."

"How are you so sure?"

"Believe me when I tell you," she said; her tone revealed inside information.

Maureen pressed. "Audrey, I don't like that look on your face, what you know that you not saying?"

"Nothing."

"Come on, don't leave us hanging."

"Yes! Tell, tell Audrey," Marcy urged.

They pulled, yet Audrey refused to give. Maureen looked at Marcy and raised an eye; they both surmised there was something Audrey was hiding.

Later, while in bed, Audrey's sisters continued to pressure her. Maureen said, "You keeping a dirty little secret." Audrey hissed, and shook her head. "Or, maybe you like him?" she teased.

"Oh, please!" Audrey protested.

"So what could it be that you can't tell nobody?" Maureen got upset. "I'm not leaving you alone until you spill the beans."

Audrey frowned.

Marcy asked, "Audrey, he did something to you?"

She flashed a stern look. "Like what?"

Her sisters quieted, waited, their eyes locked on her mouth.

She took a couple of deep breaths and said, "Oonuh is something else", shaking her head.

"Yes, your two nosey sisters," Maureen said, and she and Marcy chuckled.

In a low, agonizing voice, Audrey said, "Two times yesterday he showed me his, you know what." She rolled her eyes at 'you know what'.

"What?" Marcy asked.

"Buddy!"

"Buddy, as in penis?" Maureen asked.

"Yes. Yesterday as I was passing his side window, and again this morning hanging the clothes on the line, I saw him standing at his window with no clothes on."

"You mean he was naked?" Marcy asked.

"Yes, naked as the day he was born."

"Then he realized you saw him?" Maureen asked.

"Yes, that's what I'm telling you. He was in his bedroom with the window and curtain wide open looking at me."

"He took a chance, what if granny was around there?"

"No man, it's me he's after, 'cause he knew I was 'round there by myself. He just stared in my eyes, with his big, long hood hanging down his knees like a donkey."

"Oh Lord, then you never scream?" Marcy asked.

"No, I was too shocked."

Audrey's disclosure left the three of them in disbelief that Mr. Garrison was anything like that. "And look how he looks so quiet. Like a man who just go work and come home and stay by himself," Maureen said.

"Like a little hermit," Marcy added, with a chuckle.

"That was before, when mommy was here. Now we see the true man," Audrey said.

"So, you goin' tell Granny? She goin' be so surprise," Maureen said.

"I don't know what to do."

"You better tell her, what if him turn out to be a rapist?" Marcy said, causing the three of them to laugh with their hands covering their mouths.

"I don't know, I kinda feel shame to tell her, and I feel shame for him to," she said, and paused, as if thinking things through. "Because he seemed like such a nice man. This don't seem like the same person." Her brows narrowed. "I goin' wait and see if he tries it again, and if he ever, dog eat him supper!" They laughed.

"If him don't behave him nasty self, just let Granny deal with him," Marcy said. They agreed.

She went to bed smiling with an image of her grandmother chasing Mr. Garrison around the yard, swinging her cutlass behind him.

Marcy was in the backyard when Sandy came and told her she saw her father passing the house. "He went down the road," she said, knowing the situation with him and the family.

Marcy told Maureen he was in the area, and they went and told Audrey in the kitchen.

"So?"

"What we goin' tell him about mommy?" Marcy asked.

"Well you heard what mommy said, she don't care."

"No, that's not what I mean, how him goin' take it?"

"It goin' hurt him feelings," Maureen said.

"It going to hurt his feelings yes, but I don't know what else to tell him. You will have to tell him something if he asks, but I can't go out there now."

"Why?"

"Yeah, why you can't come, Audrey?" Marcy asked, believing she would have the right words to calm him, if necessary.

"Don't you see me seasoning the meat?"

"I can wait until you're finish," Marcy persisted. Audrey continued rubbing the curry seasoning on the goat meat without answering.

"I'm going out there," Maureen said, turning away.

"Do what oonuh want, but I can't come there now."

Hoping to stall, Marcy grabbed Maureen's arm. "Maybe we don't have to go out there now."

"What you mean?"

"I mean since he didn't see us yet, let's plan what we going to say before we go."

"We have to face him sometime, Marcy." Maureen shook off her sister's hand. "I'm going now."

Marcy caught up to her at the gate in time to see him make another round down the road. Maureen yelled, "Daddy, Daddy!" He turned and looked. They waved at him to come.

Marcy wanted an excuse to run inside the house and not face him, but he approached them smiling and her heart sank. He drew them close and hugged them. "Daddy, you gone all white now," she blurted. He nodded, still smiling. "Look how the hair on your face change," she said, avoiding the real changes she needed to discuss.

"Ah, baby, you daddy getting old." He looked older than fifty.

"I hope Mr. Fitzy not working you too hard?" she joked. He cracked a smile.

Then in a soft voice Maureen said, "Mommy gone away, you know, Daddy."

He did not answer. Maybe he did not hear, or maybe it was too much for his mind and he blocked it, the way they did when their grandmother tried to tell them. "Daddy you hear what I say?"

"You say you mada gone 'way?" His eyes grew weaker as it sank in. After a few seconds, he looked to the ground, as if thinking how he didn't see it coming. "Where she gone?"

"Mommy gone to Canada, she left over a week ago."

He stood still, silent, as if the shock had glued his mouth closed. They stared at him. No words were exchanged for a minute. Then he sighed and said, "Alright" and slowly turned and walked away. The two of them looked at each other; they couldn't let him leave like that. They had to do something.

"Daddy, Daddy, you want me follow you home?" Maureen asked.

"No, go inside." They walked behind him.

"So where you going Daddy?" Marcy asked. He didn't answer.

They followed him to the top of the road. He stopped and said, "Oonuh go home now."

When they got home they went to the kitchen and told Audrey what had happened. "Come to think of it," Marcy said, "He didn't even ask if mommy was coming back."

"Don't be stupid, him must know she's not coming back. How many people you know get the chance to go away and come back?"

"Especially somebody like mommy," Maureen added.

"Exactly," Audrey emphasized. "Who always wanted to escape the punishment he gave her."

The three of them sat in the kitchen mulling over life without their mother, and Maureen said, "If we can miss mommy so, and we know we'll see her again, I can just imagine how daddy must feel."

"Maybe later we can go see if he's okay," Marcy said.

"Of course he's okay, he has to go through this. He has to deal with it on his own," Audrey said.

"It's because you never saw him, he looked so lost when I said she was gone. Maybe he just needs one of us to keep his company now," Maureen said.

"What daddy needs now is time by himself to accept that mommy is gone and to figure out how to move on with his life." Neither Maureen nor Marcy answered, so she continued, "Maybe now he could find another woman and stop thinking about mommy. He needs to understand that he will never have her now, she is gone and not coming back, end of story!"

"Gee, that's a little harsh, Audrey," Maureen said.

"But it's the truth, don't fool yourself."

Marcy thought about it and said, "Well, especially now that he's not drinking so much, maybe he could meet somebody, you know, a nice lady."

"Right, he just needs to set his sights elsewhere," she said.

Maureen hissed and left the kitchen.

It got tense between Audrey and Maureen, but with the excitement of receiving a letter from their mother, the tension soon eased.

Saturday midday they waited on the veranda in the hot sun, listening for the sound of the postman's bell. At 12:30 he rode up to the gate and they bolted to the postbox. The postman play-acted; he pretended he was going to put the letter in the box and had his ears blasted with, "No, no." "Give it to me." "No, me!" "No. I'm the eldest, give it to me." He laughed and put it in Audrey's hand. The only problem, Audrey could not open the letter. They had to wait until their grandmother came home and she was not due until after six, which meant trying to make hours seem like minutes.

They passed around the letter, examining the red, blue and white oblong-shaped envelope. They shook it, checked the handwriting and the address, and wondered where exactly was Toronto, Ontario, Canada.

After they had finished their immediate chores, the girls cleared old, worn-out clothes from the closet, an overdue chore, just to keep their minds off the letter. Close to six o'clock, they sat in the living room with the television on, watching and listening for the gate, rather than the TV. As the gate opened, Audrey nearest the window, looked out. "It's Granny." Donovan and Marcy got up to meet her. She stopped them. "Don't go, let's pretend it didn't come and give her a surprise."

"No man, Audrey," Marcy said, flustered. She wanted to run to her and say, *guess what, mommy letter come*. But Audrey scowled at her and she sat down. Her grandmother took her time coming in, to her it seemed like hours. When she saw her in the doorway, she jumped up and yelled, "Granny, mommy write!"

"O Lawd, O Lawd, wait likkle man, make mi sit down first." Mari took the closest chair. Audrey handed her the letter as they crowded around her. "Hold on likkle," she said. She sifted through handkerchief, paper, money, medication, keys and the like, to get to the bottom of her handbag for her reading glasses. The children hovered restlessly. She found her glasses, put them on and tore open the envelope. She scanned it, then gave it back to Audrey. "Read it for mi." They knew she couldn't read well.

Audrey read, "Hello Momma, Audrey, Maureen, Donovan and Marcy, I reached safely..." She continued to say it was quite chilly and at nights she slept under a blanket. She wrote that she was not sure how things would work for now, but told Mari to kiss her darling children and to "tell them I miss them very, very much". At the end, she said she would write again in a few days. Mari asked Audrey to read it over and after she did, Maureen and Marcy asked if they could read it for themselves.

Another letter arrived by the following week and this time it had important news. She wrote that she may not return as Ms. Cynthia had helped her to find a babysitting job. Mari paused, hung her head, shook it and said, "Ah, good friend sure better dan pocket money", referring to Cynthia whom she considered a valuable friend of Rose.

After Audrey read the letter, her grandmother told her to put it in her dresser draw. That night as they lay in bed, wondering aloud what their mother might be doing, Audrey put her hand under the mattress. "Look what I have," she said, and held up a letter. "I got this from Granny's dresser draw." She sat up and folded her legs.

"What is that Audrey?" Marcy asked.

"A letter from Ms. Cynthia to mommy, when mommy was planning to go to Canada." Maureen and Marcy looked at each other, surprised at her bravery.

"Why you trouble it, Audrey?"

"Oonuh want me to read it or not?" she asked, taking it from the envelope before they answered. She held it with both hands, looking it over. "Oh, is the same flowery paper mommy wrote us on." Her sisters peered over her shoulders as she read:

Sept 2nd, 1970

Hello Rosie,

How keeping, I hope you are pretty fine. As I told you before leaving if I get a chance to help you I certainly will. You suffer long enough under Arthur. It really ruff here but if you can fight it you will get out, you can stay by me until you find a place to stay or if you want send $50 dollars I can get someone to write an invitation and I will get a room for you before you come, so speed up with it if you want to come this month, the invitation is just 3 weeks so you buy a 3 weeks ticket and bring a letter from your work place with the letter head showing you work there 6 to 7 years and recommendation and you will have your job back anytime you come and you are on a vacation, O.K. Bring divorce paper and age paper and all documents with you and don't let nobody know you have them O.K. Hide them but not in your suit case. I hope everybody is O.K. Bye for now.

Same,
Cynthia

Audrey finished reading and put the letter back under the mattress. "I still don't know why you had to take it out, Audrey?" Marcy said.

"Well, it's not like I'm going to keep it."

She thought about the content of the letter, and asked, "So mommy had to pay Ms. Cynthia fifty dollars to help her? Plus buy a plane ticket to go to Canada?"

"Yes, it cost money to go to Canada, you nuh."

"You know what I've been thinking?" Maureen said. "How Granny goin' pay the rent by herself?"

"Me too."

"The two of you forget that mommy going to send money to help her?" Audrey replied.

"No, I'm talking about now."

"Don't forget when mommy and daddy divorced and they sold the house, she got money from that."

"Oh," Maureen said, making the connection.

"And she put her money in the bank because she was at JOS. And now she's working, we don't have to worry."

Marcy never questioned her eldest sister who always had the answers. She listened as Audrey and Maureen discussed the future. Audrey planned to get a 'good job' after school, with no mention of going to university, like their mother intended. Maureen was anxious to finish high school, without adding further plans, which Marcy suspected was because she banked on going to Canada. She was glad they didn't ask her, as they'd probably laugh when she told them her secret desire was to be a dancer at the Little Theater with Rex Nettleford.

They received a letter from their mother every other week or so. By the fourth letter, there was money in the envelope. By Christmas, they received their first barrel from Canada. Although there were no doubts they missed their mother, they happily delved into the barrel for the new 'foreign' clothes, toiletries, and packed and canned foods, amenities scarce to most people in Jamaica.

Six months after Rose left, the Jamaica Telephone Company ran telephone lines on Summerfield Road. Mari applied and they got their own telephone. Rose called on Sunday afternoons. They spoke in order of age, or who was the 'lucky one' near the phone when it rang. Overall, their grandmother got the most talk time as there was always 'one more t'ing' their mother had to say to her before ending the call.

Since there was only one telephone, it was placed in Mari's room. A scheme the matriarchs 'cooked-up', according to Audrey and Maureen to find out their 'goings-on'. But in truth, Audrey and Maureen never gave the telephone a break. In the evenings, before their grandmother came home, even though they saw their friends at school they still came home and telephoned them. And on Saturdays they talked at length, both during and after their chores. They got away with it until the first telephone bill arrived.

Their grandmother realized what they were up to because she used the telephone only to receive updates on her sister Diane. So, she put a padlock on the phone and hid the key.

Chapter 17

By the following year, the allure of the telephone wore off.
The sisters grumbled that the constant searching for the key to
make a quick call behind their grandmother's back grew tiresome.

Meeting friends at the beach had more appeal. In the summer when school was out, Audrey and Maureen planned to go
to the sea, and preferred to go on their own. Marcy wanted to
go too, although she wasn't allowed to go without them. Their
grandmother sorted out that problem when she said, "Everybody go together, or nobody go at all!" She suspected something
was afoot and added, "because you never know what dem boys
at di seaside up to."

"What boys Granny?" Maureen asked, surprised at her
grandmother's knowledge of the beach scene, considering she
didn't even own a bathing suit.

She looked askance at Maureen. "You t'ink mi born yesseday?"

Marcy asked Sandy to accompany her and her mother gave
her permission to go.

They were at the beach by noon. Audrey and Maureen immediately branched off with their friends. Donovan, who had gone ahead, was diving with some older boys.

Scores of children, some from other neighbourhoods, were at the seaside. Marcy and Sandy sat on the seashore watching the splashing and diving antics of everyone else. Two boys in the water, maybe fourteen or fifteen, asked why they weren't swimming. Marcy told them they liked to sit in the sun and collect seashells. "That's boring," the light-skinned boy said. "Me and my friend," he pointed to his friend smiling with a gap in his front teeth, "We can teach you how to swim."

Marcy and Sandy giggled. "Who told you we can't swim?" Marcy asked.

"Then come in, nuh," he said, slapping the water back and forth.

Marcy looked at Sandy. "You ready to go in?"

"Yeah," Sandy said, and they met the boys in the water.

"Hey, by the way, my name is Ricky and this is Nigel."

"I'm Marcy."

"And I'm Sandy." The guy with the gapped teeth, Nigel, held onto Sandy as she entered the water. Ricky tried to take Marcy's hand, and she pulled back, her grandmother's words about what the boys on the beach were up to, coming to mind. "Take my hand, nuh," Ricky said, grinning.

I like his smile, her mind wandered, but her lips said, "No, thank you."

"I don't bite, you nuh."

"I didn't say that."

"You don't like me?"

He caught her off guard. "I don't even know you." She shrugged.

"Give it time, man," he flashed a wide smile. Marcy thought, *you're good looking yes, but you're too pushy.*

They walked out to where the sea met her chest. "This is far enough for me," she said.

"What happen, you scared you might drown?" he jeered.

"No, I just feel safer when my toes can touch the ground and the water not getting into my mouth."

"But you with me, you don't need to worry." He smiled, his eyes small and dreamy, which made him cuter. She tried not to stare.

By this time, Sandy and Nigel had moved farther away. Sandy lay over his arms as he taught her the breaststroke. Seeing Sandy so at ease with Nigel, Marcy figured to do the same with Ricky. She lay over his arms and floated on her back. She enjoyed the sun on her face. He held her in that position for a while and she felt safe. When he told her to turn onto her stomach, she did, and kept her head from going under. *So far so good.*

She pretended she was a mermaid and flopped both feet at once; she almost fell. "Oh boy, I better get off now."

He steadied himself and kept her from falling. "Don't worry, man, me have you, trust me."

She felt secure once more and relaxed. After a couple of minutes, she thought she felt his hand passing over her chest. She didn't think anything at first, just that he was struggling to carry her. Then she felt his hand brushed against her, again. This time, she definitely felt his fingers fumble her chest, as if trying to get into her bathing suit.

She sprang off his hands and shouted, "What the hell you doing?"

His face turned red. "What you mean?" he said, moving back.

"You don't know what you did?" She was shaking and her voice got louder. Ricky backed away the louder she got until he dove under the water and swam away. He swam so hard that by the time a couple of older boys came over, he was out of sight.

As she walked to shore, she looked around for Sandy and her sisters but didn't see them. She slipped on her dress and sat on the grass. While waiting, she thought about 'the liberty' Ricky took with her and vowed to be smarter.

Shortly after, she saw Sandy and Nigel coming, they were laughing and holding hands. "Where is Ricky?" Sandy asked, as if he were their longtime friend.

"Good question." Marcy frowned.

Sandy read her countenance and asked, "Everything all right, Marcy?"

She ignored her friend's question. "You see any of my sisters?"

"Yes, I saw Maureen going up the road, like she going home."

"Okay, see you later, I'm going." She picked up her towel and started walking.

"Marcy, wait for me."

"You don't have to leave because of me, Sandy." Sandy followed her anyway.

Nigel caught up to them. "She said you don't have to leave."

"Yes, but it's me and her come, and if she's leaving I have to leave too."

On the way home, Marcy told Sandy what Ricky did, and Sandy wondered if it really happened or if she imagined it. She glared at her. "Sandy, you're my friend and you don't believe me?"

"No Marcy, it's not that, 'cause if he really did that to you, then we should tell somebody and let them deal with him."

"Deal with him? You mean like get one of them bad boys from downtown to fix him business?" The two of them burst out laughing.

When she got home, Maureen and Audrey were on the veranda and Audrey asked, "Hi Misses, how was your swim?"

"Good, good," she said, and went inside to change. She kept quiet about Ricky's roaming fingers. She wouldn't want her grandmother to know she was right, and go back to chaperoned days. "How come the two of you home already?" she asked, joining her sisters.

Maureen said, "Oh, after Joanne got her first Jelly fish sting —"

"Wow, she got stung today? Poor thing."

"It spoil the vibe, so we just called it a day."

She turned to Audrey. "I was looking for you down there."

"Me and my friend Carroll spent the whole time sitting under a tree talking 'bout the NYS program; all now my feet haven't touched water." The National Youth Services (NYS) program was a mandatory on-the-job training program designed for students graduating high school, and Audrey was eligible.

"Where they goin' place you?" Marcy asked.

"At one of the government offices downtown."

"Yeah, which one?"

"Maybe the Ministry of Finance."

"Is that where you want to go?" Maureen asked.

"Well, they normally place you in the area you're strongest."

"You excited? You'll be a working woman soon," Marcy said, drawing closer to her on the railing.

"In a way, because they only pay a pittance. Thank God it's only two years."

"I'm not looking forward to it," Maureen said.

"Who knows? By then you might be in Canada," Marcy told her.

"What a day! What a day!" She clapped.

Maureen had reason to be hopeful since Rose's life in Canada was going well. On one of her last calls she said she received her landed status, and a Social Insurance Number (SIN) that allowed her to work officially in Canada. This was excellent news, as she was not limited to babysitting jobs. At one of her babysitter jobs, a child spat on her and alluding to her skin colour, asked how she knew when she was clean. It was difficult raising other people's children, especially the unruly ones, but she accepted it as her new life. And as Mari counselled, "If you want good, your nose have to run."

Now having a SIN, she worked as a live-in domestic with a couple, both lawyers, caring for their two young daughters. The new job allowed her to save more as the pay was better. And she liked her bosses. She said they were 'decent people'. They helped her to understand the immigration system and complete the paperwork. If things continued on the same path, she planned to file for citizenship in a year and a half.

Chapter 18

Since Rose left, Arthur mostly stayed in the country, and the times he was in town the children seldom saw him. Because they hadn't seen him for a while, Maureen, Donovan and Marcy decided to go and find him. A woman was raking leaves in the front yard when they got to the gate. They told her who they were and asked if she knew if their father was home. She said, "I believe so." But before she called him, she stood staring. "I can't believe Arta have dem nice children here."

When she went to get him, walking back to the gate she said, "I can't believe oonuh sweet children belong to Arta" and gazed at him with familiarity.

"Who is that Daddy?" Marcy whispered.

"Merle, Mr. Fitzy family. She come from country come help dem sometimes."

As Marcy sat on the bed, she asked, "Daddy, how you keep so scarce, you went to the country?"

"No mi never go dis trip."

"Why?"

"Mi never feel too well dem last days."

A little brown envelope with tablets was on the table. Marcy picked it up. She inspected it and asked, "Daddy why you have Phensic, you feeling pains?"

"Is Merle get dem for mi," he rubbed his chest, "for sometimes mi get a pain across here so."

Marcy noticed his eyes were sunken and he was thinner. "Them work?"

"Yeah, when dem ready."

"Maybe you should get a check up, Daddy," Maureen said.

"Mi alright, man."

Maureen picked up a letter off the table, scrutinized the white envelope with the sender's information and asked, "Who is Enid Barrett from St. Mary, Daddy?"

"Dat's mi sister."

"Your sister, Daddy?" Maureen drew back, squinted and said, "I didn't know you had a sister?"

"Of course oonuh know."

"I mean, a sister that's alive."

"I don't remember hearing about any sister," Marcy said, just as puzzled.

"No, we never heard of a sister anywhere."

"Mi coulda swear mi or oonuh mada tell oonuh."

"We know you're from St. Mary, but that's it." They never knew of relatives from either side of his family. "It's nice to know you have a sister Daddy, and that we have an auntie."

"How long since you saw her?" Maureen asked.

"'Bout a year ago."

"Where, in St. Mary?"

"Yes. She have a lickle food shop Fitzy use to supply."

"So you and her keep in touch?"

"Yes, she write mi all di while."

He said meeting his sister Enid after thirty odd years, helped him "close loose ends" in his life. He learned he had five brothers and sisters, and the six of them had four mothers between them; their father, Clarence, a man known for his big cigars, died twenty years earlier from lung cancer.

"Then how you feel Daddy, hearing you have all these relatives?"

"Well, it make mi feel good you nuh," he paused, "Mi just sorry mi never get to meet di rest a dem, for everybody scatter or dead now."

"Maybe one day you'll take us to meet Aunt Enid?" Marcy asked.

"Yes, she woulda love dat."

The children said they had homework and had to go. Before leaving, Maureen took Enid's address and promised to write her, and then she told him, "Daddy, I think I goin' have to keep a closer eye on you from now on."

"What you mean, mi dear?"

"I'm not sure you taking care of yourself."

He swore he was, and convinced them not to worry. "It's just a likkle upset stomach mi had. Mi alright, man, you daddy alright."

He walked them part of the way home. After they hugged goodbye at the corner, he crossed the street and headed in the direction of Franklin's. Marcy tugged her sister's arm. "Maureen, you see where him gone?" The three of them watched him go into the bar.

"You can believe that?" Donovan said.

"I wonder what it will take for him to wise up."

"Who knows? We'll just have to pray for him and not let him out of our sight. Think about it though, outside of us, it's only the bar he has," Maureen said.

Chapter 19

When Rose called that Sunday, Marcy told her they visited their father and discovered he had a sister, Enid, in the country. She confirmed he had a sister he spoke of around the time they met, but not much after that. Although she did not ask how he was, Marcy told her about the Phensic he took for his stomach, and that he had lost the little weight he had gained. It pleased her that her mother listened, without showing impatience towards her father. After she finished updating her mother on him, she asked her what was new with her. She said she got her driver's license and was driving for her employers. They gave her a second car they had to take their girls to school, swimming and piano lessons. Before giving her grandmother the telephone, she asked how she managed driving in the snow. "Some days better dan some. Sometimes di sun bright, bright, and when I get outside it cold as ice." She chuckled and said, "And driving on a windy day, especially if ice on di ground, I have to pray hard."

Her mother stayed on her mind after they spoke. She sat on the back veranda thinking of her bearing the elements to sacrifice for them. She sighed, rolled her shoulders to release the tightness and glanced above at specks of blue sky peeking through green ackee leafs. She smiled through tears for her mother.

Sandy came to the fence. "Hey Marcy", jolting her from melancholy.

"What?" She dabbed her eyes with the end of her dress.

"Come here."

"You come, man." Sandy came and sat next to her on the stool with the broadest smile. "Why you so happy?" Marcy asked.

She leaned in. "Remember that boy Nigel from the beach?"

"Yeah, the one from last summer you haven't stopped talking about."

"Yes, same one. Well, guess what? I just saw him again outside the patty shop."

Sandy's eyes widened, explaining Nigel had moved from the area, but was visiting relatives and friends. "Was Ricky with him?"

"No, it was him alone."

"Not that I'm interested," she said. "Just checking if he's long gone from the area."

"Well, I have you know, he is not only long gone from the area, he's migrated to America, some place name Baltimore."

"Thank heavens!"

Sandy was quick to add, "But Nigel is not like Ricky."

"I hope so, for he was a creep."

"Nigel say he wants to see me again," she said, with her ready-for-trouble voice.

"Oh, he must really like you then."

Sandy's face reddened.

"And we exchanged phone numbers."

"What if he calls and your mother answer the phone?"

"He will know to hang up."

Sandy was twelve, but sometimes she said or did something, like carry-on over Nigel that made Marcy tease her, "Sandy, how old are you again?"

Shaking her long neck and flashing her shoulder length, sun-lightened hair, she sassed, "I have you know, I'll be thirteen very soon!"

Neither of them had a boyfriend for obvious reasons, and regardless of their age, they knew 'whose roof' they lived under. Even though Rose was away, just the memory of her chilling stare, unnerved Marcy, and Sandy's mother was just as strict.

Since they attended the same high school, if they had activities after school, or on weekends, they were allowed only if the other was going. Sandy continued, "He wants the two of us to go out somewhere."

"How you going work that?"

"I want you to come with me."

"What kinda trouble you want to get me in?"

"No, no trouble." She gave her friend the 'please Marcy' eyes.

"When would this be?"

"I don't know yet, that's why he's goin' call me."

The following weeks Sandy and Nigel's communication grew beyond phone calls to meeting after school for hours at the bus stop. Because they travelled to and from school together, Marcy waited for her, barely making it home before her grandmother.

Nigel was serious about Sandy and he made it known. For her thirteenth birthday he promised her a gift. "Nigel wants to give me a pendant to go with the chain my father bought me."

"Where you'd tell your mother you got it?"

"That my father gave me."

"Sandy, you mad? What if she found out you lied?"

She took a deep breath. "Okay, okay, you right."

On her birthday, Nigel waited for her behind the bus shed. He took off a #13 pendant he wore on his chain with his own #16 pendant, and as he put it on her chain, he kissed her cheek.

Oozing from Cupid's arrow, Sandy couldn't wait to show Marcy on the bus. "You like it?"

Marcy examined the gold jewel hanging from her neck. "Yes, it's nice," she told her. "You have an answer for your mother yet?"

"I goin' tell her my friends put together and bought me as a birthday gift." Marcy's mouth hung open at her friend's audacity. "You won't tell anybody right?" Too stunned for words, she shook her head.

"Promise?"

"Sandy, you know I won't."

She squeezed her hand. "Marcy, I'm glad you're my friend, my best friend."

Having Sandy as a close friend was equally good for Marcy. She and her sisters started on separate paths to adulthood, except when they squeezed together in bed at nights. With Maureen almost seventeen and Audrey nineteen, their main interests were 'private' and 'personal'. Maureen never left the house without her lipstick and eye shadow, and she hardly saw Audrey until nighttime. It was at nights she learned of their days, like the time Maureen came home with her knees scraped off. She told their grandmother she "tumbled down, running from a bad dog", and later confessed to her sisters she fell off

Patrick's bicycle. Patrick was her friend Joanne's brother, the boyfriend she denied having. Since Maureen divulged her antics with Patrick, she wanted Audrey to open up about her guy. "Well, everybody see how you come home, change your clothes and gone again. It's obvious Audrey, there's a boy lurking somewhere," Maureen said, never hesitating to get into Audrey's business.

Marcy laughed, and Audrey asked her jokingly, "What you laughing 'bout Miss Marcy?"

"See, even Marcy knows."

"Nothing to hide my dears, nothing to hide."

"So tell me 'bout this guy nuh?"

"He's a guy from work."

"Yeah, yeah," Maureen prompted. "We want to know more, what's his name, age, and all that."

"His name is Anthony McFarland."

"Yes, don't stop."

"They call him Tony. He's twenty, finished his NYS and got full time in accounting."

"So where he lives? What he looks like? Is he good looking?"

"Lawd, inspector, you'll see for yourself." She folded her pillow and put her head down. "Me gone sleep."

"Wait, wait, what you mean I'll see?"

She raised her head. "He says he wants to meet my family."

"Woooow, things a gwaan."

"That's nice Audrey that he wants to meet Granny, I mean all of us," Marcy said.

"Yeah, he is a decent guy. I wouldn't bring him home if he wasn't."

"It sounds serious, mi sister." Maureen chuckled.

"Well, we'll see, just have to break it to Granny now," she faced the wall, "Enough, go sleep."

The following week she came into their room laughing and Maureen asked, "What you got away with now?"

"No, me just laughing at how Granny was on to me all this time." Audrey told her sisters that for days she had been trying to get their grandmother alone to discuss her and Tony's relationship, so when her grandmother came home with the groceries she met her at the door and took the bags to the kitchen. She put the groceries away and helped her to shell some gungo peas.

"Then Granny never ask how you so helpful today?"

"Wait, let me tell you, man," she swallowed and started again, "she was a little skeptical, yes, but mi never know how to come out with it."

"You were probably so nervous," Marcy said.

"You shoulda see me, me just a ramble on 'bout everything except Tony."

Audrey said she even brought up something that happened a year before. "Hear me to Granny nuh, Granny, you remember the time the big, fat, stray cat sneak through the kitchen window and eat off the fish you'd just brought home for dinner, you remember that Granny?"

"How mi coulda forget? If I did catch dat damn puss, you see."

Audrey and her grandmother had a good laugh at the past, but she needed to bring the conversation into the present. So, in the middle of their laughter Audrey slipped in her news. "Granny, I met a friend at work." Her grandmother was baffled, one minute she imagined killing a puss, and the next, getting blindsided about Audrey's 'friend' at work.

"So what Granny say?" Marcy asked.

"Wait man," Audrey slowed her down, "Me never know Granny knew what was going on, and shocked me when she asked if it was him she saw picking me up in the mornings." She said she stuttered, "Gr-Gr-Granny?" unaware her grandmother had been watching them from her bedroom all this time. She told her she saw Tony parked at the side of the house in the mornings waiting for her, and made Audrey laugh by adding, "Audrey, mi might run pass school gate, but mi never born big." The three sisters laughed at their grandmother's wits.

The following Monday, Audrey brought Tony home. They sat on the veranda with her grandmother. Maureen and Marcy planted themselves in the living room with the curtains open wide enough to see without being seen.

Maureen peeped. "Not bad, slim, big Afro, bow legs."

"And him light-skinned too," Marcy whispered.

"Pretty babies."

"Maureen, you too bad," Marcy said, and they ran from the room stifling a laugh.

Since that evening, Tony was official. He was free to come in and wait for Audrey. Mari told him, "No need hide outside in di car like a t'ief a stake out di house."

Chapter 20

One morning on their way to school, Sandy's smile was more blinding than the morning sun. Marcy knew she had news. "Yes man, give me the score on you and Nigel."

She grinned, grabbed Marcy's arm and wrapped hers around it. "Walk up little more and mi tell you. The women them just a stare," she said, referring to the street cleaners. She led her a clear distance away from them. "Marcy, come with me and Nigel to matinee this Saturday, nuh?"

"This Saturday?" She did a mental scan of her Saturday schedule.

"Yeah, me and Nigel want go watch *Love Story*. Nigel really wan' see it."

"I have to ask Granny."

"Just tell her me and you going."

"And I have to see if I have enough for show fare."

"No problem man, between me and Nigel, we will pay for you." Marcy processed her friend's request. "Come man, come," she insisted.

"All right, all right," she said, seeing how much it meant to her.

"Thank you, thank you, thank you, Marcy."

Saturday afternoon, they met at Sandy's gate. Sandy wore a red hot pants and a white popcorn blouse. "Check you out!" Marcy said.

"How mi look?"

"Just be glad your mother not home."

They headed to Cross Roads to meet Nigel at Carib theater. Getting off the bus, Sandy glimpsed him on the steps. "See him there," she said, and ran to him. Marcy caught up. Nigel walked a little ahead so no one could tell he was with them. They went to the ticket counter and the girls gave him their money. He added his and bought the tickets. Passing the snack counter, he said he was getting a roast beef sandwich and soda and asked if they wanted anything. They had already eaten and asked for buttered popcorn. Inside the cinema, they went to the back row where it was empty. Marcy took the aisle seat, then Nigel and Sandy beside him. They whispered and giggled throughout the movie. Marcy was surrounded by the love story on the screen and the one happening beside her.

As they left the theater, the street buzzed with late Saturday evening activities. They walked to the bus stop amid shoppers rushing to nearby malls and markets. Taxi drivers crawled by and honked their horns at anyone seeming too tired to wait. A young man passing on his bicycle called out, "Peanut! Peanut! Roasted or salt!" Another on foot, rhymed, "Cigarette, cigarette! Singles and pack! Get you cigarettes from Brother Mac." The woman sitting behind the bus shed, not to be left out, said, "Come get you icy mint and Wrigley's to sweet-up you mouth."

In a crowded place like Cross Roads, Marcy was surprised to see Sandy and Nigel holding hands. She leaned into Sandy. "You not afraid people see oonuh?"

She shrugged. Marcy took it as, *mind your own business.*

Nigel turned to Sandy and whispered. She turned to Marcy. "You want us go to the zoo?"

"When, now?"

"Yeah, why not?"

"Sandy, you told your mother you were going out after the show?"

"No, but-"

"Neither did I tell Granny I was coming home late, so I think we should go straight home."

Sandy and Nigel weren't please. As expected, he screwed his face and she turned her back to Marcy. Marcy felt bad and wondered if they were sorry she came. Then she thought, *well, without me, oonuh wouldn't be here in the first place.* Still, guilt weighed on her. She moved closer. "Oonuh really want go to the zoo?"

"No, it's okay, we changed our minds," Sandy said.

Marcy read the frowns on their faces. "You sure?" she asked. "Cause I will go, if oonuh still want to go."

They locked eyes, ignoring her. "Call me when you reach home," Nigel said, taking Sandy's hand.

"If I get a chance."

"All right." He squeezed her hand as he walked away.

On the bus ride home Sandy was quiet. Marcy tried to make conversation. "It was a good movie right?"

"It was good."

"I wish one day I'll have a husband who loves me like he loved her."

"At this rate Marcy, I'm not sure you'll ever get a husband."

Chapter 21

On Saturdays by midday, Marcy had the house to herself.
Once her sisters hurried through their housework, they were
gone. Even Donovan, after he swept and wet the yard was gone
for a day of soccer and sea, and at the end of the day, he and his
friends chipped in and cooked food at one of their houses. At
four o'clock, he'd run home to get ready and leave again to meet
his grandmother at the Coronation Market to help her bring
home the provisions.

As soon as everyone left the house, Sandy came over, Nigel
visited shortly after, and the house became a sanctuary for the
teenagers. Except, Mr. Garrison was home until late in the day
playing his music. And of late, he played a lot of lover's rock,
mostly Dennis Brown, as he warmed up for his 'guest'.

One Saturday, the three friends played dominoes on the veranda.
Marcy slammed the last domino on the table, winning the game.
Nigel yelled, "Kiss mi neck back! Marcy, you good!"

A voice from a silhouette passing, whispered, "Good afternoon", getting their attention. By the time Marcy looked behind

her, a tall, skinny woman with legs looking twice as long under her mini skirt, whisked by.

"Is that him girlfriend?" Nigel asked.

"I guess so, I see her a few times now and I hear him call her Michie. I think her name is Michelle."

"Boy, him must climb them pair of legs straight up to heaven," Nigel said, causing all three of them to laugh.

"She look so young," Sandy whispered.

"She look around Audrey's age," Marcy said.

"That means she's a young gal for him." Sandy chuckled.

"Or, he's old man for her." They laughed.

Not even five minutes after 'Michie' went inside his house, the music stopped and the door slammed, and the windows slammed louder. Then silence. Total lockdown. Marcy laughed to herself remembering Audrey's description of his 'donkey hood'.

After their last round of dominoes, they decided to go for a swim. As they got to the beach, Sandy and Nigel changed and ran into the water; Marcy looked for a shady tree with her Nancy Drew. Over in the bushes, she saw Beverley Campbell and hoped she did not see her. No luck, she did. "Hey Marcy, come here, nuh?" she called, in her usual husky drawl. Beverley and two boys were sitting under the almond tree, the spot she wanted. With each step toward them she regretted not diving into the water with her friends. The nearer she got to where they were, a strong bush-burning scent blew her way. She kept going for fear they would think she was being a snob, because both she and Patricia had already labelled her 'stuck-up' and a 'goody-two-shoes'. Patricia had spread the word that her father was a drunk and she was sure Beverley knew about the incident with her father and Jerry, as it was her mother, Mrs. Campbell, who came to get her grandmother. So, even though they claimed she was a goody-two shoes, with a drunkard as a father she knew they didn't view her much holier than them.

As she approached, Beverley asked, "Sandy have a boyfriend now?"

Sandy had asked her not to speak about her and Nigel, but since they were in the water gallivanting, Sandy riding Nigel's back in a jockey-ride, it was obvious to all watching. Anyway, she felt it was not her place to say, and told Beverley, "You better ask her yourself."

"So what about you? You don't have no boyfriend yet?" She grinned, searching Marcy's eyes. Marcy hissed. Beverley came closer, smelling of weed. She looked Marcy up and down, her eyes red and troublesome. Marcy sighed, certain her plan was to embarrass her before the boys. If so, she told herself, *don't give up without a fight*. Well, that was what her head said, her feet however, said, *run!* Still, she straightened her shoulders and held her stare. She knew from school that Beverley's stance intimidated others, but the rumble, tumble fights, she lost. *So maybe I stand a chance.*

The two of them locked stares with Marcy giving as good as she was getting, until she stepped back, and her breasts, squeezed into a scanty halter top, jiggled at the sides. Marcy wanted to tell her *go fix-up yourself gal*, but had a feeling that's how she liked it. She repeated her question. "So you don't have a boyfriend?" Before Marcy could answer, *what is it to you?* She said, "Or it's me you like?" skinning her teeth as though she had backed her in a corner.

"No, I don't have a boyfriend and I certainly don't want you," Marcy told her, with her hands on her hips, shaking her head.

As she plotted a way out from Beverley and her friends, one of the boys, wearing only his swim shorts that showed his bony, sea-salt dried frame, said, "You want some a dis?" He held a marijuana joint for her to take.

"No, you keep it," she sneered.

"Wait, you don't have a boyfriend, and you don't wan' taste di weed? What, you a Christian?" She ignored him. Beverley and the other boy laughed.

"Anyway, I have to go now." She turned to leave.

"Wait, nuh! I don't have a girlfriend and I looking for a nice one like you," he said, with a smug look.

"Keep looking," she said, walking away.

"Yes, run, but when you ready for a man, I'm here. Mi name Bunny, you hear, remember dat!"

With each quick step their laughter faded. She shook her head. *Nincompoops.*

She sighed and rolled her shoulders, ready for a long soak in the sea after that encounter. As she shimmied out of the shorts she wore over her bathing suit, two girls ran pass her to a crowd gathered at the other end of the beach. Marcy drew up her shorts and went to see. The closer she got, grim faces were crying out, "Oh God!" "Poor man." "Jesus, what a tragedy."

Sandy and Nigel were in the crowd. "Is what happen?" she asked, startling Sandy.

"Oh Marcy," Sandy put her hand on her chest, "I was looking for you."

She shrugged. "Long story. What happen here?"

"It look like a body float outta the water."

"A man drown," Nigel said, correctly Sandy.

She moved closer to see the body and felt sick right away. It was her first time seeing a dead body. She inspected the swollen cadaver sprawled in black swim trunks, eyes bulged, lips and other body parts not covered in sand, saltwater-ashy; she needed air. She backed away from the crowd and sat on the grass. Grief overwhelmed her for the dead man. She thought about his family, his children possibly, and how they would react to his death.

She watched people move in and out the circle studying the body, and lamenting, wanting to know where it drifted from. One woman asked, "Anybody call di police yet?"

"Yes, Delroy gone."

"Maybe we should close his eyes."

"No, don't touch him."

A man ran towards them, panting. "See Delroy a come," someone announced.

He told the crowd, "Di police on di way."

The news spread fast through the neighbourhood and more people gathered to see 'di dead body on di beach'.

An older woman wearing white gloves, maybe from the funeral home, Marcy guessed, carried a bed sheet to cover the body. "Until the police comes," she said.

But she never got a chance, as the man who announced that Delroy had gone for the police, asked, "Woman, you from di funeral parlour?" She said no and he warned, "Den leave di body alone!" and he pounced on anyone who 'set foot' near the corpse.

"Sorry, sorry," she said, stepping back. Looking pitiful, she folded the cloth she brought. "I just wanted to give the dead some dignity, man."

The onlookers murmured, wondering why it was taking the police so long to arrive. Marcy went to stand with Sandy and Nigel and asked, "The police taking them sweet time, you want to leave?"

"Yeah, me tired to wait," Sandy said.

"All right let's go,"

"I'm sure we'll hear everything by tomorrow."

As they walked home, thinking of the dead body, she said to the others, "I know I won't sleep tonight. I keep seeing his eyes bulging out his head."

"And the way his body turn blue," Sandy added, frowning at the image.

Nigel, being funny, dared her and Sandy. "Whoever reach the gate last, goin' see duppy tonight." The girls kicked off their rubber flip flops and sprinted home.

Marcy, out of breath, was the first one at the gate with Sandy close behind. "Hey Nigel," she yelled, "try not to see ghost tonight."

Chapter 22

The postman rode up to the gate as Marcy stood there with her friends. "You're late today, Mister Posie."

He smiled and handed her a letter. "Thanks." She scrutinized the envelope. It felt weighty as she bounced it in her hand. She squinted, *I wonder if it's what I think is*? Her heart skipped.

Sandy recognized her anxiousness. "What's that Marcy, your papers come?" she asked, sort of jokingly.

She nodded. "It look so, it's from the Canadian Embassy."

"Open it, nuh?"

"No I can't do that, I have to wait 'til Granny come."

She took the letter in the house and left it on the dining table. When she returned to her friends, Nigel asked, "Marcy, how comes you don't look happy?"

"Yeah, Marcy, you don't look like you just got good news."

"Well, I don't get the news yet, I have to open the letter first, right?"

After her friends left and she was alone in the house, she picked up the letter and imagined it holding her future: a new life in Canada. A life without her friends, the beach, basking in the sun on her veranda, easy access to fruits on the trees, the familiarity and comfort of 'Out of Many One People', her Jamaican heritage. She thought of opening it, by steaming it over boiling water, but knew the best thing was to wait. She set it down and went to her room. She dropped herself on the bed trance-like. *Is this really happening? Is my future about to change for good, today?* She knew it was coming, yet felt frightened, unsure and confused. She stared at the ceiling trying to understand why she couldn't see the possibilities awaiting her in Canada.

As she pondered life in the freezing cold, a mosquito buzzed at her head, upsetting her. She sprung out of bed, furious, and trailed it around the room until it pitched on the wall. Then she sneaked up on it and slapped the wall hard. She splattered it and all her frustration against the concrete. *Got you before you got me.* She smiled but within seconds, her palm reddened and burned. She winced, examining her wrist where the pain throbbed. "Damn stupid mosquito!" she muttered on the way to the bathroom.

While she washed the mosquito's stain off her hand she heard the front door open. She met Donovan in the living room. He inspected the envelope and asked, "What's this, our letter?"

"I believe so."

"You think we should open it?"

"No, leave it until everybody come."

"Canada, here we come!" he shouted, and dashed off.

Later, the family sat at the dining table discussing the letter from the Canadian Consulate. It confirmed their mother sponsoring Maureen, Donovan and Marcy. Audrey was not eligible for sponsorship as she was over eighteen, which she knew. Her mother had discussed it with her, and she told her sisters. The plan was for her and Mari to join the family at a later date. Regardless, she wasn't concerned about migrating as she and Tony were building a life together.

Maureen read the letter and handed the pages to Donovan and Marcy. The main requests of the document were to complete medical examination and photo identification. Maureen and Donovan's faces glowed from anticipation. They hugged and danced and pulled Marcy from the chair to celebrate with them. Even their grandmother's neck got squeezed in the excitement. Audrey, caught up in the merriment, said, "Boy, now oonuh make me want to come."

"Nah, you just saying that, you not leaving Tony for nothing," Maureen said.

"Well, if we got married you'd certainly see us for our honeymoon."

"Is there something you want to tell us?" Marcy asked.

"Not at the moment, my dears, but listen out for my announcement soon," she said, exuding radiance.

In the midst of jubilation, she reminded them, "One of you will have to tell daddy oonuh papers come." Marcy and Donovan looked at Maureen. Maureen was tacitly chosen to bear the news to their father that in a year or so, his three children were leaving him for good.

Chapter 23

One afternoon as Marcy came home from school, concern dimmed Maureen's eyes as she met her at the door. She had gone to see their father to tell him about their migration to Canada. Marcy thought she was going to say something like, daddy did not take our leaving well, but instead her sister said, "Marcy, I went to see daddy today and him sick bad."

His lifeless body flashed to her mind, and her body weakened. She sat in the nearest seat. "How bad?"

"Bad enough to go to the hospital, but he won't listen to me."

"So where he is now?"

"He's at home. I met him at the bar and took him home because he never look good. I tried to convince him to go doctor, but him not hearing."

Marcy sighed.

"What you think we should do?"

Marcy told her to wait until Audrey comes.

Their grandmother came home before Audrey and they followed her to her room. "What happen now?" she asked, sensing their angst. Maureen explained their father's condition and his stubbornness to get help, and asked what to do. "Anybody at di house wid him?"

"Yes, his landlord lives in the front."

"Dem know him sick?"

"Yes, but-"

She straightened the front of her house dress. "Well, at least him not alone, in case a anyt'ing."

They walked with her to the kitchen. "Yeah, but I'm worried though," Maureen insisted.

"Mi dear, not much you can do if him don't wan' go hospital, 'cause if patient don't care, what say doctor?" The girls looked at each other and back at her. "Maybe when him feel worse, him will change him mind."

Maureen and Marcy glowered; their grandmother's words were not enough.

As they left the kitchen, Maureen whispered, "I don't feel comfortable just waiting for anything to happen."

"Neither me."

"I feel I should go back up there."

"Yeah, let's go."

Mr. Fitzy's mongrels had their heads in a pan of food when the girls arrived at the gate; they barked as they noticed them standing there. Their bark alarmed him and he came out and escorted them to their father. His door was closed but not locked, so they entered. He lay on his side, hands tucked between his knees, his bare feet exposed. Maureen drew her finger on the bottom of his foot; he twitched and she did it again. He awoke and turned to see who it was and motioned them in with his head.

Marcy's greeting was stuck in her throat at the sight of his meagerness. His worn-out undershirt and pajama pants couldn't hide his frailty. She glanced at Maureen; she was just as taken aback. The lump in her throat grew and she pushed back tears. She couldn't let him see the pity in her eyes. She cleared her throat. "Hi Daddy." He nodded.

His greeting was unlike him. No *'come here make mi see oonuh'*, or *'oonuh want somet'ing to eat?'* No straightening their clothes, or extra affection. He was too weak to make prim his 'princess' and 'baby girl'. He rested his head on the folded sheets he had made into a pillow and his eyes were closed. Marcy sat on the bed beside him; Maureen climbed on the other side. No words were said. They lay with him. A picture of Jesus on the cross hung over the bed. It was new. She marvelled, musing he always knew of Jesus, just never had the need for him – until now.

All three of them dozed.

Marcy and Maureen awoke to see Donovan standing at the edge of the bed, gazing at his father snoring lightly. He leaned over and stroked his leg. He roused and nodded at Donovan, then closed his eyes again.

Maureen ushered them out. "I think we should let him sleep." They kissed him before leaving. Outside his closed door, they agreed to meet there after school the next day.

As planned, they returned the following day. Nothing had changed. He refused to discuss his poor health and flatly said, "Go doctor for what? Mi just need likkle rest."

Even so they persisted, coming in the evenings, hoping to break his resolve.

Merle, Mr. Fitzy's cousin, was in town for a few days. She prepared him porridge and soup. Her meals guaranteed him something nutritious and encouraged the children, if only for those rare days.

Thanks to her cooking, he gained some strength. He convinced himself, however, that he was better. "See, dat's all mi did need, likkle cornmeal porridge and some goat head soup."

Now that he was a little stronger, they took turns visiting. On Marcy's shift, she clipped his nails, washed underwear he stuffed under the bed, and warmed foods Merle left.

One afternoon when she came, he was not there. She fumed in disbelief and stormed down to Franklin's. She followed the laughter and banging of dominoes to the backyard and found him close to the action.

"Daddy, what you doing here?" she asked, annoyed.

He turned, surprised, and said, "Marcy."

"Daddy, you should be home."

He coughed. "Mi not too long come."

"See, you not well."

He got up and led her from the noise. "Baby girl," he took a breath, "It hard to just lay down in a di bed, day in day out, with nutting to do, mi have to come out likkle bit."

"I understand Daddy, but coming to the bar is not the answer."

"Mi know, Marcy." He pulled up a chair. "Sit down."

"Daddy, I'm not staying in the bar with you." They walked to the front. She noticed he did not smell of rum and said, "Daddy, promise you won't have anything while you're here."

"No man, mi just come to get outta di house. Mi soon gone home."

"You promise?"

"Yea, don't worry, baby, you father alright."

But Arthur didn't keep his word. As he felt better he went back to his routine of daily visits to the bar. If Marcy wanted to see him she went directly there. After school one afternoon, she visited him. Mrs. Franklin caught her peeping through the gate. "Come in, my dear," she said, and offered her a seat and a soft drink. "I'll get your father."

She sat on the porch with her eyes on the Kola Champagne bottle in her hand, as she bobbed her head to Tom Jones playing on the jukebox, avoiding glances from men passing by.

Her father came from the back. "Marcy." He had an impish smile to cover his guilt. He pulled her into him. She endured his scent of stale rum and carbolic soap for a hug.

He went to the bar to get 'a shot a whites'. White rum, his darling, sometimes chased with Coke or water, although he preferred his 'whites' straight. He got his drink and they sat in the corner, a couple of tables from the men at the bar.

Behind his back the men winked or smiled, and one glanced at her as he counted a wad of bills from his pocket. She wondered if they did not know he was her father, or didn't realize she was underage. Peeved, she thought, *my school uniform should've clued them.*

"So oonuh mother a send for oonuh to come a Canada?" She remained quiet. For one, she was upset being in the bar with him, and when he started on how "terrible oonuh mother is", she was ready to leave. She frowned. He of all persons had no right to call her mother terrible for trying to make better what he had wrecked.

"Daddy I have to go now."

"You can't spend likkle more time wid you fada?"

She got up. "I just wanted to see how you doing. And the cigarette smoke killing my eyes." He walked her to the gate.

That was the last time she met him at the bar.

She visited less, and relied on Maureen to keep her updated.

Chapter 24

Marcy and Sandy looked forward to the summer holidays, mainly because of the Independence Day celebration. Apart from Christmas and New Year's, August 6th, Jamaica's independence since 1962 was the most anticipated and eventful time of year. Stage shows and street dances were planned all over the island. The girls had high hopes of attending the street dance this year.

Although the dance took place a couple blocks outside the neighbourhood, Marcy and her sisters were never allowed to go. With their mother gone, she had a feeling she would be luckier with her grandmother. She asked her a month in advance, given that in the past her mother preferred a lengthy notice, for any occasion, which was no guarantee she'd say yes at the appointed time. So she waited until her final report to show her grandmother how well she did in school, a backup, if needed. Her grandmother did not disappoint; the only requirement was she had to go with Audrey and Tony.

Mari was scared for the children being out late at nights, and rightfully so. The politics, especially in Kingston, had become dangerous as clashes between the two political parties were heating up. There weren't only rumors of guns entering the country in barrels; reports of people being shot and killed dominated the nightly news. Political warfare was not restricted to partisan areas such as Tivoli Gardens and Trench Town, it came closer to home in the east, in places like Mountain View and Rockfort.

She knew both good and bad people came out to the dance, and warned, "Watch oonuh self, memba stray bullet don't have no eye."

Once she gave Marcy the okay, Sandy's mother gave her permission.

The Friday night before the dance, Sandy's mother put a straight perm in her hair. Sandy had soft, loose curls and when straightened, they flowed down her back. After Sandy got her hair styled, she went to Marcy's house to show her. "Gee, Sandy, you look like a white lady." Sandy laughed, running her fingers through her hair. "So, the perm never burn you?"

"Nope."

"I hear it can burn bad, and give you blisters."

"Yeah, but not the perm my mother use. The one she use don't have much chemical."

"Well, your hair don't need strong perm anyway, not like my thick head." She chuckled. "Thank God Audrey goin' press it for me."

Her mother had strict rules against permed hair. It made hair "dry and trashy," she said, and took months of olive oil steams to rebuild. Because of that, they got 'hot comb', and only on special occasions.

Saturday morning, she washed her hair and met Audrey in the kitchen. She had the pressing combs heating on the stove.

"Go get a towel 'cause you don't want to get burn." She came back with a towel around her neck and sat in the chair with her back to the stove. While the towel prevented the comb from touching her neck, she cringed as the heat came near her scalp. And Audrey, never patient with Marcy's hair, caused a few heated close calls. Nevertheless, she bore it all to have long hair in her back, like Sandy's.

She couldn't wait to see her flowing locks. *No cornrows or afro for a change.* Audrey handed her the mirror. "How you like it?"

"It look nice," she said, rotating her head to see how far it flowed. She sat forward, prim and proper, admiring her face with straightened hair. It made her feel grown-up. "Thank you, Audrey." She smiled, all teeth showing.

She went to her room to examine it closer, holding the hand mirror in front to see the back in the bigger mirror on the wardrobe. She shook her head and liked the way her hair brushed against her shoulders, and then swept the bang from her eyes. She thought of the woman in the shampoo commercial and wondered if her hair matched her sheen. And while it did shine, thanks to all the bergamot oil, it did not hang as far as Sandy's. It was slightly past her shoulders. Still, she was satisfied to have it pressed and stretched a few more inches.

Sandy readied early for the street dance and went to Marcy's house. When she walked into the bedroom, they laughed; they both had the same hairstyle: a flip with a bang covering one eye. Sandy had on red shorts and a lacy sleeveless top. Marcy wore a pink A-line dress her mother had sent. "You look nice, Marcy."

"A you look good, gal." Sandy spun around, shaking her buttocks as she turned. "Wait 'til you boyfriend see you." They laughed.

"He must be up there now waiting," Sandy said, looking at her watch.

"Where is he meeting us?"

"I told him to wait at the gate, not to go inside."

"Smart, 'cause with that crowd that goin' be there, we'd probably never find him tonight."

They waited on the veranda with Audrey for Tony. Maureen passed in a hurry. "You not coming to the dance with us?" Marcy asked.

"No, I'm going with my friends, I'll meet oonuh up there."

The street dance was a fifteen-minute walk north of where they lived, so Tony left his car at the house. He and Audrey strolled hand in hand behind the girls.

The closer they got to the venue, Sandy sped up. Marcy called out, "We all goin' the same place, you nuh."

Sandy slowed for her to catch up. "How we goin' lose Audrey?" she whispered.

"Don't worry, by the look of things, they'll lose us." The friends giggled. "She already warned me that even though she won't stick to me, I must still check in with her."

"Where she goin' be?"

"Near the DJ, she said."

"Oh good, no babysitter tonight." Sandy winked.

As they neared the grounds and the music pumped, it sunk in that they were on their way to the dance. "I can't believe we going to hear the number one sound system, Mountain Fire," Sandy said, swaying to John Holt's, *I Want a Love I Can Feel*.

"The music boom, man!" Marcy said, joining her and the two of them gyrated to the beat. "Make me show you how to do 'round di world."

"I know how to do it." And together they said, "Front, side, back, side, front, side, back, side."

"Wait, Marcy, you can wine though."

"Remember I start to take dance lessons, you nuh."

They danced in the middle of the street. "Hey Miss Marcy," Audrey called, "hold it down." For a moment she forgot Audrey was behind her. She stopped and waited for her and Tony. When they caught up, she expected a warning, but Audrey just said, "Remember where I said I'll be" and kept going into the football field.

The red shirt Nigel wore drew them to his muscular frame. He stood where they expected at the south entrance, next to four, huge, booming boxes. Sandy ran and grabbed his hand. Marcy looked away as their faces touched. Nigel started a conversation over U-Roy's *I'm Gonna Wear You to the Ball Tonight.* Sandy yelled, "It's too loud, can't hear", pointing to the boxes. They moved inside.

It was a little after eight. The place was scanty, not much dancing, only people wandering around the field. They walked to the opposite side and ended up at the food counter. Each bought a soda. There, they stood sipping their drinks, rocking to the beat and watching people come and go with plates of food. Marcy stood like a greeter, smiling as everyone went by. She watched for people from the neighbourhood, especially Patricia and Beverley. She wanted them to see that 'Miss Goody-Goody' was out on the town.

Within an hour the place was filled with revellers – single, coupled, young, old, too big in too tight clothing, and too skinny in too short. Everyone wore their holiday best to the Independence Day dance.

The girls sandwiched Nigel and they danced on the spot. Soon the crowd bunched them together and in a smooth transition Sandy and Nigel became one. Nigel had his arms around Sandy's waist and she hugged his neck, their faces buried in each other's shoulder; Marcy felt uncomfortable. To get a better grasp on Sandy, Nigel took her hand and led her to the wall. She followed them. Sandy leaned against the wall and Nigel braced himself on her and they rubbed on one another. *Oh, boy!* Now she felt really uncomfortable. She shouted over the booming music, "I'm going to get another soda, the two of you not moving from here?" Neither responded; she shook her head wondering why she asked; it was clear they weren't moving for the night.

She got the soda and coming back through the crowd, felt someone holding onto her hand. She turned and saw Bunny, grinning. She was frightened seeing him so close. She hoped he didn't see the fright on her face. "Hey, pretty girl, remember mi?" She knitted her brows as if confused. "You don't remember mi?" He continued to hold her, so she twirled her hand and he let go. He stopped grinning. "How you a gwaan like you don't remember mi?"

"Maybe I don't," she snapped, and kept walking.

He walked beside her. "Bunny from di beach, man." She wondered how to lose him. She thought of taking him to Nigel and remembered that he and Sandy were busy locked down. Anyhow, she doubted Nigel could handle Bunny, he seemed like a ruffian.

She ignored him. In desperation he stepped before her and took off his cap. "See, a Bunny, Beverley friend."

She looked at him and pretended interest. "Oh yes."

He smiled. "Yea man, a mi man."

"Anyway Bunny, I have to go, all right? See you again, man," she said, in the nicest tone and kept walking. When she realized he was still following her, she wished she knew where to find Donovan and his friends, then it came to mind to find Audrey and Tony. She scampered through the crowd to get to them and thankfully they were near the DJ as Audrey had said.

Audrey looked puzzled seeing her alone. "Where is Sandy?" she asked.

"We met some other friends and she's with them." Audrey's brows relaxed.

"Everything all right?"

"Yeah, man." She glanced back, Bunny was not in sight. Relieved, she said, "I just wanted to check in with you."

"You want something to eat? Piece a jerk?"

"All right."

Tony went to get the food and left her and Audrey at the table. "You enjoying yourself so far?"

"Yep."

"Anyway, don't leave without me."

Tony brought back a piece of jerk chicken and a slice of hard dough bread. This was her first taste of jerk. Her mother and grandmother had never used jerk seasoning, nor bought jerk for them. She enjoyed it, although unable to chew it as she'd like due to its peppery flavour.

By the time she had finished eating, Tony took Audrey's hand and said, "Let's go dance." He led her into the crowd as Alton Ellis' *You Make Me So Very Happy*, came on.

She sat by herself for awhile, taking in the music, glad she had lost Bunny, or that he had given up. She decided to stay where she was since Sandy and Nigel probably didn't miss her, anyway. She pulled the chair next to her and stretched out her legs to unwind until Audrey returned.

While she relaxed, a male voice interrupted her. "Excuse mi, can I sit here?" She turned to see. A good looking pair of dreamy eyes greeted her.

She swiftly swung her feet off the chair. "That's my sister's seat."

"I'll get up when she comes back." It pleased her that he was mannerly. "Once I eat, I'm gone."

Oh my gosh, he is so cute, and he wants to sit beside me, oh God. She wanted to say, no rush, but said, "If you like."

After he finished having his soup, he said, "By di way, my name is Manny Blackburn. What's yours?"

"I'm Marcy," she answered.

"Just Marcy? I can't get a last name?"

"Yes, but -" Although he was cute and polite, she didn't know him, and refrained from giving her last name as yet.

"Dat's all right, I respect a girl who don't give up everyt'ing too fast." He smiled, and she smiled back. She liked the way the side of his mouth slanted when he smiled. "You live in dis area?" He pushed the empty cup to the side and sat back in the chair.

Suddenly, she became conscious that Audrey might return to find him sitting with her. "I'm not sure I should be talking to you."

"Why? All we're doing is talking."

"Yes, but my sister might come back any minute." *Oh Marcy, stop sounding like a big baby.*

"All right, all right, I get di message," he said, and picked up the cup. "But I hope to see you again." Before he walked away he said, "Jack, di DJ for Mountain Fire, he's my stepfather, I play wit' him. We'll be at Beachmount Park next Saturday night. I hope you come."

She could feel him staring at her. Without looking up, she said, "I don't know about that."

"Even if it's just an hour. We start setting up at 7." She caught herself nodding in agreement, still not looking up.

When he walked off, she thought to give him a quick look-over but was frozen in place by their chance meeting. She scanned her brain to recall what he looked like - dark skin, medium afro, nice eyes, great smile – the memory was sealed. *I have to see him again. But how?*

"Marcy, you ready?" Audrey said, yanking her from her thoughts.

"Yes, if you are."

"What about Sandy?"

"Wait, I'll go get her."

Making her way through the crowd, she heard her name. "Marcy!" It was Nigel with Sandy. "We were coming to find you," he said.

"Yeah? I hope the two of you ready to leave, 'cause Audrey is ready."

"We're ready. We were just waiting for you to come back."

"Sure. I can't believe the two of you even thought about me."

"We did!" Sandy insisted.

She and Nigel hugged and said goodbye. As the girls walked to Audrey, Sandy asked, "Then Marcy, what you did all this time?"

"It's a long story."

"I was kinda worried, but figured you were with Audrey. So –"

"I have something to tell you," she said, cutting her off.

"What, what?"

"Not now, I'll tell you later." She winked.

"No, you have to tell me now!"

Because it was a secret she couldn't keep, she blurted, "I met a boy!"

"You what?"

She grinned, her face lighting up.

"You, Marcy?"

She nodded, still grinning.

"I can't wait to hear this."

She pulled her. "Yes, but keep it down."

"Where him is?"

"Quiet, I said I'll tell you later."

"But I can't wait to hear." Sandy shimmied on the spot. "Little Miss Virgin Marcy met a boy! Lord Jesus."

Chapter 25

Marcy thought about Manny every day since the dance. As she readied for school she wondered if he was awake. At lunchtime she wondered what he was having for lunch and at bedtime she pretended to be asleep to avoid Audrey and Maureen's chatter, so thoughts of him could put her to sleep.

On Tuesday morning on her way to the bathroom, she yawned and said, "I wish it was Friday already."

Her grandmother heard her and said, "Child don't wish away your life, you know how much I would love to add likkle more onto mine?" Marcy shook her head, unable to relate, because at fifteen, extra days did not matter if she weren't spending it with the boy of her infatuation.

The two friends travelled home together less from school. Marcy's dance group practiced after school and Sandy and Nigel went to the National Stadium for track and field, the Boys and Girls

Athletics Championships, or 'Champs', as it was called by most people. Although Kingston College was a favourite, watching Donald Quarry and his brothers from Camperdown run, brought a lot of thrill to the sport.

Because of this, they planned to meet the Friday night under the ackee tree. They sat on the brick wall facing their houses. Marcy said, "Sandy, I still can't believe this is happening."

"Yeah, you have a boyfriend." She chuckled.

"Well, he's not my boyfriend as yet." She paused to take in 'my boyfriend', then said, "I wasn't even looking for a guy."

"Then isn't that how things go? I can't believe you even considering him," Sandy said, raising her eyes.

"Me neither, but he's very cute!" She closed her eyes and bounced up and down, her hands and feet flipping in the air. "And don't forget nice, he's very nice too."

"I bet, for you to be so excited."

"What you think I should wear tomorrow night?"

"Maybe one of your hot pants."

"You know I don't have any hot pants."

"Well cut off the legs off one of your pants."

"You mad, Granny would kill me if I cut up the clothes mommy send."

"Well, what about one of your old jeans?"

"I don't have any old jeans." She thought for a little, and said, "Maybe I could wear my pedal pusher pants."

"No, that's not sexy enough," Sandy said. "Why don't you put on the tent dress?"

"Which one, the pink and white one?"

"Yes, the one you wore on your birthday. That's cute and he'll get to see your pretty legs."

"That's what I'm afraid of. I don't want to start nothing I can't manage."

"Ah, that's nothing if him touch your legs."

Her head spun. "Excuse me, Madam?"

"Yeah, so what?"

"You mean Nigel touch your legs?"

"And more," Sandy said, like it was no big deal. She wondered why she was surprised, considering how they 'touched' the night at the dance. "Marcy, no boy goin' want you if they can't do things with you, you nuh?" Sandy stared in her eyes, hoping she got the point.

"What you saying, that Nigel wouldn't want you if you didn't do things with him?"

"Nigel is a different type a guy, but I love him, so he doesn't have to force me to do anything I wouldn't want to do in the first place."

"Sandy, you better be careful cause you don't want a baby at fifteen."

Saturday, at 6:55 p.m., Marcy was ready to meet Manny. She checked herself in the mirror one last time. *This is it.* She sighed, squinting at her reflection. She looked out the window for Sandy in position at the gate. Everyone else had left the house, only she and her grandmother were home. Her grandmother was bathing. She stood outside the bathroom door. "I'm going with Sandy now Granny."

She heard the shower stop. "What?"

"I said, I am going with Sandy now."

"Where to?"

"Remember I told you that I was following Sandy to a youth meeting at her church?" Her grandmother did not answer. To soak up the silence she added, "It's not that far, Granny."

She had mentioned the fictitious youth service meeting to her grandmother the Sunday after she met Manny. That Sunday morning, as part of her scheme, she swept the veranda while waiting for her to leave for church. "Soon come," she said, passing her on the veranda, clutching her Bible and handbag.

"Granny, Granny!"

"Later, Marcy, later."

She was determined to tell her story while her grandmother was too busy to hear. "I just want to tell you," she said, opening the gate for her. "I'm going to a youth service at Sandy's church on Saturday."

Her grandmother's eyes questioned hers and she lowered her eyes to the imitation pearls around her neck. "When I come back Marcy, tell mi when I come back."

She was relieved to get her story out knowing she would never bring it up again, unless she had to, like now.

She fidgeted, waiting to hear her grandmother say, okay. Because, if she had come out of the bathroom and saw her in that dress, she would suspect she was too dressed up for youth service. On top of that, she had sprayed Audrey's *Charlie's* perfume all over her and put on Maureen's strawberry lip gloss. She needed to leave before she came out. "So can I go now, Granny?"

"Alright, but don't stay out too late." She turned on the shower.

"No, Granny."

She shut the gate behind her. "Let's go, let's go, it's after seven."

"Marcy, a lipstick you have on?" Sandy asked, then she sniffed. "A perfume me smell?" Marcy smiled. "Rahtid!" she said, looking her up and down. "And you even taller than me tonight in a platforms."

Beachmount Park, where the dance was held, was where Donovan and his friends played football. As she and Sandy cut across the park, she said, "Sandy walk up quick, quick, 'cause my brother and his friends might be here."

"Nah, him not over here, I saw him going down the road when I was at the gate."

"Oh." She slowed her pace. "I better take my time, 'cause I don't wan' get sweaty."

"Yeah. You look nice, though."

"Thanks."

"Marcy, me really can't believe it's you this."

She squeezed her friend's hand. "Mi kinda feel a little nervous."

"No man, just think how you goin' have a nice time."

"Remember we don't really know each other."

"Is now oonuh goin' get to know one another."

"Easy for you to say. You know Nigel, what, three years?"

"Almost. But if oonuh like each other, it easy."

"Yeah, but you know me never go out with a guy yet."

"Well, there's got to be a first, don't worry, man."

The music from Mountain Fire blasted. The Abysinians' rhythm, *Satta Massagana*, greeted them across the open land. Marcy imagined Manny looking out for her and shuddered at the thought. *Breathe, Marcy.* She composed herself.

"You can't change your mind now, you nuh," Sandy said, looking at her sideways.

"I'm not."

She spotted Manny on the stage with his stepfather. He looked up as they neared. "Marcy," he said. His smile calmed her. He jumped off the stage. Taking her hand, he said, "I'm glad you made it." Her big smile concealed her nervousness. "I see you come wit' your chaperone."

"Oh, this is my friend Sandy."

Sandy smiled and wiggled her fingers. "Hi."

"Nice to meet you Sandy," he nodded, "because you're probably di reason she came tonight." Marcy liked that he was friendly.

He took them behind the stage to sit. "Would di two of you like somet'ing to drink?"

She told him a soft drink and Sandy said the same. After he got the sodas, he said, "I just have to change di tape" and ran back to the stage.

As they waited, Sandy let her know all the things she liked about him; from his easy going ways to the Clarks on his feet, and wondered why he wore a red, green and yellow tam. "Marcy, him a Rasta?"

"I don't know."

"I wonder if him dread under the tam?"

"No, he wasn't locks when I saw him last week."

"Him cute, though, but not as cute as my Nigel," her face rounded, "maybe me and Nigel and you and Manny can go watch a show."

"Sandy, don't rush it."

They finished their sodas. Sandy shifted in her seat. "Anyway, Marcy, mi have to go home soon. You know me mother come by eight."

Manny returned during their discussing Sandy's leaving. "Sorry," he said, taking a seat. "You ladies want another soda?"

"No, we have to go," Marcy said.

"You leaving already?" He looked at his watch. "It's just eight o'clock. You not even here half hour yet."

"It's just that my friend has to go."

Manny leaned close to her. "You have to leave too?"

Before she answered, Sandy said, "Marcy, if you want to stay, stay. You don't have to leave because of me."

Even though that's what she wanted her to say, she replied, "You sure, Sandy?"

"Of course, because if I were you I wouldn't leave." She chuckled.

Manny agreed to walk with her as she followed Sandy part way home. They walked with her to the end of the field and Marcy told her not to let any of her family see her. "Have fun," Sandy whispered with a wink.

As she and Manny walked back he took her hand. "You smell nice."

"Thank you," she replied, her eyes to the ground.

"You want to go on di beach a likkle bit?"

"Okay."

No one else was on the beach and they took their time walking along the shores. "Yes, Miss Marcy, here we are." She struggled to hold his gaze. "I'm very glad you showed up tonight."

"I surprised you? Well, here I am."

"I must say you're looking very nice."

"Oh, thank you," she said, and glanced at him. *Oh God, is this me? Breathe, Marcy.*

"I like your hair."

She touched her hair. "What, my afro?"

"Yes, natural hair suits you better." She remembered having straightened hair for the Independence Day dance, the night they met.

"So what, you're Rasta?"

"Who I-man? I'm a Garveyite, conscious brethren, mi proud a my culture, you nuh," he answered, enlightening her on 'black power and black consciousness' and being 'proud to be black'. Marcy listened, nodding at each point. Although she knew Marcus Garvey, one of Jamaica's National Heroes, Martin Luther King and Malcolm X, she never knew Stokely Carmichael, was a Black Panther.

"I think," she squinted, "I heard somewhere that Nina Simone was his wife."

"Mi never hear dat."

"I like her songs."

"Yes, some singers very conscious a dem roots you nuh. Check Harry Belafonte, plenty people wouldn't know say him trod wid man like Martin Luther King Jr. Yea man, nuff a dem singer conscious."

After his black awareness schooling, he changed the subject back to her. "So you still keeping your last name from mi?" He moved closer, playing with a few strands of her hair.

"I wouldn't say that," she replied, patting her afro into place.

"It must be top secret?"

He brought his face to hers. She playfully slapped his shoulder and pushed him away. "It's no secret, it's Tomlinson."

"Well, Miss Marcy Tomlinson," he brushed up against her, "Manny Blackburn is very glad to know you."

He gazed in her eyes. She smiled and looked away. Some quietness passed. "By the way, what kinda name is Manny?" she asked, breaking the awkwardness.

"It's short for Emmanuel. I'm a junior, my father use to call mi Manny."

"Use to call you? What does he call you now?"

"My father not alive."

"Oh, sorry to hear." Surprise lined her face.

"He died when I was six." After a pause, he said, "One morning him a come in from country, tired, and crash him bike."

"Wow! That's sad."

"Yea man, it did rough, you nuh."

"You think about him?"

Manny looked out at the dark sea and took a deep breath. "Sometimes mi think 'bout him yes, especially when mi did likkle, before mi stepfada come in a mi life."

"You and your stepfather tight?"

"Yea, him cool. And him good to mi mada, you nuh."

They walked in silence until they reached a grassy area. "Make we stop here."

Marcy look at the ground. "Manny, I don't want my dress to get dirty."

He found a piece of cardboard, wiped it with his rag and lay it on the grass. "Madame, here you go." He took a seat on the grass next to her. "You comfy now?"

"As comfortable as I can be on a piece of cardboard," she jested.

"I'll give you my shirt if you want."

"No, it's all right, no naked bodies on the beach."

"Why not? We could skinny-dip."

"What's that?"

"The both of us swim naked." He chuckled.

"I don't think so, mister." She figured where the conversation was leading and changed its course. "So how old are you Manny?"

"How old you t'ink?"

"Uhm, can't tell."

"Seventeen."

"Seventeen?"

"What, mi too old for you?"

"Maybe my father might think so." She laughed.

"So how old are you?"

"Fifteen."

"Mi not dat old den. When you fada meet mi, him will see mi just right for him daughter." He grinned.

"You don't have to worry about my father, he's too sick these days to take on anybody."

"What sick him?"

"We don't really know. He loves rum, so it could be that, and he won't go to the doctor. All he does is drink first chance he gets."

"Trust mi, is not your fada alone, rum is di scourge a dis land, mi a tell you dat. Same way my mada have to be on my stepfada case. Why you t'ink mi and him a spar?" He hissed.

"So what, you mada can't get him to go doctor?"

"My mother lives in Canada, she and him divorce."

"So who you live with, den?" His eyes narrowed. She told him about her grandmother, brother and sisters, and that she was joining her mother within a year.

"So you mean, mi just meet you and you leaving mi already? You hurt mi Marcy." Playing, he put his hand over his heart.

They got quiet. Manny picked up a twig and twirled it; lost in thought. She listened to the waves splashing to shore. In their quietness, he pulled her to him. She felt comfortable with him and rested her head on his chest. He lifted her face and put his lips on hers. She opened her mouth and let his tongue in. He pressed on her, laying her back, his body shifted onto hers. Her heart raced. Her body tingled. She felt his bulge grow. He moved slowly on top of her, and sped up as his breathing laboured. "Oh Marcy, Oh Marcy." It felt good, too good to be right. Her mother's face flashed before her. "No!" she shouted and flung him off. She leaned forward, covering her face with her hands.

He knelt beside her. "Sorry, Marcy, sorry." He put his arm around her and patted her. "Sorry, mi sorry." She nodded, accepting his apologies. "I better take you home." He helped her up.

"What time is it?"

"Coming up to eleven."

"Oh Lord." She hurried across the open land with her grandmother on her mind.

"Sorry Marcy, I never mean to keep you so late, believe me," he said, keeping pace with her.

"I'm not upset with you, 'cause it's my fault too," she muttered.

"Marcy, hold on." He stopped her and they faced each other. "I like you, you nuh", his eyes penetrating, "I really like you, and I wan' see you again", his countenance serious, "Dat alright?"

She wanted to see him too and she nodded, her eyes lowered.

"When can you come out again?"

"Weekend."

"Next Saturday den?"

"Okay," she said, softly.

"We can meet here, same place. Seven o'clock?" She nodded. He kissed her cheek. "You want mi walk you home?"

"No, somebody might see us."

"I'll walk on the other side, nobody won't know."

He walked a few feet behind her until she reached her gate. She looked back and he blew her a kiss and kept going. The lights were off in the house. She opened the gate like a burglar breaking in and tiptoed to the veranda. As she got to the door it dawned on her that she had not planned how to get in without waking her grandmother.

She hid in the dark corner praying for a miracle. A dim light came on in Mr. Garrison's house. *Oh great,* she thought, *but what if his girlfriend is there*? He was her only chance. She tapped his door. He opened it wearing only a pair of khaki shorts. She was desperate to get into the house so she brushed off the image of him exposing himself to Audrey. Conscious of her appearance – crushed clothes and messy hair – she stood at his door speechless. Without words, he understood her dilemma and moved aside; no explanation needed, none given. Her head down, she walked pass him to the kitchen that separated their homes, and hoped Donovan wasn't in bed on the other side.

She slipped through the door, entering the home. Donovan was not there. *Perfect*! She doubted anyone was home except her grandmother; after all, it was Saturday and not yet midnight. She continued through the living room, creeping pass her grand-mother's room. It was closed. *Thank heavens*. She entered her room and none of her sisters were there, as suspected. She changed and went to bed. Her night with Manny replayed in her mind and kept sleep from coming.

Her grandmother had no objections to her going to Youth Service again. She actually looked pleased that one of her grand-children might 'give her life to di Lawd'.

She met Manny at the entrance of the beach. He leaned on a white truck parked not far from the streetlight. "Hey Marz," he said, reaching for her hand.

He kissed her. She shivered, feeling his lips on her face and quickly said, "Whose is this?"

"My stepfada, is it we use transport di sound system."

"Oh, not playing tonight?"

"Yea, Vineyard Town." He played with her hand, making circles in the palm. "But mi had to see you."

They left the van and walked along the shore; the breeze roughed the sea up to her feet. She eased off her slippers, tipped her toes in the water, and continued to stroll.

"I hope you never got in trouble last week."

"No. When I got home Granny was fast asleep, all now she don't know what time I came in."

He spread a towel he had in his back pocket for her to sit, and sat across from her on a tree stump. He ran his fingers through her hair. "I hope you have an afro pick after you mess up my hair," she said, teasing.

"As a matter of fact I have a pick in di truck."

"What you doing with a pick? You even comb that hair under you tam?"

"Of course mi comb it," he pulled on his tam, "but mi just love wear mi hat."

He moved closer, bringing her to sit in his lap. They sat hugging and chatting and kissing for more than an hour, then he said he had to return to the dance. "Jack no mind if mi leave, but him expect to see mi back before di crowd come."

"To relieve him."

"Yea, and make sure everyt'ing on track, you nuh."

"So, he's the main engineer and you're the backup."

"You can call it so."

"Like Batman and Robin." They laughed.

"Marcy, why you don't come wit' mi?"

"To the dance?"

"Yea."

"No, Manny, I can't come, it's almost ten o'clock. What time would I get home?"

"I'll take you home early, man."

"There is no way I can go home again after eleven. What if it get busy and you can't leave when I'm ready?"

He nodded at her reasoning, yet wished she would change her mind. "But if Granny gone to bed, she won't know what time you get in."

"Don't forget it's not only Granny I live with. I don't want to push my luck."

They walked back to the truck. "You want mi drop you home."

"Oh sure, drop me home so everybody can see me coming out of your van. Very funny, Mr. Manny."

He pulled her behind the van, from the bright streetlight and hugged her, and they kissed. She pushed him away playfully. "I can hear Jack calling."

"Alright, alright. So when I goin' see you again?"

"I don't know. You say."

"You have a phone?"

"Yes, but maybe you should give me your number, 'cause I don't know who might answer when you call."

Manny took a pen and piece of paper from the truck. He tore the paper, wrote her number on half, and two numbers on the other. He gave it to her. "My home and mi mada restaurant. Dat's where I am in di days." She folded the paper and tucked it in her bra. "Dat's your secret pocket." He chuckled.

"That's where no one will look."

"So let's plan for next weekend." He shoved her number in his shirt pocket.

"Okay."

"And Marcy, I want you t'ink 'bout staying out wit' mi likkle longer." He stroked her chin.

"We'll see."

At the fence, Marcy told Sandy she met with Manny again, and Sandy begged her to setup a date for the four of them. "You can use my phone to call him." While they talked, she said, "Marcy, ask him if he wants to go watch *Cornbread Earl and Me*. I hear it's good." Manny agreed to Saturday matinee. Sandy spoke for Nigel that matinee was good for them.

Early Saturday afternoon, the girls met Nigel and Manny at Carib theatre. As they got off the bus they noticed the guys talking on the steps of the cinema. When they got to them Sandy said, "I didn't know the two of you knew each other?" The four of them talked as they joined the ticket line.

"Yeah, me know Manny from school, he used to come Kingston College too," Nigel said.

Marcy said, "So you're a KC boy?" Manny smiled. "When did you graduate?"

"Last year."

They got to the window; the guys paid for the tickets and bought the girls snacks even though they had their own money. The theater was dark, so it was unlikely they'd be recognized. They paired up at opposite ends on the last row. Manny put his arm around Marcy and they snuggled while she munched on a raisin and nuts chocolate bar and he on a pack of cashew nuts.

The movie was intense, and when the boy got killed Marcy buried her face in Manny's chest. He rubbed her arm and kissed her forehead. "It's just a show, babes."

After the movie, they met outside the cinema. "What oonuh want to do?" Sandy asked.

"Manny has to work tonight so he's going to follow me home, then go."

"Okay. We not ready to go home as yet."

They said goodbye.

Marcy and Manny caught a bus and got seats in the back; he gave her the window seat. "So where you playing tonight?"

"Harbour View."

"Oonuh mostly play in the East end?"

"We use to live a East, you nuh, so everybody know we."

"How long now you move?"

"Three years."

He told her that after his father died his mother sold his motorcycle repair shop and bought a restaurant from his step-father, Jack. That's how they met and later married. "And dem buy a house up a Havendale."

"And now you're an uptown boy," she teased.

Manny took her hand as they stepped off the bus in down-town parade. They eased through the packed sidewalk as people moved hastily to stores soon to close, and street hagglers making a last minute sale. They headed southbound on King Street to catch the number 2 bus going East.

When the bus pulled up to the stand, people jammed the front door. Manny said, "Wait, how dem just a push so?"

He and Marcy stepped back. As soon as they did there was a scream, "T'ief! T'ief! T'ief! Mi chain! T'ief, mi chain gone!" A woman pulled herself from the dense bus entrance, holding her neck. "Him gone wid mi chain." She looked lost, spinning in every direction seeking help. "See di man a go down di road, him just grab mi chain."

A man ran in the direction she pointed, calling, "Hold him, him in a brown shirt, grab him."

Some people followed the action a block away. Marcy inched towards the mob. Manny grabbed her arm. "Marcy, where you going? Come. You don't wan' get mix up in a dat."

"Mi just curious. Mi wan' see if them catch him." She continued to go, "Come man," she said, pulling his arm. He lagged behind.

One of the men caught the suspected thief, a boy, barely a teen, thin, clothes ragged, he had no shoes. The man held the boy in his pant waist. "Hey boy, give back di woman her chain."

"It's not me," the boy said. The man holding him, wearing a T-shirt, his muscles bulging, slapped the boy's face.

Marcy whispered to Manny that he must be an undercover police. "Who knows?" he said.

"Mi don't have nutting, sah," the boy cried.

"You lie! You lie! You t'ief mi chain!" the woman yelled.

Some people going by surveyed and moved on, while others stopped to act as judge and jury. "Beat di bwoy!" said a male side-walk vender, carrying bungles of rags and towels in both hands.

"Dats all dem pick-pocket do, walk and t'ief people t'ings," said the woman beside him selling cigarettes and lighters.

"Di bwoy must get licks! Just last week one a dem try grab my chain. Mi turn 'round and lick after him and him run," said a stout, light-skinned female vendor wearing gold on her neck, hands and ankle.

The man slapped the suspect again. "Where you put it? Where you put it?"

"I beg you sah, is not me," the boy bawled, emptying his pockets.

"See di police a come," a wiry woman said, a few of her top teeth missing. She had packs of gum, peanuts and cigarettes, strung over her arm.

"Marcy let's go. Di police will deal wit' it."

A bus revved its engine, signalling it was about to leave and they scooted for it; this time there were no empty seats and they held onto the rail above. Marcy was quiet, pensive. "You alright?" he asked.

"Just glad the police came, because what if it's not the boy? What if him telling the truth?"

"You can't concern yourself 'bout dat, and I don't believe him all dat innocent."

"Sometimes you can't tell, some thieves well dressed."

In twenty minutes Marcy reached her bus stop. Stepping off the bus, Manny whispered, "Call mi tomorrow, okay babes?" He continued on to meet Jack in Harbour View to set up for the dance.

Chapter 26

Rain fell all day Saturday and into the night. Marcy and Manny had plans to meet at 7 p.m. She called him to say that their meeting in the downpour didn't look possible. He disagreed. "Why not? We can sit in di van."

"But I'd still have to come out in the rain to meet you."

"No. I can come get you."

"You know that wouldn't work either."

"Marcy, don't make a likkle ting like di rain stop you."

"Manny, it's pouring." To calm him, she promised she would if it eased.

But her sister Maureen was home, which made it more difficult. She watched Marcy looking through the window, up in the sky, wishing for the showers to cease. "How could you be thinking of going out on this rainy night, Marcy?" She had no reasonable retort for her. "Whatever is out there with your name on it can't be worth you chancing it tonight." On other occasions she would have argued with Maureen; this time she knew she made sense. "You better be careful." With that warning, she breathed in long and hard. She quieted herself and joined her sister in the living room, and on low volume, they watched *Peyton Place* together while their grandmother slept.

Marcy sensed Maureen's growing suspicion and since it was the weekend before the new school year, decided to take a break from seeing Manny. *It will help me focus on school,* she told herself, *it's for the best.*

Of course, Manny was vexed. He called her home every day and if she didn't answer, he hung up, frustrating whomever did.

She longed to see him as much as he longed for her. He consumed her thoughts. She couldn't concentrate in class and doodled 'M+M' and 'Marcy loves Manny' on her books. They pined for each other, and by October they connived to be together again.

Since sneaking in the house at nights was a challenge for her, they met during the days. They went to Saturday matinee movies, watching *Blacular, Shaft, Uptown Saturday Night,* and Manny's craze, Bruce Lee movies. She heard Maureen rave about Skateland, the 'happening place', where she and her friends skated to the latest music on Saturday nights. She told Manny about this new place.

Because it opened during the days as well, it became their spot, even though she had to cajole him into going. He thought the atmosphere was 'very teeny boppish', with too many 'schoolers', pre-teens and teens. When she countered, "But we are teenagers too", he responded,"Yeah, but we don't run up and down and carry-on like dem."

This was the only venue centrally located at Half Way Tree, where youths could meet and dance and have fun in the daytime. Knowing her choices were limited, he appeased her. After a while, he loosened up. He'd laugh as she made baby steps holding onto the rails around the rink, sometimes falling, until she conquered it and skated hands free. "Hey Marcy," he'd shout, "not bad."

The last day of school for Christmas break, Sandy left early to see Nigel and Marcy took the bus home alone. She looked forward to her holidays with Manny and thought all she needed was a good get-out-and-back-in-the-house plan. Since her grandmother knew of her dance practices at school, Sandy did not have to be her excuse anymore. She simply had to tell her the dance group had shows through the holidays. If she, Audrey or Maureen showed interest in attending, she would play down the need for them to be there, saying something like, sometimes only a few people come and the show gets cancelled, which would be a waste of time if this happens, and there was no way of knowing ahead of time. Once her grandmother accepted this, she wouldn't need an alibi for her sisters.

She stepped off the bus feeling she deserved an A+ for gumption. She chuckled at the thrill of her deception, and walking home thought, *finally I'll get to see Manny Friday, Saturday, Sunday, anytime I want, with no problem.* She hummed, *happy days are here again, my holiday plans are clear again, happy days are here again.*

Chapter 27

The whole family, including Tony, was in the living room when she entered the house. She stopped smiling upon seeing their long faces. Her mind flashed to her father; her knees buckled and she dropped her bag and took a seat. Audrey said, "It's you we're waiting for."

"Why? Something wrong with daddy?"

"Well." She sighed, her lips pursed.

"Well, what?"

Maureen answered. "We have to go to daddy tonight. We have to get him to see a doctor now, now." Her shoulders tightened. "I stopped to see him this morning and he don't look like somebody goin' live long. I left Mr. Fitzy with him. He's trying to get him to go hospital."

She changed out of her uniform and Tony drove them to his house.

When they got there, Mr. Fitzy was smoking in the front yard. "Oh thank God oonuh come." He dropped the cigarette butt and stepped on it. He opened the gate and they stood in the yard talking. "Yes, man, I had to take him because he was complaining of pain. Him fight me though, but in the end him go." They mumbled their approval. "The doctor examine him and tell him it might be him liver and give him some medications."

"That's good," Maureen said.

"Him tell him to take them for a couple a days and come back come see him."

"The doctor gave him a date, because we can't trust him to remember."

"Nor would he want to go," Marcy said.

"Him wanted to run some test on him today, but Arta tell him say him will come another time." He paused and ran his hand over his goatee. "Oonuh know how oonuh father head tough already." He combed through the facial hair with his fingers. "Boy, I don't know, I don't know 'bout Arta."

"I don't know why him won't take this thing serious," Audrey said.

"So him in the house now?" Donovan asked.

"No, when we come from the doctor, he was there for a little while, then me see him drag himself go through the gate, say him soon come." They all hissed.

"He said where he's gone?"

"I don't know where him gone."

"So you mean he's not here?" Marcy asked, grimacing.

"No, him gone from 'round a hour now." They stared at each other, then at Mr. Fitzy. "I tried to tell him to get some rest after him take the medication, but him wouldn't listen. I couldn't stop him." Mr. Fitzy, eager to fend off any blame for Arthur's carelessness, repeated, "No, I couldn't stop him."

"But daddy no easy," Donovan said, frustrated.

"Daddy definitely don't realize how sick he is," Maureen added.

"I can't believe this," Audrey said. "I really can't believe him."

The realization that Arthur, a sick man, was at Franklin's, stunned everybody. "So you mean, we have to go dig him outta di bar, when him sick and suppose to be in bed?" Audrey fumed.

"Let's not jump to conclusion 'cause we don't really know where he is," Maureen pleaded on his behalf. Audrey gave her a you-must-think-I'm-stupid look.

"So what we going to do now?" Marcy asked, facing her siblings.

"We might as well go to the bar, 'cause I can't think of anywhere else he might be," Donovan said.

"In his condition he could very well be in the hospital," Maureen said.

"Well I certainly hope so for his sake," Audrey replied. A frown wrinkled her forehead.

Everyone looked at Audrey for the next move. In frustration, she looked at Tony. And without having to instruct him, or apologize for her father probably close to death and in a bar, he, coolly said, "Okay, let's try the bar, then."

Watching Tony around the family, how he acted as if it was no big deal having a drunk for a father, or looking as if he'd rather be someplace else, made Marcy's heart contented for Audrey.

They got to the bar and Tony parked at the commissary, a couple of doors below. They were all set to leave the car when Audrey suggested, "Not everybody go, we just want to see if he's there first."

Donovan said he'd go and Maureen volunteered, "Me too."

As she waited for Donovan and Maureen to return, Marcy's insides knotted. Then Donovan came out and told them he was upstairs in one of the rooms, refusing to leave. *Daddy is refusing to leave,* she thought. *Does he know the bellyache he's putting us through?*

"The damn room upstairs makes it too easy for him!" Audrey snapped.

Mrs. Franklin had empty rooms upstairs the bar since her grown children left home. And it upset Audrey that men like her father, too drunk to go home, had more reason to get drunk because they had a room upstairs. The only problem was, like Arthur, they never wanted to leave. She opened the car door saying, "I want to see what's going on with him." Marcy followed.

Donovan led the way through joshing, dominoes smashing on tables, juke box spinning Elvis Presley, the scent of rum and cigarette, all the way to the back of the bar, then up the stairs.

Marcy kept her eyes to the floor until they reached a small, dim room above the bar. A piece of cord from the light switch hung over his bed. "Daddy," she said, pulling on the string. "The light can't get any brighter?" He made a grunt. She guessed it was no, and the room remained gloomy. The only furniture was the bed he lay on. The four of them circled him, studying his curled up, emaciated body. His complexion, normally a lighter shade like Maureen's, was now the blackest in the room. Marcy's heart hurt thinking of the tall, dignified man in his fireman uniform, the man she was proud to show off to her teachers and friends. "That's my daddy," she used to say when he visited her at preparatory school.

Their sniffles drowned hers. Welled-up tears burned her eyes. She was angry. She covered her mouth to stifle screams of *why, why, why? Why did our lives have to change? Why did daddy have to come to this?* She cried silently in her hand.

It was better that the lighting was poor, for it gave each of them privacy to handle their despair and face his fate.

Tired of shaking his head that he was not leaving, he turned away from them. Audrey brushed his arm one more time. "Come Daddy, come."

"Please come, don't stay here, Daddy," Maureen begged.

"Just let us take you home, Daddy," Marcy pleaded.

He lay still, not speaking.

Shoes scraped along the wooden floor near the room, and they quieted. It was Mrs. Franklin. The fair skinned woman with freckles, short and plumed, only wore high heels, or pumps, as she called them. One time, when Marcy visited her father at the bar, she overheard a man tease that he would pay Mrs. Franklin to walk all over his back. She laughed, throaty, and said, "Put your money where your mouth is and my pumps will walk a marathon on your back."

She marched into the room; her voice trumpeted, "Children", getting their full attention, "He's really not doing well, and if he wants to stay here, let him stay for the night."

"But he has medications at home to take," Maureen said.

"He told me they not working."

"He only got them today, he has to give them a chance," she protested.

"Well, he must know. I'm just going off what him tell me," she said. She drew close to him, pressing on the bed with her knuckles. "How you feeling Arthur, you still having pains?"

He grunted an inaudible response. She spoke louder. "You feeling any pain right now?"

A weak "no" left his mouth.

"But him don't look well, I seriously think he should be in a hospital," Maureen insisted. He groaned and shook his head.

"Let me say something," Audrey said, leaning close to his ear. "Daddy, even though you not feeling pain now, just go -"

He cut her off, forcing to speak, "No, Audrey."

"Children," Mrs. Franklin said, "don't worry yourselves, let him stay here for the night. I will look in on him and if he gets worse I will get one of the men to help me get him to the hospital." When they did not answer or move to leave, she said, "Oonuh have a phone?" They said they did. "Give me the number before oonuh leave," she said, and left the room.

They figured they might as well leave, having lost this round with him; he was determined to have things his way, even if it meant shortening his life. One after the other they climbed on the bed and embraced and kissed his warm, frail body. He turned his head to watch them leave, and they waved goodbye from the door.

Tony and Audrey cancelled plans to go out for the night, and the four of them sought their grandmother's comfort. She was in her room. She turned off the radio as they surrounded her. Audrey first spoke of his condition, then the others chipped in. "Bwoy, it don't sound good." She sighed. "I tell you man, trouble never set like rain." She shook her head. "Well, one a you better call his sister." She looked at Audrey and Maureen. "Make her know him condition critical." Maureen agreed to call and went to get the number. She continued, "For she will have to come take charge."

Maureen made the call to Enid. Her siblings stayed quiet while she relayed his illness and his stubbornness to get help. Maureen answered, "Yes, Aunt Enid", "But he won't listen Aunt Enid", and "Okay, Ma'am" a few times.

Audrey grew impatient, and whispered, "Ask her when she can come."

"When you coming?" Everybody's ears cocked. "Yes, I understand. I understand." Finally, she said, "Tuesday?" Maureen looked at Audrey. "All right then Aunt Enid, see you Tuesday."

After Maureen hung up, she explained that Enid could not come any sooner because she had no one to oversee the shop before then. "If she find that she can come before that time, she'll let us know, but for now she looking to come early Tuesday morning."

Audrey hissed. "I wish she could come earlier than that."

"She don't realize how sick daddy is," Marcy said.

"Oonuh have to understand, if she don't have the right people to leave in the shop, by the time she get back, oonuh know everything gone."

Mari's decision to call Enid was a weight off everyone, especially since none of them had ever had this experience, and it would fall on her. Despite the few days wait for Enid, as she said, "Enid coming is a blessing."

Chapter 28

Images of her father's lifeless body, and wondering if they had done everything to persuade him to get doctor's care, kept Marcy from sleeping. And when she did, she dreamed he had died. At seven o'clock in the morning, when howling echoed through the house, she thought she was still dreaming. She shot up in bed as Maureen and Audrey came to the room crying. Maureen bawling out, "Daddy gone, daddy gone" started her tears. She leaped out of bed in a daze and held onto her. Maureen fell to her knees, taking her sisters to the floor with her.

"Daddy dead? Daddy dead?" Marcy asked. Her voice trembled and her breath quickened.

As Maureen cried uncontrollably, although Marcy grieved too, she knew she had to restrain her own sorrow for Maureen's sake.

Donovan stood with Mari at the door, his eyes weak and red from sadness. Mari embraced Maureen and lifted her off the floor. "Alright, come mi love, come we go see 'bout you daddy."

Mr. Garrison offered to drive them to Franklin's. A few neighbours heard of his death and stood at the gate as they were leaving. Sandy and her mother were at the fence; Sandy was crying. They didn't stop and Mr. Garrison, acting as a shield, ushered them into the van.

By the time they were on the main road, the news of his death had spread through the area like fire on a gusty day. People were outside their yards, on the street corner; everyone was somber. Mr. Garrison stopped behind a police car and a hearse from McIntosh Funeral Home parked in front of the bar. A crowd at the gate parted to let them through, a few were amateur broadcasters. One woman asked, "Is oonuh fada?" When Marcy nodded, she whispered into the crowd, "Yes, a dem fada." They murmured, "Bwoy it sad" and "Mi sorry to hear him dead". A man commented, "You know how long I know him? We worked at the same fire station for years." A woman, looking outraged said, "Mi sorry him dead, but you see white rum, it's di devil's battle ax!" Another woman joining the crowd, asked as they reached the gate, "Is in di bar him dead?" They kept their mouths closed, head down and entered the yard.

Mrs. Franklin waited at the gate with the police. "Let them through," she ordered. "Come with me, children." She noticed Mari in the back. "This must be grandma? Oonuh come, he's upstairs."

Half way up the steps, Maureen pulled back. "I don't think I can go. I don't think I can go see him."

Mari held her. "Yes man, you can make it, you can make it mi love." They leaned on each other and made it upstairs.

Two men in white shirts and black ties waited outside the room, the same room they left him in the night before. "These men are from McIntosh." Mrs. Franklin introduced Mr. Bailey and Mr. Kent from the funeral home.

"You're the family of the deceased?" Mr. Bailey, the older man confirmed and led them into the room.

Arthur's body lay on the bed with a white sheet thrown over it. Mr. Kent pulled it down for them to see. As he did, their weeping gushed, saturating the room. Mrs. Franklin and the men waited outside. They sat on the bed beside him, touching his head, kissing his face, telling him goodbye.

After a few minutes the men returned to the room, wrapped his body and placed it on a stretcher. They walked behind them to the hearse, crying. Donovan asked, "Can we go with him?"

"No son," Mr. Bailey replied.

After the hearse left, Mrs. Franklin invited them to her house, a closed-off section upstairs. Her dining table was set with all kinds of dishes, from liver, callaloo and breadfruit, to beef soup, cake and sorrel. "Eat, eat, help oonuh self," she insisted. They told her thanks, but that they weren't hungry.

"We just want to hear what happened to daddy after we left him last night," Audrey said.

"Well after you children went home, I was in the bar 'til 1:15 when I lock-up. I check on him right after that and he was sleeping. I know he was sleeping because I saw his chest moving." She made eye contact with each of them to register her point. "It was my housekeeper who came at 6:30 and found Arthur's body." She waved her hand. "I'd say around 6:50 or so. Pearl said she called his name a few times and he never answered nor moved. She said he looked stiff and she was frightened, so she called me. And as I saw him, I knew Arthur had passed." She sighed and shook her head. "Yes man," her voice low, "I knew he was gone." Her eyes watered. "So that's when I called oonuh, McIntosh and the police."

Audrey telephoned Tony with the news. In no time he came from his house in Mona Heights. She was relieved to see him as he brought sense at the right time. When Mrs. Franklin told them to take food home, they told her they hadn't any appetite and turned it down. It was Tony who reminded them that later when they were hungry, they wouldn't have to put on a pot.

Around ten-thirty he drove them home. Audrey's first call was to Enid. She said she would come in a week as she needed time to prepare for his burial down there in St. Mary. Afterward, she telephoned their mother, but her phone rang without an answer. Mari did not go to work; she went to the market and took Donovan with her. Maureen and Marcy left Audrey and Tony in the living room and went to their room. Maureen went straight to bed and covered herself up to her head. Marcy left her alone.

She sought solace in her grandmother's room. Laying on the bed, she held the pillow to her and stared out the window, into the morning's event. Tears welled-up at the memory of her father's six-foot frame covered in a sheet leaving Franklin's, and she wondered if he had suffered; the thought stabbed her in the heart. Thinking of him dying in a bar, the only place he found refuge, troubled her. *Why?* As she slipped into thoughts of 'why' and 'what if', the things she could not change, Mr. Garrison's sound system blasted. The music brought Manny to mind and she remembered they were meeting in the evening. She glanced at the clock radio, it was 11:40. The rumble in her belly was unbearable, so she went to the kitchen.

Audrey and Tony sat at the kitchen table eating the food from Mrs. Franklin. "I warmed up the soup," Audrey said, and pointing to the oven, "the liver and breadfruit in there."

She served herself some soup and took it to the dining table. Eating it, she smiled. *Daddy would've enjoyed this.* She swallowed to clear the lump forming. After she ate, she forced herself to begin working, to put her mind on something else. She unpacked the fridge to clean it and Audrey tidied the kitchen after Tony left. The movements in the house stirred Maureen. She arose, ate and helped with the cleaning.

Later, as Marcy knelt on the veranda polishing the floor, a neighbour came to the gate with a bag, "Morning, Marcy, I have something for oonuh."

She went to the gate. "Morning Ms. Reid."

"You shouldn't even bother with that today," she said, handing her the bag.

"Staying busy helps me, Ma'am."

"It's little food I prepared. It hot, carry it go put down."

"Thanks."

She put the food away and returned to the veranda. Another neighbour came. "Morning, Mrs. Williams."

"Morning my dear. A bring a little cake and sorrell for the family." She looked at the package wrapped in Christmas paper and it dawned on her, *oh yes*, it was supposed to be 'the most wonderful time of the year'. She told her thanks.

"So how you holding up, my love?"

"I'm okay," she said, knowing neither her voice nor her face showed signs of being okay.

"Boy, it's sad about your father," she sighed, "but it's life my child." Marcy nodded. "Where the body?"

"At McIntosh."

"So is what really happen to him?"

"We not sure yet." This conversation she wanted to avoid. She pretended the bag was heavy. "I better go put this down."

"All right, say hello to the others and Granny for me. Give them my condolences."

"Thanks, Mrs. Williams."

She finished polishing and started running the polisher when Sandy came to the fence. "Marcy, Marcy."

She didn't have the energy for pleasantries, not even with Sandy. She knew she wouldn't stop calling, after all, she was her friend, so she said, "Hi Sandy."

"Come closer." She walked up to the fence. "So how you feel?"

"Take a guess."

"Well, considering your morning, things can't be good."

"You can say that again."

"Me sorry to hear anyway. Me and my mother cried when we heard." Her words touched Marcy, and she remembered why she deserved her attention.

"Thanks."

"So is what caused it?"

"What you mean, his death?"

"Yeah, how he died?"

"We don't know as yet."

"Oh." She hissed. "It must be hard, though."

"Well, yes."

"Oh, boy." She sighed.

Sandy realized she wasn't getting anywhere and played with the flowers on the tree separating them. Of course Marcy wasn't purposely trying to make it difficult, but the questions were just too soon.

They stood in silence until the gate opened; it was her grandmother and Donovan. "Sandy, see Granny come," she said. "I have to go help her with the market things."

Before she stepped away, Sandy said, "You goin' see Manny later?"

"No."

"No?" Sandy bit her lip, still, she couldn't keep her thoughts to herself. "Me know it's not my business, but I think you should go. It will make you feel better, man."

In the afternoon they telephoned their mother again and she was home. After Audrey relayed their father's passing, her first words were, "At Franklin's?" Rose too saw the irony of him dying at the bar, to which Audrey replied, "Of all places."

After she got off the phone, Audrey went to her friends waiting with flowers on the veranda. Some of the boys who played football with Donovan came to visit and insisted he come out for a game. Maureen was back in her room, in bed. Marcy lay on the settee in the living room. The thought of meeting Manny crossed her mind and she felt guilty right away. *That's a shame, Marcy.* She decided not to see him.

She went to her grandmother in the kitchen. She was seasoning the oxtail she brought home for Sunday dinner. Marcy leaned on the counter next to her. "Granny, how long it will take to get over daddy?" She teared up.

Mari wiped her hand in her apron and hugged her. "Ahh baby, ahhh," she rocked her, "it hard now, but it will ease, everyday will get a likkle better."

"I don't know if I'll ever feel better," she said, her words muffled from sobbing.

"You will, baby, you will."

In the evening, she and her sisters were at the dining table having the rest of the food from Mrs. Franklin. Audrey sat at the edge of her seat, rearing to dash off. She was only at the table for a few minutes, before announcing, "I have to get ready 'cause Tony picking me up at 6:30."

Marcy was surprised she was leaving. Although none of them said it, she assumed they were staying home, at least for the night. "You going out?" she asked.

"Yes," she replied, in a tone that implied, why not?

"Oh, okay." She lowered her gaze to hide her shock.

After Audrey left the table she decided not to assume anymore. She asked Maureen if she had plans too. "Yes," she said, another surprising response. "I'm going to Joanne's." Going to Joanne meant seeing Patrick, her boyfriend.

"I see."

It dawned on her that she was the only one staying home. The thought occurred to her that it didn't have to be this way, so she said, "One of my friends and her family invited me over later, if I wasn't doing anything."

"Who, Sandy?" Maureen asked without looking at her, which only made it easier for the lie to slip off her tongue.

"No, one of my other friends from school."

"Oh," Maureen said, concentrating on the food on her plate.

Marcy sat frozen, thinking, *she believed me,* and although she should be relieved, she was conflicted. She was free to see Manny, as none of her sisters were going to be home, yet, she wasn't bouncing in her seat with excitement, or dashing out the door. She felt guilty. "So daddy finally gone."

"Yep," Maureen said, and sighed.

"Maybe it was the best thing, since he wasn't getting any better." She sighed again. "Maybe."

"I believe he's in a better place."

Maureen raised her eyes without answering. The conversation stirred up feelings they would rather put to rest, so they stopped talking.

When Maureen left her at the table, she told herself, *Marcy, there is no prize for being a fool, seize the opportunity and go be with Manny; you know you want to.*

She watched for Maureen to leave the house and when she did at 7:15, she slipped on her dress and went to see her grandmother.

She was sitting on the back veranda with a bowl of Blackie mangoes in her lap, listening to her pigeons coo. Marcy stood at the doorway. "Granny," she said, startling her and she turned. "I'm going to one of my friend's home. Her family invited me over for the evening."

"Where?"

"Just at Outward Avenue."

She paused, as if picturing the three blocks. "Okay."

"Thanks, Granny."

"Come in before nightfall."

"Yes, Granny."

She hurried back to the room, put on Maureen's lip gloss, sprayed on Audrey's perfume and sped off.

She took the long way in case she met anyone who wanted to stop and ask about her father. *Oh shoot, daddy!* She slowed her walk. Before sinking into sadness, she rolled her shoulders, caught her breath and carried on. She checked her wrist for the time and realized she forgot her watch. *Damn!* She knew it was later than seven o'clock so she hustled toward the beach. *I pray he didn't leave. I really need to see him, I need a hug...*

When she turned onto the dirt road that led to the beach, she saw someone leaning on a motorbike. No one else was around and she wondered if it was him. The person saw her and walked toward her; it was Manny. She smiled as their eyes met. He grinned and hugged her. "Miss Marz, mi just a wonder if you tie mi out?" She pressed into his hug and he kissed her face.

"I almost never –" she uttered, and she burst out crying.

"Wow, wow, Marcy, why you crying?"

"My father dead, my father dead, Manny."

"What? When?" He brought her face up to his.

"This morning." Her tears poured and he dried them with his rag.

"What you saying to mi, Marcy?" He sat on the damp grass, and she sat in his lap. "Babes, mi sorry to hear." After she calmed, he asked, "So what really happen to you old man?" She told him her father might have died in his sleep, that it was not yet confirmed. "You mean, him get a heart attack?"

"I don't know, I don't know," she muttered.

"So anybody was wit' him?"

"Not in the room, but in the same house." She was not ready to say he died in a bar.

"So where di body now, McIntosh?" She nodded. "So who goin' look about di funeral?"

"His family."

"What about you mother, she coming out?"

"No."

"She can't travel yet?"

"Yes, but remember them divorce."

They sat quietly, embracing. Old memories, before her parents' divorce, when they were happy, brought tears. She thought it was a mistake being there. "Manny," she said, "maybe I shouldn't come tonight, I don't feel right. I feel miserable, like I wanna scream, like I want –"

"It's alright babes, mi understand, mi understand, man." Manny hugged her tighter, she didn't want him to let go.

After a while they stood, and as he brushed off his pants, he asked, "You wan' go for a ride?"

Scrutinizing the Ninja Kawasaki parked across from them, she asked, "Is it yours?"

"Yeah, a little birthday gift mi buy myself." He chuckled.

"A little gift?" she said, studying the blue and yellow monster on wheels. "Why didn't you tell me it was your birthday?"

"It gone already. And mi couldn't talk 'bout my earth day when my baby a cry." He gently stroked her face.

"Manny, you're something else." She half smiled.

"Yes, I'm your man," he grinned, "and you're my woman. I have to take care of you." He cupped her chin. "My black Cinderella."

She smiled and replied, "Yea, you better take care of me on this bike, 'cause I never ride on one before."

"You just hold mi 'round mi waist and leave di worrying to mi."

He got on the bike and warned, "Don't make you foot touch di muffler." She studied it for a few seconds. "You'll get burn." She climbed on behind him, making sure her feet were secure on the back pedals. "Now hold mi 'round mi waist." As he started the bike, she grabbed his shirt. "No, lean closer and hold on tight." His motorbike revved and sent her heart racing. She roped her arms around him, pressing tightly. "You get it now?" He chuckled.

"Just take your time with me."

Chapter 29

Manny took the long way from the beach, riding on side roads, steering clear of her street. At the top of HiLand Avenue, he turned East on Windward road in the middle of country buses filled with market vendors leaving Kingston for home. One of the bus drivers closed in on them, blocking the bike. He hit the side of the bus and pressed his horn. "Bwoy, move outta di road nuh!" Manny cut before him. "Bwoy a accident you wan' cause?" Manny sped up.

A fierce wind battered Marcy's face and her heart pounded as the towering vehicles surrounded them. She gripped Manny's waist tighter and pressed her face in his back. As he swerved in and out of traffic, it occurred to her she hadn't asked how many of his eighteen years he had been riding. Right then, a piece of cardboard flew from a truck and sailed over her head; she cowered, holding onto Manny to save her life.

The bus driver blew the horn until Manny turned onto Mountain View Road, and he continued on Windward Road.

Manny rode along Mountain View Road, slowed and turned on a dark lane. The motorbike bumped its way up the stony alleyway lined with zinc fences, lit only by the ends of men's smokes; men who stopped whatever they were doing to take stock of them passing. At the end of the path was a small house with a kerosene lamp near the front window. Manny stopped a few feet away. He got off the bike and said, "Mi soon come." She watched him walk to two men sitting on the steps of the house; both men were much older. She could not hear their conversation, only laughter as they greeted each other. One of the men, his locks high under his tam, got up and walked pass her on the bike. He stared at her as he went by; intimidated, she flinched, lowering her eyes to the ground. When he circled back, he nodded and said, "Sis." She glanced at him and nodded.

After five minutes or so of her stomach churning, Manny returned, got on the bike and asked, "Marz, you alright?"

"Yes," she answered, although she wanted to ask why they were there, but sensed it was no place to start a conversation, or linger.

Manny turned south from the lane and west on Mountain View Road, back to the beach. He didn't go to the side they were earlier, he went farther from the path. They stopped at an almond tree and he parked his motorcycle next to it. The shrub covered them from chance passersby. He laid his towel at the foot of the tree and they sat. As he fumbled with something he took from his pants pocket, she asked, "So why we went to Mountain View?"

"Mi go check some people mi know." When he turned around she saw that he held a rolled up brown paper and suspected it was weed. "Marcy, you ever try dis?"

She looked in his hand and asked, "Is ganja, right?" then looked up at him, "Is it you go buy?"

"Mi never buy it. Mi friend just gimme."

"What kinda friend that, him just have it so?"

"Cho, Marz man, just cool man." He sifted through the weed, separating the seeds. "Dis will help you relax," he said, scrunching the dried leaves with his fingers.

"I guess I don't have to ask if you've tried it," she said.

"Yea. Nutting nuh wrong wit' dis. Dis better for you dan rum. See it kill you fada."

She looked askance at him. "Don't remind me." It was a blow that quieted her. She pictured her father's dead body.

"Miss Marz, Marcy," he bumped her shoulder, "I don't like see you sad." He kissed the side of her face. "Just trust mi, man."

The strange thing is, I do trust him.

Despite not fully understanding certain parts of his life, she liked his confidence, his self-assuredness, the way he seemed to know everything. And most endearing, how he tried to please her and looked out for her like 'his woman'.

Manny spread the dried leaves on two strips of white paper he glued together with his saliva. As she watched him, her body tensed, she had never been this close to the illegal substance. *What if we get caught?* On top of that, she felt guilty because she had sworn, that she, Marcy Tomlinson, after watching her father's struggle with alcohol, would never put anything addictive to her lips, and here she was with Manny getting ready to do just that. But grieved, she welcomed anything to make her feel alive again, if only momentarily.

She crouched beside him and observed as his fingers twirled the joint into a cigarette. He licked the paper up and down before running it between his lips to smooth it. She asked what he was doing. He said, "Mi a seal it, you nuh." He flicked and shook the lighter a few times, willing the flame to grow higher. When the gas blew up in a red and yellow flame, like a skilled 'herbs man', he grinned proudly and held the fire to the joint between his lips. He pulled on it until the paper and contents sparked red and black flames around the edges. He kept puffing until the burnt weed crackled. Her heartbeat surged as her eyes trailed the sizzling weed. She leaned back as its fumes seethed in the air, letting loose a strong, intoxicating odour, and just taking it in, it relaxed her, and she slowly exhaled.

A wind rustled the waves behind her and frightened, she scanned the coast. *Good.* There were no lovers on a quickie rendezvous, and except for crickets and peenie wallies sounding their disagreement to them polluting their habitat, they were alone.

"Marcy, you wan' try some?" he asked, handing her the weed. She swallowed hard to remove the lump fear had summoned. He noticed her hesitancy. "It's just a likkle spliff man, try it." His eyes softened and his voice mellowed. She dragged on the spliff and instantly coughed. "Don't keep it in your mouth, blow it out," he instructed.

She rubbed her throat. "It a burn me, man." Both her throat and eyes itched.

Manny took the spliff. "Watch me." He pulled on it and blew it through his nose. "You get it?" After a few tries with less coughing, she got it. They took turns smoking the joint, though he did more.

Soon they shifted into their own space. Manny braced himself against the almond tree and she lay beside him on seaweed and fallen branches. By the time the spliff became a butt, he had grown quiet; she couldn't stop laughing. He drew closer, looked into her eyes and said, "Marz, mi check for you, you nuh, yea man, mi really like you." It was as if he had said, *Marz, laugh some more.*

She lay still under the headiness. The peenie wallies and crickets' noisy protest faded. She no longer heard their demand to vacate their space, nor the waves whooshing to shores. She had floated to outer space. Her head spun to its own melody as her body drifted, soaring to the sky. She danced with the stars, the moon guiding their steps through the galaxies.

She awoke with her head on Manny's chest, his head turned the other side, his eyes closed. She checked his watch. "Oh my gosh!" she yelled, at seeing the time. "Manny, wake up! Wake up, Manny!" She shook him. He ran his fingers over his eyes. "Manny, it's 11:45."

"What time?"

"Almost midnight, come." She jumped up and felt wobbly. "Wow, my head."

"Just cool, man, take it easy."

"No Manny, I have to go home now." As she straightened her clothes, she fought to stay steady.

"It's 'cause you feeling irie, man." He pushed himself up.

"No. I can't go home feeling irie."

"Go wash you face in a di sea."

She splashed and slapped her face with the seawater, hoping to get rid of the headiness and ganja smell.

Manny had gum and gave her two sticks. "Come mi take you home," he said and got on his motorbike. He revved the engine; it was too late in the night to oppose, so she climbed on. "You have mi?"

She gripped his waist. "Yes, go."

Mr. Garrison rescued her again. She was thankful, but bothered. He opened the door in only his underpants. She cringed and lowered her eyes to his bare feet. As she passed she felt his gaze following her; it was creepy. It left her feeling as though she owed him a favour, or that he had her secret.

When she got inside her house she leaned against the door and exhaled. *Marcy, that was too close.*

Chapter 30

Friday afternoon, a week after Arthur's death, Enid and her husband drove to Kingston to arrange for his body to be taken to St. Mary. She met the children at the funeral home. When she walked into the front office and they saw her, she was exactly as she described herself: short and stout, with silver, shoulder length, straightened hair. She hugged the children and commented on the distinct feature they shared with their father: "Check di likkle ears", she pulled on hers and spun each of them, "Oonuh a Arta's, for true". They laughed about it, and Maureen told her that when they were younger their grandmother always said, "Rosie never tell a lie on oonuh fada."

The attendant brought them to the viewing room; in there were tears and sniffles all around. They each had a moment with him alone. The overwhelming sadness Marcy had going into the room disappeared when she saw his body. He looked as though he was in a deep sleep, as if finally getting the rest he needed from his 'whites'. She touched his hardened face, told him she loved and missed him but understood he wanted to go. As she stood observing him in his white shirt and black and gray tie, calm and peaceful, no more suffering, she whispered, "Thank you, Jesus."

After the viewing Enid sat with them. She said she planned his burial for the following week "after di Christmas holiday". She asked how they would get to St. Mary. Audrey told her with Tony, and took the directions.

The next day, while the three sisters were in the living room, they debated whether to hang Christmas decorations. Almost everyone in the neighbourhood had hung theirs already. If it weren't for Maureen and Marcy's 'un-celebratory' mood, they would have too. Audrey argued, "The decorations would give the place a lively Christmas vibe."

"But Audrey we're not feeling the Christmas vibe," Marcy said.

"We should cancel Christmas this year," Maureen said.

"It's not oonuh one live here and some of us enjoy Christmas."

"It's not about enjoying Christmas or not, we're in mourning."

"Everybody sad that daddy died, but we didn't die with him."

"Yes, Miss Audrey, I know you don't care!" Maureen shouted.

"Did I say that? Did I say that?" Audrey lashed out.

"No, Maureen, that's not what Audrey said," Marcy reasoned.

Mari heard the quarrel and came to see. Audrey asked if she thought it was too late for Christmas decorations.

"Better late dan never," she said, and picked up the Christmas lights and strung it on the curtain rods. The sisters followed her lead, and hung bells, bows and balloons around the living room. The tension eased.

Their grandmother prepared eggnog, and the girls sipped it as they admired the lights and decorations in the room.

They heard the gate open and Marcy looked. "It's Mr. Garrison and his girlfriend," she whispered. She slid the curtain aside and they caught a glimpse of them going by. He clutched Michie's hand and led her inside his home, shutting the door and windows.

"Well at least them enjoying the holidays," Audrey said, and the three of them shared a laugh.

With two days to Christmas, festivities ripened the air everywhere. On the streets and in homes were sights and sounds, of 'Merry Christmas'. Marcy caught the holiday fever. In high spirits, she telephoned Manny to confirm their Christmas plans. To her surprise, he said he was going to the country, as Mountain Fire was playing in Portland on Christmas Eve. He encouraged her to come, but she knew going out of town meant staying overnight, which was a definite no for her grandmother. Disappointed, she settled for a movie before he left.

She met Manny at their usual spot, the entrance of the beach where he waited in his van. He suggested they go to Rialto Theater because it was close to home. She reminded him, "That is the reason why we can't go, it's too close to home."

"What about Harbour View Drive-in? Dat far enough for you?" He chuckled. "And they showing *Harder They Come* again." They agreed on the drive-in.

On their way to the movies, she stared out the window. *If he's going to country, what kinda Christmas will I have?* She sighed into a sour mood and withdrew. Manny picked up on her moodiness and nudged her. "Hey, how you so quiet tonight?"

"I don't have anything to say."

"No man, I know you, somet'ing wrong."

"Nothing's wrong, it's just life," she said, still looking outside.

"Marz," he said, and turned her face to his. "Talk to me, what's up?"

"It's... it's just that I was expecting me and you to spend

Christmas together."

"Me and you can spend Christmas together, it's up to you."

"But you goin' country."

"Yes, and I told you to come."

"But what would I tell Granny?"

"We can figure out somet'ing."

"But you leaving in the morning."

"Yea, I can come pick you up."

She thought about it, losing concentration during the movie. *What story would I give Granny?*

Driving back from the show, he asked, "So you make up your mind yet?"

"Manny it not that easy. I don't feel comfortable always lying to granny, and this would be the biggest one."

"You wan' mi ask her for you?"

She slapped his arm. "Very funny."

"No, for real. It's about time Granny know mi."

"Get serious Manny. And I tell you all the while, it's not Granny you have to worry about, it's mommy, and somehow she would know everything all the way in Canada."

"Boy, mi don't even like hear 'bout Canada," he squeezed her hand, "'cause mi no ready to lose you."

They drove in silence until they reached the beach. He parked and they stayed in the car. He put on a Curtis Mayfield cassette and took her hand as *So In Love* played. He entwined their fingers and gazed at her with conviction. "Marz, mi love you, you nuh. Mi love you bad." His words flowed with Curtis'. She knew he cared, but hearing him declare his love with such feeling, shook her up. She trembled as he drew her closer and kissed her lips. He pushed back the seat and they continued kissing. He caressed her shoulders, her arms, and dotted her face with little kisses, melting her. As she succumbed to his tenderness, she felt him fondling her breast. She had a limit she didn't want to cross, and pushed his hand away. "Oh Marcy, please," he begged.

"I can't," she whispered. He slid on top of her, moving his body around. "Oh, Marcy, please."

"Stop!" she said, "I don't want to go that far, Manny."

"No Marcy, I wouldn't do that."

"Well get off me then." She pushed him.

He eased off and they straightened up themselves. "You not mad with mi, my sweets?"

"Manny, we just have to take our time."

"All right." He held her face, stared in her eyes and said, "But mi want you know mi really love you." She nodded. He kissed her lips.

"Anyway, mi have to go home now." She put her hand on the door.

"So you a come a country wit' mi?"

"No Manny, it's too short notice. I don't know what to tell Granny."

He hugged her and said he'd call when he returned in a couple days. He drove behind her until she reached her gate and waved goodbye.

Before she went in she prayed for the courage to knock on Mr. Garrison's door. Remembering how he ogled her the last time, she shuddered. Nearing the veranda, she noticed the living room door was slightly opened. Her immediate thought was a break-in, then Donovan came out. "Don't shut it, don't shut it," she said quietly, running to the door.

"Where you coming from at this time?" he asked.

"Where you going to at this time?" she mouthed, as he kept going.

The next day she awoke to carols streaming into the house from the neighbour's radio. She thought of Manny, and Christmas without him. *Have a Happy Jolly Christmas* came on. *Ahhh, I wish I could block out that stupid song,* she hissed, *and the whole Christmas Day excitement.* She rolled out of bed to find everyone else busy. Maureen was mopping the veranda, Donovan was sweeping the yard, and Audrey and her grandmother were in the kitchen. She stopped at the kitchen. "Good morning."

"You're right on time to set the table and squeeze some orange juice," Audrey said, handing her the plates.

Mrs. Bartley, the elderly woman next door, came from the country to spend the holidays with her son and daughter-in-law. She saw them in the kitchen. "One of you come get dis," she said, lifting a bag. Mari went to the fence for the bag filled with avocados, cho-cho and yam, right on time for breakfast. She sliced a few avocados to add to the ackee and codfish, fried plantains and Johnny cakes.

Shortly after the children sat to eat, their mother telephoned. They were expecting her, and the reason Mari was in her room. While the children had their breakfast, she updated her on Enid taking Arthur's body to St. Mary, because his father had a family plot there.

Marcy was the last to speak with her mother and it surprised her how much she longed for her; her warmth, her smell, her special care, and she cried. "Mommy, I miss you, I wish you were here."

"Very soon we'll be together again, my love."

She quieted and dried her eyes. It was the first time she wasn't distressed by that fact.

They sat on the veranda afterward. Her siblings shared their Christmas plans. She had none and wished instead to go to sleep and wake when it was all over.

In the evening, she and Sandy met at the fence and exchanged Christmas cake. Sandy wanted to know her plans since Manny was not in town. "Right here in my bed."

"So because Manny gone country you staying home?"

"Yeah, I'm not fussy."

"But it's the holiday, everybody going somewhere."

"It's all right with me."

"Well, you can keep Granny company." Sandy laughed. "Or you can come out with me and Nigel."

She groaned and said, "I don't know, I have to think about it."

As the evening grew, and her brother and sisters prepared for the night, she became restless. She watched Audrey and Maureen get dressed in holiday outfits and felt like getting dressed up too, only she had no place to go. She went to find Sandy. "All right then, get ready by eight," Sandy said.

A little after eight the girls were at the top of the road. "We meeting Nigel here?"

"No, we going to his house, his friend keeping a party."

They took a taxi to Nigel's home in Patrick City. He and a group of boys were two doors down; music rocked from the house. Nigel left the boys and greeted them. When he kissed Sandy on the cheek, the boys roared, "Wooow, Nigel" and "Gwaan, Nigel". Nigel beamed like 'di big man in town'.

He took them inside his house and they sat in the living room. He brought them rum punch, without the rum. "Mi mother don't drink."

"So this is rum punch cousin," Sandy said, laughing.

"This is fine with me," Marcy said. He told them his parents were out for the evening. "Then you're alone here?"

"No, my big brother in his room."

It wasn't long that he and Sandy disappeared in another room. She relaxed and listened to the music from next door, getting into the party mood as she waited for them.

She noticed Nigel and Sandy were gone for close to an hour and got impatient. A clock on the wall gonged at 10:00 and she went in search of them. She knocked on a door she saw them go into, there was no answer. As she turned from the door she bumped into Nigel's brother coming from his room. She averted her eyes and hurried to the living room. He followed and sat beside her. "You is Sandy friend?" She nodded. "What's your name?"

"Marcy."

"Marcy, I am Paul, Nigel brother. "

"I know."

"What a pretty girl like you doing all by yourself?" He stared at her intently.

She gave him a 'get lost' look which didn't deter him. Paul was in his early twenties, stocky, and his gaze made her uneasy. Her look was icy, but he didn't feel the chill. She got up to leave. "I better go find Sandy."

"Why you rush off so?"

She went to the room again, her heart on rapid beats. She opened the door without knocking and walked in. The room was dark but she made them out in the bed. They scurried, pulling the sheets over them and she looked away. She felt awful barging in and hoped they didn't think she did so out of spite. "Sorry, I had to. But if the two of you not going to the party again, tell me so I can go home," she told them.

"We going, we going," Sandy said.

They got off the bed and Nigel turned on the light. Paul shoved his head in the room. "Pappa and mamma come."

Nigel, not looking like 'di big man in town' anymore, said, "My parents come."

"How you said they weren't coming for now," Sandy grumbled.

"I don't know what happen," he said, looking helpless. "Oonuh stay, me soon come."

Sandy trembled. "Oh my God, Marcy, how we goin' get out?"

Nigel returned to the room. "My mother got sick, that's why they had to come home."

"So how we going to leave?" Marcy asked.

"Their room is in the front, so we can't walk through the living room." He blinked as if figuring it out. Sandy and Marcy stared at each other. "Come, follow me," he whispered.

Nigel led them to the back veranda. He carefully opened the gate and they slipped out. Sandy tripped over something. "Rahtid, is what that?"

"Shhh, stop you noise," he said.

The girls tiptoed behind Nigel to the other side of the house. As they turned the corner, two dogs laying at the front barked at them, preventing them from getting to the gate. Nigel hushed the dogs, but they continued to bark. He said, "I don't want my father come out, so we have to walk next door."

"You mean climb over the people them fence?" Marcy asked, giving him 'the eye'.

"Yes, the dogs won't move, and I don't want my father come catch us."

At this point, Marcy was too livid to worry about his father or the neighbours catching them, and that they might have dogs.

She just wanted to get out. Nigel pressed on the wire fence and she climbed over; thankfully, she wore pedal pushers. Sandy did not do as well; her hem got hitched on the fence. She examined it under the street light. "At least my dress don't tear."

She and Nigel still wanted to go to the party and Marcy told them, "I'm not in a party mood" and that she wanted to leave.

Sandy was torn between wanting her boyfriend and offending her best friend; she said, "Marcy, just stay little longer, nuh?"

"Sandy my vibes dead and me just wan' go home." She walked off.

"Wait nuh?"

"I said, I'm going home." She kept walking.

"You one goin' walk on the street in the middle night?"

"Yes, I'm going to take a cab," she replied, assured of her plans.

She heard Sandy's sandals catching up. "Okay Marcy, wait for me."

She stopped. "Don't feel you have to leave on my account. Stay with Nigel if you want."

She stopped the cab, then realized she hadn't enough money. She needed Sandy's portion to get home. It was clear she couldn't have gone far without her friend and got off her 'pumps and pride', sitting quietly for the ride. Sandy nudged her. "Marcy, mi sorry how things turn out."

She locked eyes with her, saw in her friend what she could only hope to be, and squeezed her hand. "It's okay."

They rode in silence for awhile, then Sandy said, "It's the worse Christmas I ever had." They laughed.

"I'm just glad the dogs never bite us." They laughed harder.

It seemed more like weeks than days to Marcy, waiting to hear from Manny. And when he called, he told her the dance was one of the best. She said, "Well you know it's Christmas, what you expect?" not letting on that she was sorry she wasn't there.

"I wish you'd come," he said, "but tell mi what you did."

"Oh, it's too boring to tell," she said, avoiding his 'you should've come'. "Let's plan from now what we doing for New Year's."

"Marcy, mi have to tell you somet'ing."

"What? You sound so serious."

"Mi have to go back to country."

"What?"

"Yes, babes."

"Oh, Manny, you killing me, man."

"Babes, just come wit' mi."

She contemplated his words and told herself, *Marcy, you don't want a repeat of Christmas.* "I'll come, I'll come."

She got off the phone. She sat at the edge of her grandmother's bed and wondered how to pull off a country run with Manny. She hadn't used the dance group excuse as yet, maybe this was the perfect time. Or, even better, the one about her friend and her family going to the country and inviting her, even though going to the country and getting back in time for her father's funeral could make her grandmother skeptical. *If I practice saying it with a straight face, it could work.*

Over the next few days, she set out for her grandmother. Since the trip was on Saturday she planned to tell her by Thursday. She wanted her alone, when Audrey and Maureen weren't around to plant doubts in her mind. Her radio show started 8:30. Five minutes before it began she entered her room. Her grandmother was in her usual nighttime spot, the chair by the window. She had not decided which plan to use, until she walked in and began, "Granny -"

"What happen now?"

She crossed her fingers behind her back and came out with, "Granny, can I go to St Ann with one of my friends?"

"Wid one of you friends?" She stared and Marcy held her breath, trying not to look away.

"Yes, my friend Ayoka and her family going and she asked if I wanted to come with them."

"When dis?"

"Saturday, Granny."

"And come back when?"

"The next day."

"Mi know dis friend?"

"No, Granny."

She didn't answer and Marcy hoped for an answer right away, so as not to lose sleep wondering.

Her radio program started and she shifted her eyes to the radio in front of her. Five minutes into the show and she paid her no attention, so she walked away.

She didn't know what to think, was it a 'yes', so she could phone Manny with the good news, or 'no' so she could come up with plan b.

Friday night came, and no word from her grandmother. She had already told Manny she'd meet him Saturday, midday, two bus stops from her road.

Saturday morning she got up with a plan to be in her grandmother's sight from she awoke. She knew she liked her coffee shortly after waking, so she made it, adding the right amount of condensed and evaporated milk, remembering to add a pinch of salt, and took it to her. "T'anks, mi love," she said, reading her Psalms. "Put it down." She rested it on the bedside table and left. When her grandmother went to the washtub, she went to rinse a few pieces and made small talk, only getting a nod here and there. By the time she got dressed for work, she was there too. "Let me zip you up, Granny."

Her grandmother took a last look in the mirror, picked up her handbag, and said, "Not here."

That's all, not here! Marcy followed her out the door. She believed she had done everything to permit a *'Yes, Marcy, you can go'* but got nothing, not even a *'Make mi t'ink 'bout it'*.

She was devastated, but not defeated. She went to find Sandy. They sat on the wall as she told her of her predicament. "So what you goin' do?"

"I don't know, but I want to go."

"I woulda go," Sandy said.

Marcy rolled her eyes at her. "Yeah, but I'm not you."

"Well, you nuh can stay then."

Marcy hung her head in thought, and said, "I can't just disappear like that."

"But you told her you and Ayoka and her family going to country, so she will just think that's where you gone."'

"You make it sound so easy." She sighed and shook her head.

"But it's easy, for you already gave her a story. By the time she thinks about it, you're gone."

"Yeah, and when I come back?"

"By that time she'll be so glad you never ran away, she'll take anything you say." She chuckled.

"Sandy, I wish I was as confident as you."

"Granny love you man, she not goin' say anything."

"All right, walk with me up the road at 12 o'clock. I will signal you and you wait for me at your gate."

"Yeah man, just call me when you ready."

She hid her toothbrush, rag, comb, and underwear in a bag. Audrey was not home, so she watched for Maureen and when she was busy in the back, sneaked out with the folded plastic bag under her arm. Sandy followed her to the bus stop where Manny waited. He sat in his mother's car, the car they used for deliveries. "Sandy, please don't say anything."

"No man, go on, go enjoy yourself." She knew her friend wouldn't tell, but she was nervous and had to say it.

"Drive, drive fast," she told Manny, stepping into the vehicle. "I just want to leave the area."

Manny kissed the back of her hand. "You keep your word."

"At what cost, though?"

"For a good cost." His face lit up.

"Yeah, but all now Granny don't know say me gone."

"Marcy, just relax, you're wit' mi and I'll bring you back safe and sound to Granny."

Chapter 31

Manny drove with the windows closed and the air conditioning on. After half hour of driving with the windows closed, she asked him to open them to let in natural breeze. She breathed in long and exhaled with a stretch, curling up on the seat. "Yea man, that's how mi like when you relax."

"Where is your stepfather?"

"Him and mi mada gone down from dis morning."

"You mother goin' be there too?"

"What you 'fraid? Mi mada don't bite." He chuckled.

"No, but what she goin' say about me?"

"What can she say? You're mi girl." She sat quietly and he continued, "You will like her, man."

"What's her name?"

"Faye, Faye West."

"West, that's Jack's last name?"

"Yea."

As they got close to Flat Bridge, she sat up. "I remember this place. My father drove here on the way to Dunn's River Falls."

"You 'fraid to cross?"

"Well driving with you, yes."

"No man, mi can handle dis."

"That you say, but I don't know if you buy your license."
She smiled at him.

Before they crossed the bridge, Manny pulled over. He
bought coconut water and sugar cane from the vendors. They
drank the coconut water on the side of the road and ate the cane
while driving. The bridge didn't scare her anymore. Once they
passed, she lay back into the ride and enjoyed the country road.
She told Manny, "From a child traveling with my family, I loved
this area, I liked how the water trickle from the rocks into the
stream," she exhaled, "I feel totally at ease on long drive outs."
She emphasized the long.

"Dats 'cause you not driving."

"Maybe." She smiled and winked at him.

Manny kept quiet as he drove, and after awhile she pushed
back her seat, closed her eyes and let him handle the road.

As he made a swing and began ascending, she felt light-
headed. She sat up as the car climbed the winding hills of St.
Ann. The higher they ascended, the sicker she became. "Manny,
I don't feel so well."

"We soon reach."

"No, stop, stop a little."

He drove a bit further, stopping at a safe spot. She clasped
her head with her hands, steadying herself. A few minutes of
her sitting still, he asked, "You alright now?" She nodded.

Once they continued up the hill, the spinning started again.
She told him to keep going since they were not far from their
destination.

By the time they reached, she felt queasy. Manny took her
inside and the women swarmed her. "What happen to her? She
feeling sick?"

"Yes, coming up di hill."

"Bring her come lie down," the elder woman instructed.

Manny led her to a bedroom and soon someone handed her a cup of tea. She nodded her thanks. She took a few sips and then closed her eyes.

She stirred about an hour later and Manny and one of the women stood over her. "Marcy, you feel better?" Before she answered he asked, "You want somet'ing to eat?"

"Get her a cup of mannish water," the woman said.

Manny left her and the woman she suspected was his mother. She was pretty, the female version of him, a shade lighter, similar full eyes, with what Jamaicans called 'pretty hair' - naturally straight with a little wave.

She sat up and leaned on the bed board, feeling a bit self-conscious with only the two of them in the room. "You're Marcy?" she asked, pleasantly.

Oh God. "Yes."

"So it's you my son going mad over?" She smiled broadly.

She smiled back. *Manny where are you?*

"Your last name is Tomlinson right? I know some Tomlinsons, you nuh. Where your parents from? Your father?"

Oh gosh not my father, please. "My father -" Manny came back to the room.

"I was just telling Marcy that I know some Tomlinson from St. Catherine."

"No Momma, Marcy come from Kingston."

"I know, but I talking about her parents."

"Oh, Momma, let her rest, man."

Manny sat on the bed next to her as she had the soup. They began talking, and quietly his mother left the room. "You saved me."

"What she said?"

"Not much. I'm just trying to guess what she might be thinking. She know my age?"

"What dat have to do wit' anyt'ing?"

"Who knows, she might think I'm too young to be your girl-friend."

"Is not what my mada t'ink. Is what I want and I want you."

He kissed her. "Mi love you, you nuh."

"I love you too."

"While you're here, don't worry 'bout nutting."

Shortly after, his mother knocked the door. "Dinner ready."

They joined the family in the backyard; uncles, aunts and their children sat under a leafy mango tree. The surrounding was filled with all types of fruits and ground provisions; and breadfruit, banana and coconut hung from the trees.

One of the women came from the house serving curry goat. "Grandpa kill a goat yesterday," he said, filling her in.

As they ate, he pointed out each person and their relationship to Jack. "It's down here Jack and him brothers and sisters born and grow, and every year dis time everybody come up here. Some not even here, dem live a foreign."

His Aunt Peggy, carrying a tray with cups, announced, "Who want juice?"

"Me." The children raised their hands. "And me, please."

"What you have?" someone asked.

"Plum, guava, lemonade."

"Just a coconut water for mi," Manny's grandmother said. One of the men chopped the top off the coconut and handed it to her. After she drank it, he chopped it in half and she ate the jelly inside.

Across the street from their house, the drum and base of Sly and Robbie blasted. "Jack a warm up," Manny said. His mother left the group to join Jack, taking two cups of goat head soup with her.

"Where the dance keeping?"

"On di school grounds in front." Manny told her that the one-room school Jack and his siblings, and his parents before had attended, was in poor condition. For the last few years, he said, Jack had held a dance at the school to raise funds to refurbish it. This year, the funds was for purchasing paint and doing some repairs. "Come, let's go," he said.

They walked a few feet up the hill, and typical of the hilly country roads, it was unpaved. She kicked off her sandals as the rocks twisted her ankles. "Marcy, why you do dat?"

"Because I don't want to burst my slippers."

"But you could get cut."

"It's all right. What if I never had anything to wear?" He looked at her sideways and shook his head.

His mother saw her coming. "Be careful," she said, "something might run in your foot."

"See what mi tell you," Manny said. She took heed and put on her shoes.

Manny relieved Jack at the sound system, and he went to sit with his wife on the steps. Marcy stood beside him watching him 'at di controls', impressing the men who gathered.

Manny was caught up in the men requesting songs and she said, "I'm going to see what the children doing" and wandered to the other side of the yard. As she took a seat on the steps of the school building, her eyes trailed the murals behind her. Pictures of the Coat of Arms, the map of Jamaica divided in its fourteen parishes, and the Doctor Bird, drawn on the concrete wall atop the seven National Heroes - Marcus Garvey, Paul Bogle, Sir Alexander Bustamante, George William Gordon, Samuel Sharpe, Norman Washington Manley, and the lone female, Nanny of the Maroons. Observing the chipped paint on each hero's drawing, she agreed a fresh coat of paint would brighten their distinction.

The children performed in the center of the yard for the women and older children who cheered them on. They played hoola-hoops, skipping, braided strings around the maypole and different classes raced each other. Two races brought the most cheers and raised the most funds: 'egg and spoon', where the children balanced an egg on a spoon and raced; and the 'crocus bag', where they ran, or tried their best to, with their feet enclosed in a bag, tripping over each other with laughter in the dusty school yard.

After two more sodas, Marcy went to find the toilet. She asked a woman tending to the children where it was and she showed her where to go. It was a small, two-room shed for male and female. Inside the female's, sunlight streamed through the top to provide light. She didn't bother to look for the light switch, and chose the nearest stall. She jolted upon opening the door, as she stared into a black, bottomless hole. After steadying herself, she laughed. *Oh, so this is the outhouse Granny said she used as a little girl in the country.* Gingerly, she did her business. Not looking beneath, she maneuvered around the abyss and hurried back to join the others in the yard.

By night fall, it was a different kind of fun. All the children went home, clearing the grounds for the 'big people' to 'throw down'. And this they did, coming out in droves with their contribution.

Jack freed Manny, taking over the turntables. The music went from rocking to mellow, with The Isley Brothers, Teddy Pendergrass and Smokey Robinson drawing the men to the women. Manny and Marcy 'rented a tile' and slow grind on the spot. Al Green's *What a Wonderful Thing Love Is* came on and he took her hand and led her behind the school. They ended up in the bushes. He leaned her against a tree. "Lord Manny, it dark 'round here."

"Dats di idea," he whispered, kissing her neck.

"What if a guinea pig run out on me?"

"What if you nose was a door post?"

"Where would I put the inches?" She finished the phrase. They laughed and kissed.

"You enjoying yourself?"

"I can't believe I'm having so much fun at country."

"You see, you town girls have to come country more often." They kissed some more.

"So when we going back to Kingston?"

"Thought you said you having fun?"

"Yes, but-"

"Don't worry, man, mi will get you home on time."

As they headed back, the crowd counted down New Year's and sang *Old Anzine*. Manny pulled her under the street lamp. "Happy New Year's, my sweets." He kissed her with his heart. "Mi love you, you nuh. You love me?" Trembling, she nodded. "You sure? You sure, sure, sure?"

"Yes! I'm so sure, I sneaked out of my house for you, that's how much I'm sure."

They walked back to the school holding hands. The crowd swelled onto the street and Manny went to see if Jack needed help. Marcy sat with his mother at the gate. She asked how things were going so far. "I'm having fun, I surprise myself."

"We do this every year, and sometimes on a smaller scale with just the family," she said. She took a sip of her beer. "It's nice to get away from town sometimes." Marcy nodded and smiled.

Around one o'clock she felt her body and eyes drooping. She was tired, but didn't want to bother Manny, who was occupied with Jack. His mother caught her nodding. "Marcy, you ready to sleep?"

She yawned. "Yeah, but Manny busy."

"I will take you over."

She let Manny know she was turning in. "Go on wit' momma, she will set you up." He winked and squeezed her hand.

Faye had the sleeping arrangements figured out. She led Marcy to the room where the children slept. Pointing to the bed with the girls, she said, "You can sleep with them." She picked up on Marcy's hesitance. "You have anything to sleep in?" In her planning she forgot her night clothes, and of course, Faye had one.

Sleeping with the girls reminded her of her younger years when Audrey and Maureen complained of her feet landing on their backs. She slept at the edge of the bed and was happy to see daylight. She rose before they did and went to the bathroom. They were still asleep when she returned to the room. She wandered through the house hoping to see Manny and strayed into the kitchen. His grandmother and Aunt Peggy were cooking breakfast. "Come in mi love, take a seat," his grandmother said. She sat on a stool. "You want likkle tea?"

"Thank you, Ma'am." She was used to having tea first thing in the morning and was glad she offered.

"You want mint or green tea?"

"Any one, thanks."

"We have cerasee too, if you want." She took that as a joke and laughed. "I'll have mint, please." Not even her mother's threats of "oonuh not leaving dat table until dat cup empty" got the children to readily gulp down the bitter cerasee bush.

Breakfast was a range of foods from the backyard, and served as brunch since almost everyone slept until late morning. Manny hadn't mention their leaving, so she checked in. "What time we heading home?"

"I hear Jack say dem want to go beach."

"Then is what time we would reach Kingston?"

"I don't know yet. I don't even sure what going on."

"Oh Lord, Granny must be going mad. I wish there was a phone."

"Not up in dem area."

"You remember tomorrow is my father's funeral?"

"Rahtid, a tomorrow?"

"Yes, I told you."

"Mi did forget, man." He scratched his forehead. "Where him a bury?"

"I told you that too. St Mary, where he's from."

"I will get you home on time, man."

After eating, they followed Jack and his brother into the bushes to pick fruits to take home. But after fruit picking, Jack was ready for the beach. By then, it was passed midday and Marcy could foresee their celebration going another night. All she could think of was her worried grandmother, and so the sooner she got home, the less stress for everyone. "Manny, we can't go to the beach, you have to take me home."

"Is you fada you a worry 'bout? Make di dead bury di dead, man." He chuckled. She was speechless. *How could he think that was funny?* She gave him a dirty look and walked away.

She went to the bedroom, cursing under her breath. *I know I shouldn't have come. I knew he wouldn't take me home as he said.* She sat on the bed with her plastic bag in her lap, thinking how to get to Kingston on her own, and then he came in. "Marcy, mi never mean to say dat."

"You said it though." She frowned.

"Sorry, mi sorry." He sat beside her. "You know what mi t'ink, you stay down here 'til tomorrow and go straight to di funeral."

"What? No!"

"Why not? Dat easier."

She turned to face him. "First of all, I don't know where in St. Mary the funeral is and I don't know if you notice, I don't have a change of clothes. And you forgot, I never told Granny where I was going? And worst of all, she never gave me permission." She hissed. "I can just imagine how she's fretting."

Manny left the room. She gazed out the window, the sun piping through, *I really wish I could stay, but I can't. If Manny could just understand...* He came back to the room. "Marz come."

"We leaving?"

"Just come."

She grabbed the bag, slipped her feet into her sandals and scurried behind him. His mother and grandmother were in the living room; she told them goodbye. "Bye, bye Marcy, sorry you couldn't stay longer," his mother said.

"I am sorry too." She made a sad face, which was genuine, because she would've stayed had she gotten permission.

Manny drove all the way to Kingston without stopping. As they neared her house he wanted to know what she intended to say to her grandmother.

"I have no idea. I hope she'll be so happy to see me that nothing else will matter."

"Wishful t'inking."

"Since I told her my friend Ayoka invited me to country, I might as well stick to that."

"What if she want to double check with Ayoka?"

"Well, that's another story… by the way, how is your girly accent?" They laughed.

"No, seriously, what you goin' tell her?"

"Manny I don't know, I really don't know." She mulled over his question. "At least I made it home in time for the funeral."

"Anyway, call mi first chance you get."

He pulled off the main road close to where he'd picked her up. He kissed her. "Don't worry, man, Granny goin' be too glad to see you, she won't get mad."

"From your lips to God's ears." She opened the car door. "I better go face the music."

"Yes, go on, go get you beating from Granny." He chuckled. She trembled, pretending to be scared.

But she turned serious once she took the corner on Summerfield Road, counting each step, sweat pouring from every crevice. Closer to home, she feared, *How me goin' face Granny now*? She got to the gate; no one was in the front yard, nor on the veranda, not even Mr. Garrison's music greeted her. She tried the living room door and it was locked. She went to the back and the backdoor was locked too. She remembered it being Sunday; Granny was at church. She stood on the steps. *Where is everybody else?*

"I don't think anyone is there, you nuh," Mr. Garrison said. He was dressed and about to leave. "You want to pass through?"

"Yes, yes thanks."

She moved around the house checking for answers to her pressing question: *where could everyone be*? Usually, when her grandmother went to church, Audrey and Maureen helped in the kitchen until she returned, but nothing was cooked or even seasoned for dinner. She went to find Sandy. Sandy was with her mother in the backyard. She waved and went back inside. As she changed into her house clothes, she heard the gate open; she hurried to the window and saw her grandmother. She grabbed the mop and started mopping around her. Her grandmother entered the front room; she kept her head down. Her grandmother stood there looking at her. She exhaled long and hard, shook her head, and carried on without saying a word. Marcy looked up after she passed and watched her go straight to her room. She continued mopping with a smile. She felt lucky and thanked the Lord, until her grandmother called, "Marcy, come here?"

Oh God!

She dropped the mop and clasped her sweaty palms in a quick prayer and crossed her fingers behind her. "Yes, Granny?"

"Zip down dis for mi." She unzipped her dress and turned to leave. "So where you was misses?"

"Granny, remember I told you one of my friends invited me to country?"

"Yes, but I didn't say you could go. What if somet'ing did happen to you? Is mi woulda get in trouble."

"Sorry, Granny." She hung her head.

"Yes, you should be sorry. What if you mada did call? What mi woulda tell her? Mi here worrying miself wondering where you coulda gone." She pulled her house dress over her head.

"It won't happen again, Granny. Please, I promise."

"And you miss you fada fineral."

"What you mean Granny?" She looked at her, puzzled.

"Maureen and Donovan gone."

"How?" Her eyes darted, her brows narrowed.

She told her they left in the morning and might not have gone at all due to Tony's accident. "What accident Granny?" Her head spun. She walked with her to the kitchen.

"Mi dear," her tone softened, "car run in a Audrey and Tony dem night before last."

"What? Them all right?"

"Yes, Audrey a likkle shake up, but Tony worse, and di whole a him car back mash-up."

"Oh my gosh, him in the hospital?"

"No, him at home. Audrey wid him."

"So Granny, how Maureen and Donovan gone?"

"Well, dats somet'ing again."

She explained that because of the accident with Tony and his car, everybody put off going to the funeral. Maureen, however, wanted to go. She checked with Mr. Fitzy and although he was going, he was taking the family and had no room in the car. She called Enid and told her their dilemma and she sent her husband for them. "But the funeral is tomorrow," Marcy bemoaned.

"Yes, but dem wouldn't have time tomorrow, so dem come dis morning."

Her head was on overload; she went to lay down. She stared into space, unsure which was more upsetting: missing her father's funeral or leaving the country early. She thought of sneaking a call to Manny, then changed her mind; she wasn't ready for his reminder, 'make di dead, bury di dead'.

Later on Audrey telephoned and she answered. "Marcy, where you disappeared to?"

"I went to the country."

"With who? Did you tell anybody?"

"Yes, I told Granny."

"That's not true, because Granny was looking for you. You know her pressure not good, and you have everybody worrying and wondering what happened to you, where you gone. We were going to report you missing today if you didn't show up." She held the phone from her ears while Audrey ranted, until she called her name. "Marcy, Marcy!"

"Yes."

"Where's Granny?"

"Outside."

"I guess you heard what happened."

"Yes, how Tony doing?" She told her Tony was better, though it pained when he moved, and was bedridden for a few days. "So what about his car?"

"That done. He was thinking of getting something better anyway."

"Oh. So when you coming?"

"A little later, tell Granny for me."

"All right."

Since she had the phone, she made a quick call to Manny. She stayed just long enough to let him know 'so far, so good', that Granny didn't beat her, as he had joked. She told him about Tony's car, and left out the part that Maureen and Donovan were gone to the funeral. No need for him to know she had spoiled his fun.

She went and told her grandmother what Audrey said, and stayed in her room for the rest of the day.

It wasn't until the next morning that she saw a 'blingas' on Audrey's finger and asked, "What is this I see, my dear?"

"Oh, Granny never tell you?"

Mari answered from her room. "Never memba mi child."

"It's the same night Tony proposed and we coming from the restaurant the car got hit."

"Oh." She turned Audrey's ring finger. "It's nice though, I like it. So him propose in the restaurant?"

"Yep." She smiled, brighter than the diamond.

"I'm happy for you, my sister."

In the evening, Maureen and Donovan returned home from the funeral. She expected them to be mournful, instead they were inspired. Donovan said their father looked "dignified" in a jacket and tie, and could not remember seeing him "so sober looking", which made them all laugh. Maureen was thrilled to meet the extended family, and brought home names of cousins to stay in touch with. A little jealousy tugged at her, hearing all that she missed. Yet, she was thankful the spotlight was off her.

Chapter 32

By January, she was busy with school again and for two weeks Manny hadn't seen her. He was sullen and needed a solution to his frustration. One afternoon after school while she waited at the bus stop, he appeared, offering to drive her home. The bus stop was crowded with girls from her school, and they watched and whispered. She was embarrassed and pretended not to see him. He blew his horn, which drew more attention. She quickly got into the car. "Manny, what you doing?"

"Mi just come to carry mi baby home."

"You acting like a fool, you nuh. You want them girls go talk 'bout me at school?"

"You don't t'ink dem have man to? Mi sure plenty a dem a do more dan you."

"Manny, all I asked for was a couple weeks until I catch up."

"Marz, mi only a give you a ride home, what's di big deal?"

"You don't understand, man."

"Mi understand say mi long to see you. You don't long to see mi?"

"Don't give me no poor-ting eye. Of course I long to see you."

"Den how you treat mi so? You don't love mi."

"Manny, sometimes even love have to take a break."

"Mi don't know 'bout dat."

"You ever hear absence makes the heart grow fonder?"

"Well, dats why I'm here." She shook her head. He continued, "And you ever hear, outta sight outta mind? So mi don't wan' you forget mi." She felt his love.

"I wouldn't, I couldn't, Manny," she said; his words melted her and she softened under his gaze.

He caressed her fingers and brought his face up to hers. "I coulda kiss you right now."

She wanted to kiss him too but pushed him away. "Yeah, you just keep your eyes on the road."

"Meet mi later nuh?"

"Manny, you know I can't, it's a school night." He gave her the sad eyes again. "I will see. If I get a chance I'll call you."

"What about weekend?"

"I'll definitely try."

Manny turned on a side street to let her off. "Mi can't wait to see you, babes."

"Me too."

"Den give mi a kiss, nuh?"

"Manny, you see how close we are to my house?"

"Alright, alright, see you soon."

She came home to news that their immigration papers had arrived. Maureen and Donovan were elated after months of looking out for the letter. Donovan met her as she entered the house. "Marcy, guess who going to Canada?"

"Yes, my dear, we are approved!" Maureen waved the letter at her. They walked to her room.

"Canada here I come!" Donovan said.

"Not sure Canada ready for you," Maureen teased.

"Donovan, you not goin' miss your little clique?"

"Most of the guys them gone, and who don't gone abroad, move, or gone live with them baby mother. So me kinda ready to leave too." He left the room pumping his fist in the air, "Yes! Canada, I'm coming!"

She turned to Maureen. "So when do we have to leave?"

"The letter says within three months."

She thought of Manny. "Only three months?"

"What you mean only three months?" Maureen looked at her cockeyed. "Look how long we been waiting? I have dreamt to see Canada with my own eyes for so long. I am ready for the high life baby." She shimmied.

"Yes, Miss Posh," Marcy joked. "You just too high class for me."

"Can't help it if I have big dreams, my dear." She stuck out her chest.

"Well, the only thing I'm anxious about is seeing mommy again."

"Of course. And all the foreign things I see on TV, I want some a that." She laughed.

"So, what about your friends, you not goin' miss them?"

"Yeah, but I'll keep in touch," she said, flashing her hand like it was no big deal. "There is just too much opportunity awaiting me, and now daddy gone, I'm free to fly away myself."

After Maureen left the room, Marcy's mind stayed on what she said regarding opportunities. She wondered if her 'big dream' was here on the island with Manny.

Saturday night as she entered the path to the beach, Manny saw her and flicked the light on his bike; she ran to him. They hugged and kissed their hellos. They sat by the tree and she leaned on him. They looked out into the open, peenie wallies serenading. She hesitated disturbing the moment with her news. She knew telling him of her immigration papers would ruin the night before it began. Still, it had to be done sooner than later. "Manny, my papers come."

"What papers?" She stared at him, as in, *you know what papers.* "Oh, you leave-mi papers." He sighed, grew pensive and out of the blue, started singing Ken Boothe's *My heart is gone, and I need, I need someone to cry on.*

"Manny, don't make it sound like that." She felt her tears forming.

"How else mi can put it? My girl a leave mi for foreign." He reached in his pocket and took out a spliff.

"You really have to do that now?"

"After what you just tell mi," he ran it through his mouth, "mi need somet'ing to calm mi head and mi heart right now."

"You knew it was coming."

"It don't make it any easier."

He lit the weed and pulled on it. She fanned the smoke from her face. "You want to try it?" He asked.

"Nah, not tonight."

"Why? Just take a draw nuh?"

"Manny, we never needed that. Look how relaxed we were."

"Mi want you share it wit' mi, man."

"You know I can't really handle it, it makes me cough."

"Alright try it dis way." He pulled on the spliff, lifted her head, covered her mouth with his and blew the smoke down her throat. She coughed and pushed his hand away. "Just go slow," he said and did it again. This time she held the smoke, and her body mellowed as she exhaled. She inhaled the smoke a few more times, until her eyes closed. She sunk to the ground, laying flat on her back. Her head spun. She felt his lips on her face, neck, chest then breast. "Marcy, Marz," he said, shifting himself on top of her. "Marcy, mi love you, mi love you, you nuh." Passion crackled his voice. She wanted to say she loved him too, but he locked his mouth on hers.

His body rubbed hard against hers, and although her head spun she sensed a difference, a forcefulness in his approach. She murmured, "No Manny."

"Why, you don't love mi?"

"Yes, but -"

He pressed into her and shoved his tongue deep in her mouth, his hand creeping up her dress. With her head in circles, her body pinned under his, his tongue gagged her call to get off; she stopped wrestling. He pulled down her underwear and his fingers fondled her. She felt him fumbling to unzip his pants and realized what was happening. All her senses and strength rebounded. She fought him off, his mouth still locked on hers, stifling her scream, and with all her might she bit down on his tongue. He recoiled, holding his mouth. Frightened, she slid from under him and stood trembling as he groaned.

"Marcy," he said, and mumbled something about her biting him. He looked pained; her eyes watered. She panicked, believing she must have done him serious damage. She took off. She ran without looking behind as she listened for his bike, expecting him to catch up to her.

She never stopped running until she got close to her gate and saw the light on in her grandmother's room. To avoid alarming her by opening the gate, she climbed over the wall and crept to the veranda; the living room door was ajar and she sneaked in. She went to the bathroom to wash her face and brush her teeth, and while there stared at her reflection in the mirror. Her eyes burned with welled up tears, and she counted her blessing of a narrow escape. She chucked back tears and willed her eyes to smile before leaving the bathroom. The clock in the living room showed 8:20. She felt pleased to be home sooner than her grandmother's bedtime and walked boldly into her room. She was changing into her nightie. "Good night, Granny."

"Good night, mi love."

She fixed herself a tall glass of milk and corn flakes, a slice of bread with cheese and settled before the TV to block out the night's event.

A month passed and she and Manny had no communication. He never checked in, not even to call and hang up, his usual stunt, nor showed up at the bus stop to offer her a ride home, and although she missed him, she never called either. Sometimes when alone, she'd laugh remembering their last night together, how she sprinted home from the scene. But mostly when she reflected, she felt terrible, fearing she had injured his mouth and now he hated her.

It was February, two months since they had any contact. It was also days away from her sixteenth birthday, and a month from the date of her leaving. She spent more time in the kitchen with her grandmother, giving her rest off her weak hands and knees. Although her grandmother didn't tell her, she was pleased that she stayed home at nights. And on her birthday, she surprised her with a Walkman cassette player. "From mi and you mada," she said. The Walkman became her new best friend and Michael Jackson, her new love. She had another surprise that day. When she came home from school, there was a postcard on the table with her name on it. She opened it and her heart skipped as she saw Manny's name inside. The card, handwritten, simply said,

> *To Marz,*
> *My girl, the one I'll always love, happy birthday,*
> *Manny Blackburn.*

The birthday card brought tears; her heart ached. She needed to see Sandy, and watched for her in the backyard with the card. About half hour of waiting, she left.

Her mind stayed on Manny. She thought of calling him, then talked herself out of it. *Why bother start up things, when I'm gone in a few weeks, anyway?* Agonized over their fate, she shut herself in the bathroom and cried in the shower.

The next day, she showed Sandy the card as they rode on the bus to school. "Manny sweet, him is a sweet guy." It pleased her and she smiled open mouthed. "That's nice, man." Her friend didn't know she and Manny were no longer together. Marcy withheld that information because she knew Sandy would want them to work it out. But how could they? She was leaving. All she wanted was her heart to heal in peace. She smiled while Sandy talked. "So where you keep the card, under your pillow?" She laughed, knowing she was right.

Her final week at school was a time of well wishes for her migration to Canada. Every day a classmate treated her to lunch and told her, "Me goin' miss you, Marcy" and admonished, "Don't forget me, make sure you write!" Some students said they wished it was them getting the opportunity to live abroad. A girl who never spoke to her before, told her, "I would love the chance to go to a foreign country, even if I didn't live there, just to have the experience, to see what snow is like."

Even teachers were encouraging. "Continue to take in your books." Mrs. Hyatt, her history and geography teacher, told her that a former student who had migrated wrote to her of her new style of learning. Mrs. Hyatt said, "She wrote that she could get away with just cramming and memorizing" but "I advise you, Marcy," she drilled, "try to understand what you're learning and when you need that knowledge, it will be there."

Audrey spent most of her time at Tony's house, so the announcement of their November wedding was no surprise. They 'dropped by' every day for dinner, and she took a change of clothes. Because she was often away and her siblings were leaving, with her grandmother's swollen, stiff joints, she hired a helper, Daphne, twice a week to wash and clean; she would begin work the week after her siblings left.

In their final week, Maureen, Donovan and Marcy cleared out and packed items they were taking to their new home. The day before Marcy's leaving she sorted her suitcase one last time. Sandy was at her house and she told her to pick the clothes she wanted. "But you not carrying much."

"No, my mother said she'll have warmer clothes because it's dead cold over there now."

"You know me only want the sexy ones them." She chuckled.

"Well, you know you come to the wrong house."

She picked through and took a few pieces. "By the way, you going to see Manny before you leave?"

"Not sure, yet." She still had not told her they weren't friends anymore.

"Why, Marcy? Manny is a nice guy, how you treat him so bad?" She didn't answer. "And me know him love you."

"How you know that?"

"Me not blind. Him nice, man."

She kept quiet about the last night they were together, and changed the topic to Sandy's guy, her favourite subject. "So how things with you and Nigel?"

"Good. Me can't wait for me and him to finish school, then we can live our life."

"Well, you have just a few more months until you start youth service, because you say you not going to university, right?"

"That's what I'd like, but me father want me to go to CWI." The College of the West Indies, a prominent university in Jamaica and the Caribbean, was where many parents aspired for their children after high school.

"That sounds good."

"Me and Nigel wan' do our own thing."

"But don't Nigel going to CAST? You'll still have to wait." Nigel had two more years at the College of Arts, Science and Technology.

"We'll see, I'll write and tell you."

"Sandy, do the right thing. Your father has the best idea for your life right now. You know how many children would love that opportunity to go CWI?" Sandy shrugged. "Anyway, you coming to airport tomorrow?"

"Of course."

After Sandy left, Marcy joined the family on the veranda. They were in the midst of congratulating Audrey and Tony. "What's all the excitement?" she butted in.

"You're going to be an auntie," Maureen announced. "Yes, there is a bun in Audrey's oven." Everyone laughed.

"Yes, my dear, I am expecting."

"That's good news, how long?"

"Two months."

"So oonuh going to have oonuh hands full. Wedding in November, and baby same time."

"Well you know you can't plan these things," she caught herself, "Well you can but – "

"We don't mind putting off the wedding until next year," Tony said.

Marcy thought, *yes Tony, you may be the baby's father, but what would mommy say about the baby coming before the marriage?* "Well, congrats, you two!"

She turned to her grandmother. "Granny, you have a great-grand on the way as we're leaving."

"You won't miss us then," Donovan said.

"How you mean, I goin' miss oonuh yes."

Marcy sat next to her, hugged her and rested her head on her chest. "I goin' miss you Granny, I goin' miss you so much, I can't wait until you come to Canada." Her grandmother had no words. Her chest heaved under Marcy's head, holding back her tears.

The next day Audrey and Tony arrived to take her siblings to the airport for their one o'clock flight. The three of them had one small suitcase each, which fitted easily in the trunk of Tony's new Ford Cortina. Mr. Garrison met them on the veranda to say goodbye and wished them a safe flight. As he shook Marcy's hand, she remembered 'their little secret'. "Thanks for everything," she said quietly. With a sly smile he nodded.
Her grandmother walked them to the gate. Marcy waited until Donovan and Maureen said their goodbyes. Her eyes watered, her spirit was broken. She felt her heart would stop beating. "Bye, Granny," she said, as tears flowed. Her grandmother embraced

her, Maureen and Donovan hugged them, and they huddled at the gate, crying.

"Come on, oonuh don't want to miss oonuh flight, oonuh will see Granny soon," Audrey said, fighting back tears.

Sandy met them at the car. Marcy gripped her hand, glad for the support. They squeezed beside each other in the car, holding hands, not talking, the lump in Marcy's throat barring all words. She stared out the window driving along Windward Road, Rockfort, and Harbour View, wondering if she would ever see those streets again. And turning on the airport road, she looked out into the sea and thought of Manny. Thoughts of their time at the beach stabbed her heart and she squeezed Sandy's fingers. Sandy muttered, "Me know me dear, me know." She glanced at her friend, and she too was teared up.

They reached the airport. Tony drove up to the doors and they took their suitcases from the car. As Marcy picked up hers and turned to enter Departures, she stopped, her brows narrowed. She thought she saw a silhouette she recognized across the street. She looked behind her; it was Manny. Her heart quickened. She turned around. He was sitting on his bike. They locked eyes. She couldn't tear herself away, and in that moment she wished her leaving was a dream. "Marcy, come on," Audrey called.

Manny nodded, his smile strained. She shook her head, bit her lip, and forced back tears. "Come on Marcy!" Maureen called, and she hurried to keep up. In the airport she gave Sandy a how-did-he-know look? Sandy smiled, crookedly. Marcy looked at her sideways, smiled and shook her head. *That's why you're my best friend.*

After they checked in, Audrey and Tony said they weren't staying to see them off, so they hugged and said they'd call when they reached. Marcy said goodbye to Sandy, and she said, "Make sure you write as soon as you reach, you nuh."

"As soon as I reach, like tonight you mean?" she teased.

"You better." They hugged and she peered over Sandy's shoulder to see if Manny was still there, but he was gone. Maureen and Donovan yelled for her to come.

"Go on, go catch your plane."

"Bye, my friend."

Lightning Source UK Ltd.
Milton Keynes UK
UKOW02f0059021216
289018UK00001B/88/P